IMPRESSIONS OF ARVO LAURILA

Impressions of Arvo Laurila

Lauri Anderson

NORTH STAR PRESS OF ST. CLOUD, INC.
St. Cloud, Minnesota

ISBN: 0-87839-208-4

First Edition, July 2005

Printed in the United States of America by
Versa Press, Inc., East Peoria, Illinois

Published by
North Star Press of St. Cloud, Inc.
P.O. Box 451
St. Cloud, Minnesota 56302
northstarpress.com
nspress@cloudnet.com

1 2 3 4 5 6 7 8 9

Contents

Arvo's Daughter's Teacher

The Portage Gazette, June 12, 1885

On Saturday afternoon, at the Osceola mine, Jussi Ahola
accidentally blew himself up while stamping blasting powder
into a charge hole full of dynamite. Apparently Mr. Ahola
created a spark with the bar he was using. Mr. Ahola, who was
nineteen, leaves grieving parents in Finland. What remained
of him was buried in the Finnish cemetery behind the Lutheran
church on Sunday.

Coach had spent most of his time avoiding one thing or another while he was growing toward manhood in Coppertown. In the halcyon days of his youth he had avoided making his bed, cleaning his room and splitting wood. If his mother found a daylong task for him, he would disappear into the woods for hours. In high school he avoided learning anything, and after graduation he avoided finding a job, getting married and settling down. Coach's dad had wanted Coach to join him as a logger, but Coach was no fool. He saw how woodswork had worn down his dad. Already the man looked ten years older than his actual age. So Coach had joined the Army and had gone to Vietnam, where he had avoided actual combat. The Army had made him a supply clerk. Each day after the supply depot closed, Coach sat on a bar stool, drank cheap beer, and avoided any thought of the war.

When Coach returned home, he'd gone to college on the G.I. Bill. To avoid hard classes, he'd majored in Elementary Education. He took easy math and science classes that existed specifically for future teachers. Plus, he didn't have to take a foreign language. For a while he thought he might have to teach when he finished, but he avoided that by specializing in audio-visual aids. By properly utilizing his A-V knowledge, he could avoid actual teaching most of the time, for most school libraries contained an amazing number of films, slide sets, and other aids that could fill up a school day.

Coach graduated from Northern Michigan University in 1974 but delayed looking for a job until it was too late to get one near home. In late August, he accepted a position in a middle school in central Wisconsin and from then on taught eighth graders all day year after year. One year he made a mistake and married a woman who expected Coach to be responsible. She was always trying to get him to do something. "You're not my mother," he'd reply to her badgering.

"I'll bet your mother never got you to do anything either," Coach's wife would say. Fortunately the marriage lasted only three years.

3

Coach taught in Wisconsin for thirteen years, but then an eighth-grade social studies position came open in Coppertown, and Coach returned home. He became the coach of the eighth-grade girls' basketball team and gained his nickname, but he could never tell if he was called "Coach" out of derision or respect. His teams were never particularly successful, and nobody paid much attention to junior-high-school basketball anyway, especially the girls' teams. Plus he didn't get paid anything for his extra duty. The high school coaches all made bundles of money, especially the hockey coaches. Those guys were always put at the head of the line at the barber shop and bank. People spoke of them with awe in their voices.

None of that ever happened with Coach, but he gained a girlfriend who had a son, he continued to teach, and the years passed. In 2002 he'd put in twenty-eight years as a teacher but those thirteen years in Wisconsin had ruined his chance to retire early because his position on the pay scale had not transferred to Coppertown. He'd lost a bundle by changing jobs, so he still had years to go before he could end his frequent forays into the library to find A-V aids to fill up each day.

And so he had arrived at June 3, 2002, and all day he had been trying to avoid his girlfriend. She wanted him to accompany her to the eighth-graders' graduation from Middle School. Her son was graduating, and Coach's presence would make them appear to be a family. Maybe it meant that she wished they were married. Whatever the case, Coach wished to avoid the entire process. He'd put up with the little bastards and their hormones all year, and now he hoped never to see them again. He felt this way at the end of every school year.

Graduation was at seven in the evening, so Coach began to drink at one in the afternoon. The first six Coors lights went down smoothly, and then he switched to shots of Kessler's whiskey. By seven he was too drunk to notice that he was drunk, so he drove to his favorite bar (the Ramada), sat on his usual stool and ordered a beer. He tried to do the crossword puzzle from the evening paper, but the words kept rearranging themselves all over the page. Soon the phone behind the bar rang, and the barmaid brought it to him. It was his girlfriend. "Yes," he said. "I'll be right there. I have a one-hundred-dollar bill for your son, a present."

Then he handed the phone back to the barmaid. "Tell her I'm not here—that I left—if she calls again," he told her.

He finished his beer and the Kessler's and ordered more just as Ethel Sarkkinen burst through the doorway, stumbled, caught herself and weaved to the bar. Gator was right behind her. His eyes were big and round and protruding. They had given him his nickname. "God, am I glad to see you," exclaimed Ethel. "I was afraid I was the only teacher skipping the graduation of my students." Ethel was sixty pounds overweight and fifteen years younger than Coach. Her boyfriend, Gator, was fifteen years younger than she. A couple of years earlier, before he'd begun to drink heavily, Gator had been Coppertown High School's best hockey player. Since then he'd failed at a community college, had lost three jobs, and had had two cars repossessed. In addition, Ethel had discovered that Gator could barely read, but he was still great looking, and Ethel had jumped at the chance to drive him around and buy him his drinks in return for some good sex later. After all, it wasn't easy for a fat, thirty-six-year-old, single woman to find a date with anyone, let alone a twenty-one-year-old hunk.

The three had several rounds of whiskey, with Coors lights on the side. Then Gator staggered off to the bathroom. Ethel immediately leaned over from her stool and rubbed up against Coach. "God, I'm glad he's gone for a few minutes. I just can't talk to him. He doesn't seem to know anything at all. But he really likes the way I look," said Ethel, fishing for a compliment. When Coach didn't respond, she became more direct. "Do I still look good, Coach?"

"Honey, you've always looked good to me," he replied. He put his arm around her shoulders and fondled her right breast. She squeezed more tightly against him, and it dawned on Coach deep within some recess of his mind that Ethel's big breast didn't mean a damned thing to him. He might as well have been squeezing a grapefruit. At least the grapefruit would be good for breakfast, he thought, but aloud he told Ethel she was one of the prettiest women in the town.

"It means a lot when you say things like that," said Ethel. "You know that I've had a crush on you for years."

Gator came back. His eyes were even bigger. He had a haunted look, like an animal about to be slaughtered. "Where we going from here?" Gator wanted to know.

"There are lots of parties," replied Coach. "Maybe over to Wally Keskala's?"

"Do you suppose those two girls from L'Anse will be there?" asked Gator.

Ethel had a dreamy look now, as if she were floating away on a cloud; but her big rump still sat heavily, burying the stool seat.

"Which two girls are those?" Coach asked, pretending innocence.

"Those two that were in here last night—the two you kept staring at," said Gator. "They're related to Wally. Cousins I think."

"Those two are high maintenance," said Coach.

Gator laughed.

"High maintenance, my ass," said Ethel. "They were making a play for you, Coach, and you weren't fighting them off."

"High maintenance," repeated Coach but he liked the idea of those two young girls making a play for a fifty-plus-year-old man.

"You leave those young girls alone," said Ethel.

The phone rang. It was Coach's girlfriend. She flat out didn't believe that he had left the bar. "You put him on the line or you've made an enemy for life, girl," she said to the barmaid.

The barmaid brought Coach the phone. He listened passively to his girlfriend's tirade. The whole bar could hear her as she screeched into the phone. Ethel shook her head and raised her eyebrows, indicating silently that she was with Coach in his hour of need. When the girlfriend paused for breath, Coach said he'd be there shortly and hung up. "Let's go to Keskala's," he told Ethel and Gator.

Gator had no money, not a dime, so Ethel tried to pay their bill with a credit card, but the machine rejected it.

"I hate those goddamned machines," said Ethel.

"I can try again," said the barmaid.

"No . . . no. It'll just do it again. That card is full up. So are all the others. Listen. See if you can get the manager to run me a tab," Ethel said. "I'll be in tomorrow to pay it."

The barmaid had dealt with Ethel before, and she seriously doubted if the manager would be open to such a suggestion, but she dutifully disappeared toward the manager's office anyway because something had to be done.

"Let's get out of here," Ethel said to Gator, and they got up to leave.

"Why don't we just go to the casino," said Coach, suddenly remembering that it was thirty miles away and out of reach of his girlfriend. Plus Ethel would agree. She seemed to spend half her evenings there and was on a first-name basis with everybody who worked in the place.

Ethel and Gator thought the casino was a great idea. "Plus, I can get gas with this," she said and grabbed the tip that another customer had left at the bar. She and Gator disappeared just before the barmaid returned. The barmaid had once been one of Ethel's students, but that was years before.

"She left," said Coach.

The barmaid shrugged and gathered up Ethel and Gator's tabs.

"You can give me my bill too," said Coach.

The barmaid quickly totaled the tabs on the machine and handed Coach his bill. As he reached for his wallet, one of his eighth-grade students appeared at his side. Coach tried to remember the girl's name but couldn't. The alcohol had fogged his memory. The girl had been the back-up center on Coach's basketball team. Coach liked to think she had a crush on him.

"You weren't there!" the girl said so loudly that heads turned in their direction. "You missed your own students' graduation." The girl was visibly upset, but the sharpness in her voice brought her name into focus. She was Charlotte Laurila, the daughter of a professor at Coppertown College. Charlotte's parents were divorced, and Charlotte floated back and forth between them. She looked a lot like her mother, Tiltu, whom Coach often saw in the casino. Sometimes the mother was with one guy and sometimes with another. She got around.

Coach tried to defend himself by lying. "I was standing in the back by the door," he said. "But I was there." Then he realized how he must appear. He fumbled at the rear of his pants, but was too drunk to locate the pocket. The girl watched in horror for a few seconds and then reached into Coach's pocket herself and withdrew the wallet. She handed it to him with a look of disgust. "You can't be here, honey," he said to her. "This is a bar. You're not supposed to be here."

"It's also a restaurant," said Charlotte. "So I have every right to be here. I came in with my dad. He stopped to talk to a friend, who is sitting right over there." The girl pointed in the general direction of the tables in a far corner.

Coach looked in that direction but saw no one he recognized. Then he refocused to discover Charlotte's dad, Arvo Laurila, not more than five feet away. The professor was staring at Coach in disbelief. Coach wondered if the professor was in the PTA. Would he cause trouble? Coach waved weakly in the professor's direction and turned back to the bar. He threw two twenties down on the shiny surface and told the barmaid to keep the change. Then he weaved his way toward the door. Charlotte Laurila was now with her dad. The professor was giving his daughter an affectionate hug because she looked upset. At the door Coach turned and waved to them, but both gave him very angry looks. Coach pushed against the door and fell out into a cool early June evening.

Casino, here we come, he thought.

He wondered how the dice would fall.

Arvo's Friend Sulo

The Portage Gazette, January 15, 1888

Last Monday at the Catholic church in Atlantic Mine, Mr. Lenni Wiitala, whose family attends the Lutheran church, married Kathleen Sullivan after she accused him of fathering her child. On Monday Mr. Wiitala went missing and no one has seen him since. Last Wednesday Josephine Wercinski announced to authorities that she too is carrying Mr. Wiitala's child. The engagement of Mr. Wiitala (announced in the paper on January 8) to Ann Seppala is apparently off.

In mid-January while gales whipped the Lake Superior shoreline into an eerie deathscape of jumbled ice and freezing spray, Sulo was trying to get a roof on the snow-packed frame of the log house he had been slowly building for the last few years. Sulo was dressed in his warmest clothes—long underwear, a red wool cap with ear muffs, a green wool scarf, a yellow and black checkered flannel shirt, heavy green wool pants, high maroon-and-grey wool socks, and brown leather work boots—but the winter cold penetrated to the bone anyway. The coffee in the mug that Sulo had set on the ledge of a vacant window opening thirty minutes earlier was now ice.

"This damned house will be the death of me," Sulo said aloud to himself. He perched on the ladder at the edge of the roof and wrestled another piece of sheeting into place while the wind tried its damnedest to rip it out of his hands. The frigid wind had blown steadily out of Canada since early December, picking up moisture as it crossed the lake and dumping the moisture as snow on the Keweenaw Peninsula. Sulo was certain that every moisture-laden cloud aimed itself directly toward his unroofed home-to-be. The building was surrounded by huge drifts that climbed halfway up the outside walls, and the inside flooring was buried under four feet of the white stuff. Even now snow swirled thickly about Sulo, and his breath streamed in a cloud out of his open mouth. Already the unnailed piece of sheeting was coated with a thin veneer of white. Sulo reached into the front pocket of his leather carpenter's belt and pulled out three or four nails. In the cold his ungloved fingers had lost their pliancy and feeling, and he immediately dropped two. They struck the edge of the roof and sailed out of sight into a drift below. Sulo pulled his hammer from the side belt loop, rechecked the alignment of the sheeting, and hammered the nails home.

Sulo had spent his adult life building houses for women. Periodically, whichever house it was would be lost, along with whichever woman it was, and he'd start the process all over again. Sulo could never decide which was the more self-defeating—always to lose both the house and the woman or to lose the woman but retain the house. That was the pattern with Sulo's best friend, Arvo. Arvo had taken out a small mortgage, combined it with his life savings and bought a modest older home in town when he and his first wife had married. When that wife left Arvo for another man, who already had a house, she'd loudly proclaimed that she wanted money, not the house, for her half of their assets. So Arvo had remortgaged the house and paid her off. Then when Arvo's second wife also left to live with another man, Arvo had taken out a third mortgage. "Jesus Christ, Arvo!" Sulo had shouted at his old friend. "How many times are you going to sell your own house to yourself before you wise up?"

But Arvo had never wised up. Already he had fallen in love again, this time with a woman twenty-one years younger who was a chronic gambler, a heavy drinker, and a prowler after men. It was obvious to Sulo that sooner rather than later she would take Arvo for every penny he had. Then she'd demand half of their remaining assets in cash and Arvo would be on his fourth mortgage.

"You're a damned fool, Arvo!" Sulo had shouted at him when he could see as plain as day what was about to happen once again. "You've got a fifty-thousand-dollar house and one hundred and fifty thousand dollars' worth of mortgages. I don't understand it. Why does the bank keep letting you borrow more and more money when you have no security? Are they too fools?"

"It's because I have a great credit rating," Arvo had replied.

"Well, one of these days you won't be able to make the payment, and then you'll lose the house and be left with nothing. To hell with your latest bitch. Just give her the house and let the bank take it from her. You can come and live in the trailer with Taimi and me. Or live in a goddamned tent. Even in January it'd be preferable to taking on another mortgage!"

Arvo had looked sheepish because he knew that everything Sulo had said was true. Arvo had a secure job as a teacher, with benefits; so it wasn't entirely his fault that attractive women kept wanting to marry him. This latest one certainly had an unbelievable number of psychological problems and physical addictions, but she also had bright green eyes full of laughter, long brown hair with tinted strands of blonde scattered through it, large full breasts, a small waist, large hips, and the kind of large thighs that Arvo found ideal. On the other hand, she had run through half a dozen men in less than a year before she appeared one morning in the back row of Arvo's class and had shortly thereafter informed Arvo that he was the great love of her life. Of course, he knew that he couldn't trust her, but he'd married her anyway because she was young and beautiful and crazy, and already their marriage was a wild ride. She drank too much, gambled away thousands of dollars, drove too fast, and was incapable of concentrating on anything that required intellectual effort. In compensation for her inner chaos, she kept herself and their house neat and orderly, but the orderliness was clearly a false front, and everything seemed to be careening toward another divorce. "Maybe I'll take a second job. Or a third. Anyway, a mortgage is only for thirty years," Arvo had said.

"In thirty years you'll be eighty-eight," Sulo had replied. "A house isn't worth so much grief. Neither are women, especially your latest one. She's nuts!"

"How's your building coming along?" Arvo had asked.

That was a week earlier when Sulo had accidentally run into Arvo in the parking lot at Walmart. Arvo had gotten up off the pavement, had brushed himself off, and had walked over to the driver's-side window of Sulo's pick-up. Sulo had rolled down the window, and they'd talked about the useless-ness of their lives. "We're both charitable institutions for dysfunctional women," Arvo had said.

Sulo had agreed. He'd certainly been charitable to his first wife, and now he could hardly remember her. She'd been tall and stately, with a thick mass of ash-blonde hair that fell nearly to the back of her knees. For a long time after their estrangement, he'd remembered the weight of that hair in his hand. And he'd remembered the smell of her flesh in bed beside him at night. But now he only remembered disconnected facts about her. The actual woman was gone. How had she gone so completely out of his life? Maybe it was because in those long-ago days Sulo drank a lot. Even then he'd seen her through a haze of love and booze. Naturally, they'd met in a bar—a noisy place crowded with college kids in Durham, New Hampshire. She was a New England Finn from Fitchburg, Massachusetts. Sulo had gone East from Michigan's Copper Country to New England to work construction. For a while after he and Ruth married, he'd repaired roofs and run a tree service in and around Boston. People back home in the Upper Peninsula didn't believe how much money he made. Michigan loggers would have to fell enough trees to fill a logging truck twice over just to earn what he got for dropping one diseased tree into someone's backyard, cutting it up, and carting it away.

Ruth had dreamed of owning riding horses ever since her childhood. So Sulo bought land in Cornish, New Hampshire—not far from where, since 1953, J.D. Salinger had lived in self-imposed exile. He and Ruth lived in a trailer while he built her a house, a shed, a barn, and a corral. He bought Ruth a pair of horses, and she seemed happy. Days he removed trees and repaired leaky roofs and nights he carpentered. Weekends he drank.

Sometimes he'd saddle up the Morgan (the other was a palomino) and ride over to David's place. David was Jewish, from Manhattan. He'd moved to rural New Hampshire to commune with nature and to farm. David quickly learned that crops required physical labor and daily care, so he'd tried animals—mink, rabbits, goats—but animals were worse. They required lots of care and stank. So David started a tree farm. Trees were easy. Once they were planted, they took root naturally. David spent every non-winter afternoon sitting lotus fashion on an old khaki Army blanket in his back field. He ritualistically popped pills, washed these down with scotch, and cleansed his palate with a joint. In the heat of mid-summer he sat each day motionless for hours, watching his trees grow.

Sulo would race the Morgan across his own field and into David's. "How's our Jew?" he'd shout, and David would come out of his drugged meditations.

"Don't call me that!" he'd cry. "I don't shout 'Hello, Christian' at you."

"So how's the Jew?" Sulo would insist.

"I'm okay."

"Are your parents still sending you money?" Sulo would ask, knowing that the question irritated David.

"Have a joint." David would reply, offering Sulo a little bag of the finest weed and a package of ZigZag wrappers.

On a Saturday in June, Ruth and Sulo had had dinner and drinks at a friend's. When they got home it was pouring. Sulo had parked in tile driveway, and they'd run to the front door, soaked from the moment they'd lunged out into the storm. They'd hardly gotten inside before Ruth said she was leaving. "What do you mean?" Sulo had asked. "It's really pouring out there."

"I don't mean it that way," she'd said. "I want a divorce. I've found someone else."

Sulo had walked right back out the door and into the downpour. He'd chosen the oldest of their three vehicles and driven away. He'd never looked back, and even now, decades later, perched precariously on a ladder in the middle of a raging snowstorm, he didn't know how or when their divorce had ever become final.

All he knew was that two days later he'd arrived in Michigan. In a kind of trance caused by a combination of exhaustion and adrenaline, he'd driven through Marquette and on into the Huron Mountains. He'd found a narrow and rarely used side road, had driven until he came to a steep drop-off, had parked on its edge, had gotten out, had put the car in neutral, and had pushed it over the edge. It had crashed down through brush and small trees for a hundred feet before it slammed into a birch that crumpled the front. Sulo had removed the number plate and registration and had walked back toward Marquette.

A day later he was in Houghton, drunk. He'd stayed that way for a week. When he sobered up, the past was dead. He'd found a job in a lumberyard and settled into a new life.

Three months later he accompanied a buddy out West. They helped build million-dollar homes around Lake Tahoe and Jackson Hole. Those were aimless years but full of delight. Then he returned to the Copper Country, got an engineering degree, and met his second wife in a Houghton bar.

Sulo hammered another piece of sheeting into place and cursed because the wind, which had been threatening all day to blow him off his ladder, was picking up. It now bore down upon him with the roar of a freight train. The weatherman had indicated that there could be blizzard conditions before morning—as much as fourteen new inches of snow accompanied by winds powerful enough to knock over an unwary man. *Only a damned fool would still be putting on a roof in a January blizzard*, Sulo thought, but it was preferable to sitting in the trailer and getting drunk or driving to the casino to look for wife number three. Sulo loved wife number three dearly. She was the great love of his life. But he hated the way she gave away a dollar to the Indians for every one that he put into their future home. How could a family ever get ahead under those circumstances? Would he ever find enough money to be done or would he die with the house incomplete, as Sulo's Uncle Toivo had died with his boat incomplete? Uncle Toivo had been the kind of little man with big shoulders and huge arms who could hoist himself into a handstand on a tree limb, but the motorboat he'd spent years building had killed him the first time he'd taken it out. From the dock, his wife and two teenaged sons had watched as he tested the boat's seaworthiness by running it in a sharp circle. Somehow, to their horror, he'd fallen overboard. From the shore they couldn't tell how. Then the circling boat had struck Toivo in the head, sending him instantly to the bottom. The older boy had swum out from the end of the dock and had dived for his dad until the boy was exhausted. It had taken a team of professionals two days to find the body in the thick mud of the bottom.

Sulo hammered a couple more nails and then set the hammer carefully down on the sheeting and thrust his numb hands deep into his jacket pockets. The ladder was shaking from the force of the wind. Sulo thought briefly of wife number two, but even that brief thought caused his stomach to heave. He quickly tried to remember wife number one but with little success. Of course she would be in her fifties now, and he only remembered her as a twenty-four-year-old beauty. Recently an old friend had called from Boston and had filled Sulo in on her life since the 1960s. Apparently she'd had a hard life since Sulo had left. She'd married a wealthy businessman and had had a daughter who had died of cancer at age seven. The businessman had withdrawn to his own part of the house, and she and he had lived alone. She

16

had money though. She'd held onto the house and land that Sulo had left her and recently had sold it to a developer for two million dollars.

Sulo met wife number two in 1983, right after finishing his civil engineering degree at Michigan Tech. She was living in a dingy second-floor apartment over a restaurant in Hancock. She'd only been in the Copper Country for a short time. A month earlier she'd come to Hancock from Fairport Harbor, Ohio, with a boyfriend who had local relatives. In the middle of the night without telling her, he'd disappeared back below the bridge. When Sulo met her in the B and B Bar, she was very angry toward men, and Sulo mistakenly thought the anger was directed only toward her boyfriend.

They hadn't been together more than a month or two before she became pregnant. A Justice of the Peace married them at Agate Beach, and four months later their daughter, Erikka, was born. Erikka was fine, but wife number two had nearly died of septicemia and other complications. The hospital bill was over one hundred thousand dollars and Sulo had no insurance. For a while he sent the hospital ten dollars a month. By then Sulo had his first engineering job, but it was with a local construction company and didn't pay a lot. The hospital's collection agency had called one evening to ask if Sulo could pay more per month. "No," Sulo had told them. A week later the hospital sent word that the bill had been forgiven. All charges had been dropped.

Eventually Sulo had gotten a job with the state—good pay and good benefits. He had gotten a loan from the bank, used it to purchase land in Misery Bay, and set out to build a log home. Neighbors had been wonderful, They had brought him tools, logs, and their own skills.

Sulo and wife number two had lived in a tiny trailer while he built in the evenings and on weekends. Erikka was either with a sitter or with him or at school because wife number two was rarely home. She spent afternoons and evenings at the local shelter for abused women and had always been in court early each morning. If any domestic violence had occurred overnight, she was there to ensure that the judge got a restraining order on the guy. In those rarer instances where a woman had been the violent one, she was there to support her. "She never would have hit him with a stick of firewood if he hadn't been such an asshole," she'd said concerning one case.

17

"But she nearly killed him. He's in the hospital with broken ribs and a broken skull," Sulo had retorted.

"He was drunk and abusive," wife number two had replied.

"So was she. He was asleep on the couch when she went after him," Sulo had said.

"She should have finished him off," wife number two had said, ending the argument.

And so it had gone. He had worked during the day and had come home each workday afternoon to take care of Erikka and to build their log home. Wife number two had gone to court each morning and to the shelter home for the remainder of the day and into the evening. While Sulo was building for the family, wife number two was tearing apart other families. She had always tried her hardest to ensure that any woman with a problem marriage got a divorce rather than counseling. "Counselors try to keep people together," she had told Sulo, "and probably they should be apart."

Sulo had challenged her on this point on a rare evening when she had stayed at home to help him lay cement. "If you hate men so much, why do you always have to have one around?" he had asked her. "Admit it. All of your adult life you've lived with a man. You've told me that yourself. And how do you think it makes me feel to hear you bitch constantly about men? What have I ever done to you? I'm a good father to your child, a pretty good lover, a provider. Plus, I'm building you this house."

Two year's later, just when Sulo was about to finish off the inside of their log home, wife number two had left him and moved back to Ohio. As part of the divorce settlement, Sulo had sold the unfinished house and sent her the cash value.

So here he was again, trying to roof a third house for a third wife. Icicles were hanging from his nostrils and ears as a freezing wind whipped past him. The ladder was vibrating against his booted feet and against his waist, where he leaned heavily into a rung. He waited for a moment between violent gusts to hoist another piece of sheeting into place, but he wasn't fast enough. The wind tore the sheeting from his grasp, and it rose into the wind and sailed across the yard, out over the pasture, and disappeared over treetops into the woods. He would have to hunt for it tomorrow. Right now he was cold to the bone. Only a damned fool Finn would try to get a roof on during such a storm. He climbed down the ladder and tried to lower it to the ground but the wind did that for him. It ripped the ladder from his grip and slammed it into a drift. A cloud of snow shot away from the point of impact.

Sulo plowed his way through drifts to the trailer. Inside, a warm cup of coffee awaited him. He'd fry a potato sausage and eat it with some of wife number three's homemade rye bread. She'd be home soon from the casino, or she'd never make it. The plows would be out all night trying to keep the roads clear. Along the lakeshore visibility would be zero. Sulo was worried. Wife number three was the great love of his life. Everything about her was attractive to Sulo, even her crazy stubborn streak. He just wished she didn't gamble so often or so much.

The potato sausage was just about done when wife number three swung their rusting Bronco into their driveway and plowed her way through a foot of new snow to a parking spot. Sulo would have to go out just before bedtime and shovel out their parking area. That way there'd be less snow to move when he got up at dawn. As wife number three pushed through gathering drifts to the trailer, the lights brightened for a split second. Then the comforting hum of the refrigerator ceased and the electricity went out with a loud pop. Thank God they burned wood. Otherwise the trailer would be ice cold by morning, and the pipes would be frozen because in this kind of storm, work crews would not get the electricity back on line for hours. Sulo liked to be immersed in darkness. He found the silence of the dark to be comforting. Plus, he liked when the place rocked from wind gusts, and the whole world was blurred from rushing snow.

The door snapped open, and wife number three came into the dark out of the dark. She fought against the wind and closed the door. Then she stamped her feet and left a little pile of snow on the welcome rug. "All the way home I kept thinking about what I wanted to eat—pizza, dill-flavored potato chips, and a brownie," she said.

"A little potato sausage will have to do," Sulo told her.

That night as the blizzard roared outside and Sulo lay curled up beside wife number three in the warmth of their bed, he had a nightmare about

Uncle Bob. Uncle Bob had come home from the Italian Campaign of World War II unusually quiet and withdrawn. He'd seen too much death and dying to be comfortable with normalcy. It was as if he had all sorts of emotions bottled up inside that he couldn't express in words, and there was no other way to get them out. So he just kept them buried and walked softly as if a jolt would cause him to explode.

For a few months Bob would cry quietly at unexpected times—over a chicken dinner or in the middle of listening to a Lone Ranger drama on the radio. Sometimes he talked about crabs on a North African beach crawling in and out of the mouth of a dead GI. Once he talked about brain tissue and blood pocking his face and getting into his eyes and beard.

After a couple of years, Bob withdrew right out of the Copper Country world he had grown up in and moved to Detroit. He rented a single room in a boarding house and got tool-and-die work at General Motors. Until his retirement, he earned good money every day at General Motors and lived quietly alone at night. His room lacked a closet, but he kept his clean clothes stacked neatly against a wall. Each evening he washed his dirty clothes in the little sink and laid them on the radiator to dry. Fastidious about his appearance, in the morning he pressed them before he left for work, folded them neatly, and added them to the clothes stack.

Bob cooked his meals on a single hot plate plugged into a wall outlet. The hot plate sat on a small low table. Nearly every day he ate what he called "herk." Herk consisted of a half pound of hamburger fried with onions and then mixed in the skillet with a can of Franco-American spaghetti. After the mixture was heated through, Bob ate it with a fork straight out of the skillet. Then he washed the skillet and fork in the sink and set them back on the hot plate for the next day. He bought the Franco-American by the case and bought the half pound of hamburger daily on his way back from work.

Bob always drove second-hand vehicles with high mileage and no perks. If he wanted to listen to the radio, he'd park a small battery-powered Philco on the passenger seat.

Sometimes Bob wore a cowboy suit—a huge white sombrero, a red shirt with white arrows on the pockets and fringe on the sleeves, and chaps and boots. Other times he wore a Tigers' baseball uniform with the number nine on the back. Once he wore the cowboy suit on the long drive home to the Copper Country for a vacation. When he crossed the straits on the ferry, everybody stared.

In the summer of Sulo's sophomore year in high school, Uncle Bob gave Sulo driving lessons. Uncle Bob wore his cowboy suit for the lessons, complete with a toy six-shooter loaded with caps. Every time Sulo made a mistake, Uncle Bob shot him. When Sulo made a very narrow left turn, Uncle Bob shot him twice. Each time the cap gun fired in the closed space of the car, the report sounded as loud as a real pistol's. Sulo's body would jump instinctively and the car would swerve. "Stop swerving the damned car!" Uncle Bob would shout as he shot Sulo again, causing another swerve.

Every time Uncle Bob returned to the Copper Country, he asked Sulo's mother to make him herk for supper, and she always did. Usually he'd eat her *pulla* with it, but he also loved Durkee's packaged Snoball cakes, especially the pink ones. "Hoppy's world is the only one that makes much sense," Uncle Bob would explain to Sulo as they ate. "If you ever feel the need for a role model, don't choose anyone from this shithole place, and don't ever choose a politician or a general. Hopalong Cassidy's way is the right way. Or Jesus', I suppose, if you've come to that."

When Uncle Bob died unexpectedly in his early fifties, he left $410,000 in a half dozen bank accounts. Sulo wondered where the money went because neither he nor his mother ever saw any of it. They only heard about it from relatives, some of whom barely knew Uncle Bob.

And now, as the blizzard roared, in the nightmare Uncle Bob was in his work clothes and shooting Sulo with real bullets from a real carbine. The crack of the rifle echoed through the trailer and spread out through the night, and Sulo awoke knowing with absolute certainty that the roof of his unfinished house was gone. In the cold trailer, Sulo was sweating profusely, trickles of water running down his forehead and into his eyes. He rolled out of bed and crept through the dark into the kitchen. He poured himself a cup of cold, stale coffee from last evening's pot.

The power was still out, so he sat at the table and sipped in the dark. The only gift from Uncle Bob that he still owned was a Hopalong Cassidy lunchbox from forty years ago. It sat on a shelf nearby. Sulo stared at it and thought of his childhood—of coming alone to America at the age of five. In a bedroom drawer he still had the handwritten tag his real mother had attached to his coat pocket when she put him on the plane in Helsinki. He hadn't seen her since. Briefly a ghostly image floated through his mind—his mother was at work in the Helsinki train station; she was down on her knees scrubbing the floor; he couldn't see her face. He tried to picture himself, his parents, and his three siblings in the one room they inhabited on an island near Helsinki. He remembered shitting in a bucket and his sister cleaning him up. Who am I? He wondered.

Sulo checked his watch. It was nearly three-thirty. Outside the wind was still ripping at the eaves and rattling the windows. Sulo walked to the outside door and opened it a crack. Cold air and snow swirled in. A huge drift blocked the doorway.

In the morning the sun beat brightly out of a frigid, silent sky. Sulo had shoveled his way out of the trailer, and now he stood in the middle of his yard, surrounded by glare from the sheet of snow, which had coated nearly everything—the road, the driveway, trees, the picnic table. Sulo sipped from a cup of fresh coffee and stared at the open space where the top half of his new house used to be. He shifted his gaze to the log base of the structure. It looked out of plumb. What kind of wind could move logs? he wondered. "Jesus Christ!" he muttered as he observed the wreckage. He would have to start all over and if he didn't get done by midsummer, the bank would take it all anyway. It's a good thing I'm a patient man, he thought to himself as he picked up a board that had blown from somewhere and now lay nearby on top of the snow. Sulo carried the board over to the remains of his new house and swung it as hard as he could at the log wall. He swung the board again and again until it shattered into a short stump. He threw down the stump and attacked the logs with his gloved fists. "Heyuhhh!" he screamed, but the logs didn't care. They were indifferent and impervious. "Jesus Christ! I'll break my hand!" he screamed to himself. "You're losing it, man," he

22

added. Sulo fled through the drifts to the trailer and sat at the table drinking more coffee. The splintered and twisted pieces of frame lay somewhere out in the pasture, already buried. Little of it would be salvageable.

Sulo rose and went to the window that looked out toward the remains of the new house. He stared out the window for a long time. Wife number three got up and joined him, still in her nightgown. She got herself coffee and together they stared at the damage, trying not to think about lost time and lost work. "A second frame will go up faster," Sulo told her. "Plus, it won't contain so many mistakes." The power was still out. "Thank God we burn wood!" he said.

By early afternoon Sulo was on his eighth cup of coffee. He'd used a scoop and a shovel to clear four feet of snow from the floor of his roofless house. He was almost ready to hunt for lumber beneath the drifts when he heard the roar of engines and a caravan of pickups turned into what normally would be his driveway. His old friend Arvo was in the lead truck. "You need help?" Arvo shouted as he stepped out of his pickup into the surrounding whiteness.

Sulo stood in the unframed doorway of his house project, a shovel in his right hand. "Well, I've lost the roof and the wall frames. But you can see that. They're a bunch of toothpicks somewhere under the snow out in the field. And the logs have moved an inch or two and are threatening to collapse. Other than that, I'm okay," Sulo replied. "But I could do with another cup of coffee and maybe a sandwich."

"We brought our own tools," said Arvo. "Do you have enough lumber somewhere under all of this damned snow? We'd like to go right to work, rebuilding this goddamned house."

"Who you got out there?" asked Sulo as he surveyed the crowd milling around their trucks. Wife number three would already be worrying about feeding so many Good Samaritans. Sulo himself was wondering how he'd get enough lumber to rebuild. He'd already borrowed to the hilt—from the bank, his retirement, his friends—but the money was nearly gone. "God doesn't like me much," he said to Arvo.

"I can't help you with God, but I rounded up everybody you and I know—which isn't many—and a lot of people we don't. They're all willing to help as long as you keep feeding them more coffee."

23

Sulo noticed that the Lutheran minister had come. Sulo had only been to the man's church once—for a meeting about life insurance that had for some odd reason been held in the church basement—but apparently that was enough. The minister had brought the men of his congregation. Other friends with carpentry skills were also ready to help.

Arvo walked into the broken shell of the house to inspect the damage. "How long have you been building yourself a house?" he asked Sulo.

"This house?" asked Sulo.

"All of them," explained Arvo.

"Since the 1960s," answered Sulo.

"And it's now 2002," replied Arvo. "And in all of that building, how long have you actually lived in one of your creations?"

"Not long," said Sulo.

"Well maybe this time you're actually going to finish it and then live in it for a long time," said Arvo. "Hopefully you'll die one day peacefully in your own bed in the bedroom of your goddamn creation."

"And still with wife number three," said Sulo, who could feel the need for more coffee and a cigarette.

"You're too old to swap wives anymore," said Arvo. "That's why we're all here. We're going to help you rebuild this thing. We're here to cheat the bank. Soon you and wife number three will be sitting inside your new home, watching the deer feed outside your picture window."

"And what about you and your current wife?" Sulo asked Arvo. "How's that going?"

"She wants a leather living room set," said Arvo. "But I think she's having an affair with a logger from Watton and some guy named Keith from Tapiola."

"It looks like you're going to get another mortgage," said Sulo.

"Sure," said Arvo.

Arvo and Tiltu

The Portage Gazette, April 23, 1888

On Thursday morning Lars Ponkala and Amy Keskimaki were in circuit court charged with adultery by Mrs. Keskimaki's husband. Mrs. Keskimaki stated to the court that her time with Mr. Ponkala was spent constructively and that she still loved her husband even after he threw away her clothes.

Arvo had never liked phones. He viewed them suspiciously as an invasion of privacy. If pressed, he would begrudgingly admit that they served a purpose if somebody far away had to be reached, but, for the life of him, he could not understand how someone could talk for hours on end to someone else who was nearby. "Why not just go over to their house?" he'd say.

On the other hand, Arvo' s young wife, Tiltu, could talk all day on the phone. Sometimes she'd call her neighbor, Maija, and the two would discuss the trivia of their lives from just after breakfast until just after lunch. They'd talk with the phone jammed between shoulder and cheek while they fixed meals, dusted, or drank coffee. At some point Tiltu would invent pressing business and hang up but immediately call someone else, usually one of her numerous friends in South Range. She'd talk to a bevy of them through the afternoon. After supper she'd drive off to visit them—sometimes in their homes and often in a bar. She'd come back by midnight with incredible stories of what someone had done. "Helmi got drunk and sprinkled vodka on Keith's belly. Then she sprinkled salt on it and licked it off."

"Who's Keith?" Arvo asked.

"Just a guy we met in the bar," said Tiltu. "He's from Elo and logs."

Periodically Arvo would try to get Tiltu to stay home for a quiet evening with him and their daughters, but Tiltu was nearly always resistant. Sometimes she would stay home to play mindless card games such as Slapjack or Cribbage or a board game like Pictionary. She generally enjoyed Hollywood romances like *Maid in Manhattan* or comedies like *Green Card*. On television she liked *America's Most Wanted*. She would travel hundreds of miles to a mall in order to shop in Pier One and Younker's. Watching sports bored her though she cross-country skied in the winter and played tennis very badly in the summer. She also kept in shape at a local gym. She occasionally read *People* and *Woman's Day*, but she was especially bored by anything that required a lot of thought, such as books, though she occasionally read *True*

Crime. She liked reading about serial killers, serial child molesters, and serial rapists. She especially liked reading about someone who was all three. "*True Crime* is real," she'd tell Arvo. "That fiction you read and write is just crap."

Arvo taught literature at the small college in Coppertown. His favorite writers were too numerous to list but included Dostoevsky, Camus, Hemingway, and Duras. In the evenings, Arvo sometimes wrote stories. Many had been published as collections in books, but Tiltu had never read them. She wasn't even aware that Arvo sometimes wrote about her.

If Tiltu was forced to watch television, the show was *Cheers* or reruns of *Cheers.* "I love its realism," she'd say. She imagined that's how it was in the South Range, Houghton, and Coppertown bars where she spent a lot of time. Her favorite bars were the Cozy Corner and the Monte Carlo. She knew every bar fly in the Copper Country—male and female, young and old. She knew their personal histories too. Sometimes Arvo would go into a bar with Tiltu, and she'd toss back one beer after another. Then she'd start telling him about the other patrons. "See that woman at the end of the bar? She used to be married to the guy at the pool table—the one playing alone. But he had an affair with the woman talking to his ex-wife, the one next to the end with the bleach-blonde hair. So she took up with a Rintala. He's a prison guard and makes good money. But he was already married and with two kids, so . . ."

Sometimes Tiltu would agree to stay home with her family in the evening, but she'd pout and then put a BeeGees tape into the machine and turn the stereo up so loud that the walls vibrated. She'd dance alone for a while and then begin to pace, and soon she'd be out the door or, becoming depressed and angry, she'd go upstairs and into her bedroom, shutting the door behind her.

At such times Arvo wondered why he'd married her. After all, her own mother had warned him against it. "Stay away from my daughter. All she'll cause you is grief," his future mother-in-law had told him over the phone, the first time they had spoken.

"She likes to play the field, and she never makes a commitment. When she moves on to a new boyfriend, she always keeps the old one dangling.

28

Usually she has two or three hanging out there while she plays with her latest catch. I hear good things about you, and I like you, so I don't want you hurt. Tiltu will destroy you. She's a lot like her father. He was a drunk and abusive. Whatever demons drove him, drive her, too. When she was a girl, she used to try to protect me from him, but now she's become him."

But Arvo knew why he'd married her. Unfortunately, the reasons were all too obvious. Tiltu was twenty-one years younger than he and very beautiful. She had long brown hair, mischievous large green eyes, and a wonderful explosive laugh. She was also clean, neat, and orderly, with a quick sense of humor. She knew how to dress to emphasize her appeal.

She also came to him with a history. She'd become sexually active with a married thirty-seven-year-old neighbor when she was thirteen. The neighbor had children Tiltu's age, but that didn't faze her. She secretly met him where he worked and they had sex until Tiltu's mother found out. Then she'd moved on to her freshman biology teacher. He'd drive her for the weekend out to his farm, where they'd have a good time. At fifteen she'd moved out of her childhood home and moved in with her twenty-seven-year-old motorcycling boyfriend, but he'd refused to put up with her continuing promiscuity. They broke up, and she'd had an abortion. She'd moved back in with her mother and slept on the couch. For a while she'd harassed the motorcycling ex-boyfriend and his new girlfriend—slashing their tires, keying their car hoods and doors. In the ensuing six months, she had gone through a string of new boyfriends while she cashiered in a grocery store. She'd decided to become a nurse, but it didn't work out. She took classes on most weekdays but cashiered on free days, in the evenings, and on weekends, and partied nearly every night after work.

In class she was only half awake, and she never seemed to have time to prepare properly. One day an instructor drilled her on all she didn't know, and shortly thereafter she was tossed out of the program. That had happened years earlier, and Tiltu still hated that instructor with unalleviated passion. "The bitch didn't drill anyone else, just me," Tiltu still argued. "Some of the other girls liked to party too, and she didn't drill them."

Years later Arvo still wondered if Tiltu' s ignorance had been singled out because of him. Coppertown was one hell of a small town, and she had been one of his students at the college. They were dating when Tiltu was expelled from the nursing program. Arvo's first wife had been a college professor of French, with her own career. She'd been teaching for years in lower Michigan and then in southern Indiana when Tiltu appeared in the back of his class, flirted outrageously with him, and told him after a class that she was in love with him. He should have known right then what kind of woman she was. How could someone fall in love from the back of a classroom?

So he had divorced. He had married Tiltu. It was the biggest mistake of his life, but he now had two wonderful daughters, so the relationship had not been entirely monstrous.

Right from the beginning Tiltu'd thrown tantrums several times a week. She'd slammed the back door so hard that she'd shattered all of the glass. She'd kicked a watering can through a window. Several times during the week, she'd down a bottle of merlot before dinner, another during dinner, and begin a third in the early evening. On weekends, she'd consume two six-packs and then go to a bar or a friend's. Arvo couldn't believe that a five-foot, three-inch, one-hundred-thirty-five-pound woman could consume so much liquid, but she managed it again and again. Late in the evening, glassy-eyed and swaying, she'd get verbally abusive. "What are you doing here?" she'd shout. "I'm here all day, taking care of this damned house. I clean and cook and take care of your daughters. What do you do? I know what you want. You want to trap me in this goddamned house, but it won't work. I'm going to go out whenever I want to, and this is one of those times." Then she'd head for the bars. The next day, because she was hung over and tired and Arvo had time between classes, he would do the cleaning and cooking and then take the girls to a park.

Early in their marriage, she'd had only one affair. When the girls were infants, she'd ostensibly gone on a Saturday to visit a girlfriend over near Ironwood. In actuality, she'd driven only four blocks, to the house of an ex-boyfriend who was a drug counselor at Mental Health. The ex-boyfriend raised marijuana in his attic under infrared lights. He and Tiltu had spent the day naked in his bedroom, smoking dope and having sex. In the late after-noon Arvo had driven his daughters four blocks to Laurn Grove Park so they could play on the swings, slide, and monkey bars. The red sports car which he had bought Tiltu was parked two houses away in front of the ex-boyfriend's two-story. The ex-boyfriend's car was in the driveway. Arvo had hustled the girls back into his car over their protestations, had driven the short distance to the ex-boyfriend's, and had parked directly behind Tiltu's Daytona. He'd left the girls in the car, with the window open, and had walked to the ex-boyfriend's front door. He'd pounded on it for five minutes and had given it a few dozen kicks, but no one had answered. He'd gone around to the side of the house where sliding glass doors gave him a view of the entire downstairs area. Tiltu was not there. Neither was the ex-boyfriend. They were obviously upstairs on the other side of an open window. Arvo had yelled. Then he had screamed. No one had answered, but his little girls had stared at him out of the open car window. They clearly had thought something was seriously wrong. Arvo had then driven the girls home, and five minutes later Tiltu had arrived, hair and clothes disheveled, and her eyes wild with anxiety. "We were just smoking dope," she'd said. "I know you don't believe me, but we were just lying on his bed getting high."

Arvo had almost divorced her that time—had refused to sleep with her for about a week. But he'd given in, and then she'd redecorated the house and had cooked some wonderful meals and baked pies and cheesecakes. She'd been especially receptive in bed.

And so, with time, he'd forgiven her. Years passed. During those years he and Tiltu were in love and did nearly everything together. They fixed up their home—papering, painting, carpeting, and buying new furniture. They fixed gourmet meals together and worked out. They entertained their children together. Arvo applied for summer teaching and research at Phillips Andover near Boston and took his family to New England. They visited historical sites in Boston, Concord, Salem, and Fall River. They spent days at Salisbury Beach and in the White Mountains of New Hampshire. Arvo got other grants and took his family to Maine and Quebec. They'd been married nearly ten years before the serious trouble began.

Tiltu was introduced to the casino by her mother, and soon she was going there several times a week. Tiltu had a job as a receptionist and pseudo-secretary for the principal of a rural elementary school, seven miles out on the Portage Lake Canal Road. The job was not full time and didn't pay a lot. The real secretary, with whom Tiltu shared an office, had gotten her the job. The real secretary was a party girl like Tiltu. They'd met at the Eagles' Club bar, where a third woman had just won a one-hundred-dollar bet from three hunters from Wisconsin. The bettor, a close friend of the secretary, had bet that if she went down on the hunters, she could bring off each within a minute. She and the hunters had gone into the pool room and shut the door. Then she'd gone to work. The first two had been quick but the third, an older man, had taken fifty-eight seconds. Tiltu had done a quick calculation in her head. "One hundred bucks for three minutes of work equals two thousand dollars per hour. Hell, I'd do anything for that kind of money."

"I just did," the bettor had replied.

The real secretary was a fake blonde in her mid-forties. She had a boyfriend in his twenties who still lived with his parents and often broke their dates or showed up late. But she professed to love him dearly. On the other hand, she liked to party at men's clubs like the Eagles' and she'd had affairs with several members, including one long-term affair with the live-in boyfriend of a woman who worked as a nurse in the maximum security prison at Baraga.

The secretary had quickly recognized that Tiltu was a woman much like herself, and so she had made sure that Tiltu became the receptionist in the same office. Tiltu was delighted to receive a paycheck, which she spent at the casino every week.

From then on, Arvo noticed that his wife was very patterned. On payday, she came home from work full of energy. In the next two hours, she downed a bottle of merlot. Then she always offered to take the family out for pizza or some other inexpensive fare. On the way to the restaurant she went through the drive-in at the Ripley branch of the South Range bank, where she had her checking account. She always took out several hundred dollars in cash and put the remainder in her account. Then they ate at the Loading Zone in Lake Linden, Quincy's in Dollar Bay, or the Ambassador in Houghton. Over dinner Tiltu polished off another bottle of merlot or a cabemet. By the end of the meal, she was smashed and clearly agitated. "Well, I'm going to the casino now. Do you want to come?" she'd say.

If a babysitter could be found on short notice, sometimes Arvo accompanied her to Baraga or Watersmeet. Usually , though, he stayed home with his daughters. If he did go, he sat for most of the evening at the casino bar, drinking free soft drinks and watching a ball game on the overhead TV. He rarely gambled. He couldn't afford to. Tiltu almost always had lost all of her cash by nine o'clock. Then she cashed a check, withdrawing most or all of the money from her checking account. When that was lost, she charged on a credit card. By then it was midnight, and she was usually down by four or five hundred dollars. Sometimes she temporarily won big. One night she won the jackpot—forty-six hundred dollars—but lost all of it in a few hours. Several times she quickly won and lost around twenty-five hundred dollars.

After midnight she was always in a strange zone, her movements dreamlike and jerky. She caromed rapidly and randomly from one slot machine to another and soon on to others. She fed the machine twenty-dollar bills and played until they were gone. She cashed out and played the quarters three at a time. She hit the button, fixated by the spin of the wheels. Other times she pulled the arm. Sometimes she alternated these actions repetitively. Always she grew angry and desperate because her losses were mounting. She'd snap at Arvo. She'd curse him for peering over her shoulder. "Leave me alone! Christ! You're always hanging around me!" she would say, her eyes on fire.

So Arvo would retreat to the bar. Later she would come by and really lay into him. "Why did you come with me? You've ignored me all night! You're such a bastard!"

By one in the morning, Tiltu was almost always broke, so she went after Arvo's money. "Let me borrow a hundred. I'll pay you back. I'll show you a really good time on the way home." She'd sidle against him flirtatiously, but her words were slurred, and she could hardly stand after drinking for hours. If he refused to give her more money, she immediately turned on him. "You're such a cheap bastard!" she would say. "You blame me for everything that goes wrong but you don't offer me anything. All you want is sex, but it'll be a damned long time before you get any, you cheap bastard!"

Sometimes Arvo capitulated just to shut her up. Other times he gritted his teeth and bore the endless barrage of her words.

On the way home in the early morning hours, Tiltu often slept. Then Arvo would turn on the radio, lower the volume, and listen to the mournful lyrics of Patsy Cline, Jim Reeves, Hank Williams, or the country tunes of Ray Charles.

Eventually Arvo stopped accompanying his wife to the casino. To protect his assets he got separate accounts, but that didn't always work. Tiltu still spent all of her own money and found ways to spend Arvo's. The daughters' college fund was nearly drained by her. Arvo began to hide money so that he could pay bills. Tiltu began to spend more and more time at the casino, coming home later and later as the months passed, and then years.

Arvo had been with Tiltu nearly fourteen years when Tiltu's lifelong best friend, Danielle, asked Arvo if he could loan her fifteen hundred dollars. She was getting divorced from her philandering husband and needed the money for the lawyer. Arvo felt sorry for her. Her husband was apparently having half a dozen affairs simultaneously. "Get a good lawyer and take him for a ride! Take as much as you can get from the self-centered son of a bitch!" Arvo told her as he handed her the money.

Danielle paid him back two weeks later, after her family pooled their funds to help her.

A few months after that, another of Tiltu' s friends, Cherie, asked Arvo to loan her money for a lawyer. She too was getting a divorce. "I'll pay you back in a month," she said. Again, Arvo loaned the friend the money—two thousand dollars. One morning a month later Tiltu' s two closest friends, Danielle and Heidi, came over to visit. Danielle thanked Arvo once again for the loan of fifteen hundred dollars. Tiltu and her friends sat in the kitchen, drinking coffee and talking about renovations all three were making to their homes. Tiltu talked about how she wanted a new home out in the country, where she could garden. "You've spent the price of a home in the casino," Arvo said. He stuck around a few more minutes to be polite and then went out to the garage to lacquer a table that earlier had a large stain sanded out of its surface. When he came back into the kitchen, Tiltu cooed at him. "Can you get me another cup of coffee, Hon?" she asked him. He did, and he later brought her a piece of pecan pie he had baked the night before. She gave him a kiss on the neck. "He's a keeper," she told her friends, and they giggled.

A couple of days later, Tiltu' s two friends came to see Arvo while Tiltu was at work. "We need to talk to you," Heidi said They appeared nervous, and Arvo wondered why. "We might as well get right to it," said Heidi, the more talkative of the two. "We watched Tiltu being so warm and sweet with you the other morning that her performance made both of us sick. She was just playing a game. She has the two thousand dollars that you loaned to Cherie Heinonen. We don't know why Cherie returned the money to Tiltu instead of to you. Anyway, the point is that Tiltu is going to use the money to get a lawyer. She's divorcing you."

"That doesn't make sense," said Arvo, who felt like he had just been kicked in the head. "I know she has a serious gambling problem, but I love her and I've been really good to her."

"She's having an affair," explained Heidi. "Every time she goes to the casino, she meets a guy named Dub Santti, from Watton. They've been seeing each other for months."

"Are they having sex?" Arvo asked

"That's what an affair is," said Heidi. "They meet at the casino and then they go somewhere and do the dirty. She's been to his house and met his kids. He's divorced. Dub Santti is a logger and a school drop-out. I can't imagine what she sees in him. He's a total loser."

"How do you know all of this?" Arvo asked. He felt like he was going to choke. His mouth was dry all the way to the back of his throat, and beads of sweat had popped out on his forehead and nose.

"She talks about him all of the time. It's like listening to a high school girl with a crush," said the other woman, recently divorced from her philandering husband.

Arvo was devastated, and yet it made sense. Why else would Tiltu sometimes go to the casino with only fifty dollars and be gone until the wee morning hours? If she were just gambling, she would have run out of money within an hour. Arvo thanked the women, and after they left, he waited anxiously for Tiltu to come home. When she did, he told her what he knew. He was hoping that she would confess and beg him to forgive her. Instead her eyes narrowed, and her voice took on an icy edge. "Who told you?"

Arvo refused to say, so she refused to admit it was true. Then he told her his source, and she began to shake with fury. "Those bitches! I'll never trust them again!" she said. "Okay then, it's true," she added. "But I don't love him. He's just someone to have sex with. But those so-called friends—I'll never have anything to do with them again! They were supposed to be my friends. Friends support each other. They keep secrets. Friends don't betray friends! It's unforgivable!"

"And wives don't betray husbands," said Arvo.

Knowing he was a fool, Arvo set out to save his marriage, but his life just got crazier and crazier. He tried to buy Tiltu's loyalty with expensive new outfits. He took her for the weekend to an old Victorian mansion, the Laurium Manor Inn, that had been converted into a bed and breakfast. Tiltu loved the elegance of the place, with its elephant-hide wallpaper, its tinted windows, its horsehide couches. "We ought to get new leather furniture," she said as she ran her hand over a couch cushion and pressed against its firmness. Her voice was full of enthusiasm. "And a new house out in the country where I could have a garden."

Arvo wondered how they'd do that when she was still spending thousands of dollars at the casino. Plus, he had to learn to trust her again.

When they got back from the wonderful weekend, Tiltu went out jogging. "I had a great time with you, but I need exercise," she said and kissed him hard on the lips. "I'll be back within an hour," she said and headed out the door and disappeared down the street.

Two minutes later the phone rang and an operator asked if Arvo would pay for a long-distance call to a Dub Santti in Watton, Michigan, from a pay phone down the street at the Citgo. Tiltu was furious that the operator had called Arvo. She said that she was going to switch her phone service. "I'll never use that company again!" she said.

Arvo and Tiltu went shopping for three days in Appleton, Wisconsin. They bought Tiltu several new outfits, swam in the motel pool, made love on the motel bed, and ate wonderful Italian meals at the Olive Garden and Victoria's. They returned home close to midnight, and as they entered the front door with their luggage, the phone rang. It was the boyfriend from Watton. He had been diagnosed with gonorrhea. "You certainly know how to pick 'em," said Arvo, who realized that he could be talking about himself too. "What did you expect from a casino barfly?"

"He doesn't drink anymore," said Tiltu. "And I'm sure he's loyal to me. He must have caught it from his former girlfriend—the one that preceded me. He says she was a slut."

In the morning, Tiltu and Arvo went to the doctor's for shots. The nurses, former students of Arvo, acted as if the disease were Arvo' s fault and that Tiltu was his victim. Arvo withdrew into the deep silence that all Finnish males are capable of entering when they have been publicly wronged.

Then Tiltu broke up with her Watton boyfriend. "You're the one for me," she told Arvo. "I want to be with you forever. Plus he has terrible body odor."

So that he would trust her, Tiltu insisted that Arvo go with her to the casino. He hated being there, especially when all of the cashiers presumably knew of Tiltu' s transgressions. They'd obviously seen her there with other men, probably making out with them. Plus she continued to throw away large sums of money. Then one night she went alone because Arvo was insistent. "I hate the damned place," he said. But at one-thirty she called. "The van's in the ditch," she told him. We won't be able to get it out until tomorrow. Come and get me. I'll meet you by the side door of the casino."

From their brief conversation, Arvo assumed that Tiltu had started home, had slid on ice into a roadside ditch, and had walked back to the casino to call him for a ride. Arvo drove the thirty miles to Baraga in trepidation and found Tiltu standing alone in the casino parking lot. For reasons that Arvo never understood, Tiltu had driven their van behind the casino bingo hall. Probably because she was very drunk, she had then backed the van very fast over a sheer drop-off that formed the wall of a drainage ditch. She'd dropped the van thirty feet through the air and it had miraculously landed upright in a stream. Arvo saw the Watton boyfriend standing by the casino entrance, watching as Tiltu climbed into Arvo's car for the drive home. It took most of the following day for a wrecker to get her van out. "You're lucky to be alive," Arvo told her when he brought the van home.

A few weeks later, Arvo received a Saturday night call from Tiltu's Watton boyfriend while Tiltu was at the casino. "I just want you to know that your wife is wrecking my life," the man said. "She lies to me all the time, and I can't trust her. Now she's seeing another guy, a Maki from Elo. She met him at the bar in the casino a couple of hours ago. She refused to talk to me and only had eyes for him. Then they went outside. He got in his truck, and she got in her van and they drove away. I followed in my truck. They went to his place, and they've been inside for over an hour. I'm sitting outside, watching his house and talking to you on my cell phone. I don't know what she sees in this guy. He's dorky-looking, with an ugly, pitted face and a beard to cover up some of the pits. He's skinny as hell and awkward."

The boyfriend went on to tell Arvo how Tiltu had made him so distraught that he could no longer hold down food or get his work done. "If I didn't work for myself in the woods, I'd fire me," he said. "I'm not worth a damn any more."

The man talked about his pain and suffering for an hour and a half. Arvo detested the man and probably would have killed him if they'd been face to face, but distance allowed him to sympathize with another poor fool in love with Tiltu the Betrayer. Then Santti made a mistake. "But don't get me wrong," he said finally. "I'm no wimp. I was trained as a killer during the Vietnam War."

"I have people like you for breakfast," said Arvo, who had been an all-state athlete three times in his youth. "I don't feed them—I eat them." Then Arvo hung up.

A month later, Arvo had an opportunity to back up his threat. He was at the casino with Tiltu when she attempted to pick up her Watton boyfriend right in front of him. She and the boyfriend were sitting together at the bar. At first Arvo didn't know who this man was, but when they continued to talk, it dawned on him that this must be the boyfriend that he had never seen close up. Arvo grabbed the man's hair from behind and yanked him off the barstool with such force that the man fell to the floor on his back. Before Arvo could kick him in the ribs and step on his face, the boyfriend scurried away crab fashion, got to his feet, and dashed out the door. "You had no reason to do that," said Tiltu, who was drunk as usual. "We were just sitting at the bar. You might have hurt him."

"Let's go home," said Arvo.

"No," said Tiltu. "I'm staying here."

Arvo left her there without a vehicle and drove home alone. His daughters' cousin, Sam, had been babysitting the girls that night. Arvo explained to Sam that Tiltu would not be coming home that night.

"Sometimes I hate my aunt," said Sam.

The next afternoon, Tiltu called from her mother's home in Chassell. The Watton boyfriend had left her there. "It was a mistake," she said. She was crying. "I was drunk. I cried all night and wouldn't let him near me. I kept thinking that if you left me, who would buy me macadamia nuts and Sayklly's chocolates on Christmas? I still love you and want my family."

But her drinking and gambling continued.

One Sunday night when she was very drunk, Tiltu threw the cordless phone at Arvo as he sat in the living room reading student papers. The phone struck him harmlessly in the chest and dropped into his lap. Tiltu retrieved the phone and thrust it violently into Arvo's face, shouting "Call a lawyer! I want a divorce! I've already got money for one of the very best lawyers from a boyfriend. Call a lawyer!"

Instead, Arvo tried to call Tiltu's sister, who was married to the sheriff. Arvo wanted the sister and the sheriff to come over and calm down Tiltu. Tiltu tried to yank the phone out of Arvo' s hands, and they began to wrestle with the phone. Arvo realized how idiotic this was and let go. Tiltu fell to the floor with the phone grasped tightly in both hands. Then she got up, ran into the kitchen, and ripped the phone station from the wall. She ran outside and disappeared down the street.

Arvo's daughters were silently standing on the hall staircase. They'd heard their mother's shouting, and now they were frightened. Arvo gave each a hug, assured them that everything was going to be okay, and that he'd be right back Then he drove the short distance to his office at Coppertown College and called Tiltu's sister. She wasn't home, but the sheriff was, and Arvo explained that Tiltu was drunk and acting crazy. The sheriff said he'd be right over.

But when Arvo returned home, Tiltu had already called the Coppertown police and two officers were waiting to take him into custody. They were neighbors and knew the actual situation but had to arrest Arvo anyway. "Michigan law states that anytime a domestic abuse accusation is made, the accused is automatically locked up for twenty-four hours, no matter what," they explained to Arvo. "Your wife already knew you'd be automatically locked up when she called us. She's probably known how domestic violence laws work since childhood. We used to get called to her parents' home often. Her dad was always beating up her mom."

At the jail Arvo spent several hours in his brother-in-law's office and then was booked by one of his former students, a criminal-justice major. Everyone was very nice to Arvo. They brought him coffee and books and gave him his own cell. They called it the penthouse.

In the morning Arvo went before the judge, who was another friend. A woman from the Shelter Home was sitting in the front row of the courtroom. She asked that Arvo be slapped with a restraining order. "Otherwise he's apt to beat up his wife again or run away with his daughters," the woman argued. But the sheriff, Tiltu's sister, and Tiltu's mother were all willing to testify against Tiltu. So, a few days later, all charges were dropped. During the interim, however, Arvo stayed at the sheriff's home. Tiltu cried for three consecutive days and tried multiple times to see Arvo. Eventually they met clandestinely at a sister's home and Tiltu pleaded for Arvo to return home. "I don't want to divorce you yet," she said.

After his return home, as a kind of last resort, Arvo applied for a grant to spend the summer in Hawaii, doing research on Pacific Islands' writers such as Albert Wendt of Samoa and Epeli Hau'ofa of Tonga. He found his family an apartment on Waikiki Beach, about two hundred feet from the water. While Arvo did research at a think tank called the East-West Center, near the University of Hawaii, Tiltu was supposed to explore Oahu with their daughters, but she refused. She and the girls spent their days in the apartment, bored. Arvo went with Tiltu and his daughters to climb Diamondhead, to visit the aquarium, and to boat out to the Arizona Memorial, but she refused to go anywhere on her own. Arvo arranged to meet her and their daughters at the palace of the former Hawaiian monarchy, but she didn't show up. The East-West Center arranged a bus tour of Oahu's north shore, but she didn't go. When their diabetic daughter, Charlotte, became ill with food poisoning after eating shrimp, Tiltu used the illness as an excuse to return to Michigan. "I hate Hawaii," she said. "It's boring."

The day after her arrival back in Coppertown, Tiltu left her daughters at a neighbor's house. "I have to run to the mall. I'll be back in an hour," she told the neighbor. Then she headed for Baraga and Watton and the casino. Hawaiian time was six hours behind Michigan's, so Arvo called all night, beginning at 6:00 P.M. when it was midnight in Coppertown. By midnight in Hawaii, Arvo knew that she had once again betrayed him. Then he had a panic attack. He knew with certainty that he would never be able to leave Hawaii and that he'd never see his family again. He knew, in fact, that he was going to die, that the immense canopy of the Pacific was going to smother him in its weight. At three o'clock in the morning he crawled on his hands and knees out of his apartment and down the hall to the elevator. He reached up and hit the button to open the doors while remaining on all fours. When the elevator arrived, he scurried inside, reached up, and hit the button for the lobby. As he rode it down, he got to his feet with great effort and leaned, breathless, against a wall. When the elevator stopped and the doors opened, Arvo ran across the lobby and out into the warm night air of Oahu. He stood for a moment to let the breeze blow against his face. Then he wandered out into the silence of the street. He followed it a short distance, cut through an alley, and found himself on the beach. Stretched out on a nearby bench was a homeless native Hawaiian. Arvo woke up the man and told him his story. The man didn't say anything but sat up at one end of the bench and motioned for Arvo to sit at the other end. Arvo kept talking until the darkness receded momentarily from his soul. But it was still there, all around him, ready to swallow him up again.

41

Early in the morning, Arvo returned to the apartment and called Tiltu. She had just gotten home from sex and gambling and hadn't slept all night. "I've booked a flight to Chicago," he told her. "I'll arrive there at 5:30 A.M. If you're not there, I'm divorcing you. If you are there, I still might. I love you. You're the one great love of my life, but you drive me crazy. Why do I have such a passion for you when you treat me abominably? Why am I always giving to you when all you do is take? I'm losing it. I'm turning into someone like Uncle Lenni." Arvo's Uncle Lenni had lived for years in the pantry of the farmhouse that Arvo's Finnish grandparents had built when they came from Finland in 1904. He had lived all of those years alone, a recluse with a pitchfork ready to attack trespassers.

Tiltu was outside O'Hare at 5:30 A.M., and that day they drove back to the Upper Peninsula. The drive took about eight hours. Tiltu had not slept for days. Neither had Arvo. Each was stunned and silent.

A few months later, in March, Tiltu sued for divorce. She and Arvo lived together for several months after the divorce papers arrived. Living together was convenient for Tiltu because the apartment she was renting from her mother in Chassell would not be empty until June. "I'm doing this because I don't want to hurt you any more," Tiltu told Arvo. "What kind of man do you think I'll have next?" she asked him in the same breath.

She agreed to walk away from her marriage for thirty-five thousand dollars in cash. Arvo drew up a contract to that effect, and she signed it. Arvo took the contract to his four-hundred-pound lawyer. The lawyer, who was unusually useless, even for a lawyer, said that the judge wouldn't accept it. "I'll draw up a proper one," he said. Unfortunately, his secretary had quit, and he himself was too lazy to draw up the divorce papers himself. Weeks passed, Tiltu eventually moved out, and the next time she spoke to Arvo she had upped the ante to fifty-seven thousand dollars. Arvo was furious and wanted to sue his mountainous lawyer for ineptitude but that would require the hiring of another lawyer who would want another hefty fee and who probably wouldn't do anything to a colleague anyway. One lawyer suing another lawyer would just lead to further ineptitude. So Arvo let it go.

In the divorce proceedings, no one seemed to be concerned about Tiltu's losses in the casino. "The seventy or eighty thousand dollars that she lost is simply no longer part of your assets," Arvo's lawyer told him. "Under Michigan's no-fault divorce laws, her three affairs don't count either. The judge will simply divide your assets and hers."

"She doesn't have any," said Arvo.

The lawyer shrugged his shoulders and handed Arvo a hefty bill.

In the final settlement, Tiltu got over fifty thousand dollars. Arvo got their former home. "I can get myself my own home now," Tiltu said gleefully. Arvo wondered how their daughters would ever have money for college. "Nobody gave me money for college," replied Tiltu, "and I'm doing okay."

On a Saturday morning, Tiltu moved furniture into her apartment while Arvo was away at a friend's. She took as her half of the furnishings every piece of furniture and every item that she and Arvo had bought together, though she left him some pictures of the girls. "Arvo will be able to buy replacements because he makes more money than I do," Tiltu explained to her sister as they loaded a new rolltop desk into the truck bed.

Arvo had had to take out a second mortgage on the house in order to pay off Tiltu. "He should be able to pay it off by extra work in the summer," Tiltu explained to her sister. "In fact, I hope he does work summers because every increase in his pay increases my child-support money."

Tiltu's tiny apartment was eleven miles from Arvo's house. Their daughters spent most of their time with Arvo. He had custody every other week, but they also came often to his home after school during the other week because they considered his place to be home—their friends and school were nearby.

Time passed. Tiltu fought often with her Elo boyfriend, but they stuck together because she hadn't yet lined up someone else. While they were swapping the children on a Sunday afternoon, she told Arvo that the guy was too possessive. "He doesn't trust me," she said, "and I hate that."

Alone in his house, Arvo felt the darkness closing in. He became afraid that he was going to die young like his Aunt Lemppi or become a drunk like his Uncle Toivo or become a paranoiac recluse like his Uncle Lenni or end up nuts and locked away for years in a state mental institution like his Aunt Aina. Arvo was approaching sixty and had little hope that another vivacious young woman, like Tiltu but minus her sociopathic personality, would ever again enter his life. He no longer felt a pleasurable rush of adrenaline at the thought of finishing his life in Michigan's Copper Country. Now the region represented a shattered family, lost dreams, and broken promises. He remembered how Tiltu had once cried for three consecutive days at the thought of losing him and that she had then chosen to break every single bond that had united them. *Women are strange creatures*, he thought. But in the early morning hours, the darkness tunneled into his mind, displacing thought with a suffocating blackness without shape or end. Often he would bolt out of bed with a silent scream choking the inside of his head. Nothing could help. He felt without foundation and no one cared. Well, his daughters cared. But they weren't always there and, anyway, it didn't matter because the jarring of his sanity persisted. He was sure that he wasn't going to make it. He felt right on the edge of a bottomless pit. He had gray November in his soul. He knew he had to stop loving Tiltu. *A man has to be strong not to love because the world gets colder and colder every year*, he thought.

He remembered Aunt Aina sitting on the well curb and nodding her head back and forth to the ticking of a clock. He remembered Uncle Lenni, alone in the farmhouse pantry, ready to attack with a pitchfork anyone who stepped onto his property. *Those long-dead people were crazy, but they are my roots*, thought Arvo, and so he decided to seek meaning and rediscover a definition of himself by journeying with his daughters for two and a half days to the little Finnish mining town in northern Maine where he had spent his youth.

The town still sat along the shore of Lake Hebron. The lake itself, with its heavily wooded shoreline and its many inlets, was still pristine and beautiful, but the town was nearly dead. Main Street was littered with the hollow shells of former businesses. The slate quarries were no longer worked. One old man who lived by the main highway gathered pieces of slate from tailing heaps and sold these to tourists from the front porch of his home. Otherwise, the industry was gone. One small store remained open, selling beer, soft drinks, bologna and other over-priced items to the occasional customer who couldn't be bothered to drive twelve miles to the nearest supermarket. Arvo toured his past. Fields where he once played were now forest. His Finnish grandparents' farm was now a cemetery. The farm buildings had long since been razed, and Uncle Lenni was buried where the farmhouse once stood. The outer fields were now poplar forest. Arvo visited his own family's former home in the village. It had become a weathered shell. The school he had attended had been torn down. The gym where he had sought basketball immortality still stood but was now a dead monument to past glories. A high school girlfriend from forty years earlier had become a drug-addled, broken-toothed, and shapeless hag. Other high school friends had moved away—to Massachusetts or Connecticut or Colorado—leaving no ties to the past and no forwarding addresses.

Arvo took his daughters to visit their grandparents' graves. His daughters had never met them. Both had died before they were born. "When I die," he told the girls, "I want you to cremate my remains and scatter my ashes on your grandparents' graves." They promised to do that.

When they returned to Michigan, Arvo was still depressed. "I'm a ghost," he told his friend Sulo.

"You've got to believe in the mystery," said his friend.

Arvo didn't know what that meant. Because his children were with Tiltu that week, he felt utterly alone. To fill up an empty evening, he drove to Blockbuster to rent a movie. He chose a film called *Matewan* and found a new hero—Sheriff Sid Hatfield. During a coal-miners' strike in West Virginia, Sheriff Hatfield had prevented company thugs from evicting mining families from company housing. "I don't care if it is company property; these are my people, and I won't let you do this!" Sid had said.

"But we have the law on our side," the leader of the thugs had said.

"There's a higher law," Sid had replied.

When the thugs came back later to force the evictions, Sid had shot the leaders dead. But Arvo didn't have anybody that he needed to shoot. His life was smaller than that and less dramatic. Plus, it was a mess. "Just like a soap opera," he said aloud. His voice sounded hollow in the silence of his home.

The next morning Arvo heard on NPR an old folk song that intrigued him. The song was about Frankie Silver, the first woman hanged in North Carolina and one of the first women condemned in the entire country. Something about the song haunted Arvo, so he made a copy, and then through interlibrary loan he received several books about Frankie's trial. Soon Arvo was so drawn to the case that he couldn't sleep at night. He kept thinking about Frankie Silver on the scaffold. Arvo packed suitcases for himself and his daughters, and the family drove south for three days. In the southern Appalachians of North Carolina, Arvo located Frankie's grave in a disused churchyard cemetery. "They buried her in 1831," he told his daughters. "Earlier, they hanged her for killing her husband, dismembering his body, and trying to burn it in the fIreplace. He was killed at Christmastime in 1830."

"That's terrible," said Charlotte.

"There were lots of questions about what actually happened in their isolated cabin," said Arvo. "Frankie's husband was a large man who drank heavily. He could occasionally be abusive. Frankie, though, was very small. At the trial they called her *petite*. She was nursing a newborn that Christmas. Maybe her husband's actions endangered the baby. Maybe he struck the baby or her. Maybe there were other extenuating circumstances. Maybe she had help. Some people at the time thought she had. No one will know now."

"We love you, Daddy," said Charlotte.

"On the scaffold, facing a gloating mob, she was given a chance to speak, and she stepped forward to do so, but her father, who was in the back of the crowd, shouted over the heads of the others, 'Take it to your grave, Frankie!' and she did. How could he say that?" Arvo wanted to know. "The words that scream the loudest were never spoken. How could a father condemn his child to silence in the moments before she hanged? He should have taken her place or died trying to save her."

At that lonely gravesite Arvo felt acutely the indifference of people to each other and the indifference of the universe to everything. Arvo felt a need to embrace and comfort the long-dead Frankie Silver, but he turned away, threw his arms around his vibrantly alive daughters and led them back to the car. On the way home, they visited the grave of Sid Hatfield. Sid had been gunned down by company assassins a year after the confrontation on the streets of Matewan. Matewan itself was depressing—a broken and polluted place whose glory had long faded away.

The long drive back to Michigan's Upper Peninsula was uneventful. Somewhere in Ohio, Lucy suddenly said, "You're weird, Dad, but we love you for your weirdness. Nobody else's dad would drive for days just to visit two strangers' graves in another part of the country."

Maybe I am weird, thought Arvo, but he didn't feel weird. He just felt the great weight of a sadness.

"Let's stop at a motel with a pool," said Lucy.

A few days later, back in Michigan's Copper Country, Arvo came out of emptiness and into a waiting room of the emergency room at the hospital. He had a cloth hat on his head. Wires protruded from it. "What's going on?" he asked his friend Sulo, who was sitting nearby, looking worried. A nurse, one of Arvo's former students, also sat nearby.

"They just gave you an MRI and an EKG," Sulo explained. "You've been away for a while, but now, thank God, you're back."

"Where'd I go?" asked Arvo.

"I don't know," replied Sulo

Through the open door to a hallway that led to another waiting room, Arvo could see Tiltu. She was dressed to the hilt and looking extremely beautiful in a black outfit that Arvo had once bought her. Draped over a nearby chair was the long black dress coat that she wore to work because it made her look sophisticated and urban. "She's the one who put me here," said Arvo, staring at Tiltu through the doorway. "Get her out of here. Now!"

The nurse went out to tell Tiltu to leave, and a doctor came in. "The tests came out negative," said the doctor. "You don't have anything physically wrong with you. I conferred with a couple of my colleagues. We think you've had traumatic amnesia caused by extreme stress. Your brain just overloaded and short-circuited and took you away for a while. How do you feel now?"

"Like I want to die," said Arvo.

"I'll give you some pills for that," said the doctor. "They'll block the chemicals that cause your depression. They take about three weeks to reach full strength in your body. Then you'll feel fine. You may even be euphoric."

Arvo thanked the doctor but vowed to himself not to take the pills. *If all I have of Tiltu is pain, at least I have that,* he thought.

A week later, after a sleepless and panic-filled night on the suffocating surface of his empty bed in an empty room, Arvo rose early to go to the college for the first day of a week-long summer literature class for senior citizens. The topic was Finnish-American Writers, and thirty-two old folks had journeyed from all over the country to take it. Their RVs filled the parking lot in front of the college dormitory. Arvo had taught classes of seniors before, and they were always wonderful students—inquisitive and full of questions. They brought a lifetime of experiences to the discussions. As usual, Arvo stood by the building entrance to help if any of the seniors had trouble with the stairs that led to the classroom. As they approached across the parking lot, a hefty woman stumbled over a curb and fell hard onto tarmac, smashing her left knee, spraining her left ankle, and breaking her right. "I'm so angry at myself," the old woman said immediately. "Three months ago I fell and broke my shoulder and now I've done damage again."

The woman hunched on the tarmac for what seemed a long time. One of the seniors placed a notebook by her so that she wouldn't tear her knees when she tried to get up. Eventually she put her knees on the notebook and, with Arvo's help, she got to her feet. For a while she couldn't move because of excruciating pain. Arvo held the woman firmly under her good shoulder. Finally she baby-stepped over the offending curb and stood patiently until a van arrived to take her to the emergency room at the hospital. "I'm so angry at myself," the woman said again. "But I can make it."

Yes, you can, thought Arvo as the van took the woman away. Arvo led the remainder of the seniors into the classroom building.

In his youth Arvo had fulfilled a number of romantic and improbable dreams. Back then he had greatly admired Jack Kerouac's *On the Road* and *Dharma Bums*. Arvo, too, had wandered across the country after graduation from the University of Maine. He'd gone to graduate school in Michigan and

California and had then taught briefly in Vermont. Later still, he had worked as a Peace Corps Volunteer in the West African country of Nigeria, had taught English on the profoundly isolated Island of Moen in Truk Lagoon in the great emptiness of the Pacific, had traveled through Asia and had chaired the English Department at a women's college in Turkey. He had summered in Provence and Paris and roamed through Europe.

Now, with his summer teaching done, he sought new meaning in his life by recreating that past. He decided to again visit faraway places where he had once been acutely alive, starting with Nigeria. When Arvo had Peace Corpsed there in the late 1960s, one and a half million Nigerians had died in a civil war, in massacres and from starvation and disease. On the day in 1967 when the Peace Corps had ordered Arvo and his first wife (she, too, a Volunteer and eight months pregnant) to abandon their village because it was too dangerous to remain there any longer, Arvo had stuffed their few belongings into a backpack and had thrown the pack into the back of a U.S. Government van that would take them to the capital. In the meantime, the villagers had gathered around Arvo's wife, pleading with her not to leave. "If you stay here, we are safe," one of the villagers had said. "If you leave, the Nigerian Army will kill us all. We will have to hide in the forest or cross the river into Biafra, where our people are building a new nation."

Arvo and his wife had gotten into the van and ridden away, never to hear anything of those people again.

Now he wondered if any of them had survived the horrors of those days. Arvo had kept up with events in that unhappy country through an organization called Friends of Nigeria. He knew that Nigeria was now probably the most dangerous country in the world to visit. Large numbers of people were killed in grotesque ways. In the Niger Delta people punched holes in oil pipelines in order to steal and sell the oil. With the end of a crowbar or the blade of an ax, they smashed the line until oil poured out. They caught the oil in jerry cans and sold it in the market. Hundreds of people multiple times had been incinerated when the oil spills ignited. In one case the oil had spilled out of the rupture for months, forming a vast lake that exploded into a firestorm when an oil thief tossed a cigarette. In that same region kidnappings and tribal warfare were common. Oil executives and engineers lived in walled compounds with armed guards. In Nigeria's north, the Muslim authorities had declared Sharia law. Villagers routinely stoned to death women accused of adultery. They cut limbs off thieves. Mobs of Christians had fought mobs of Muslims. Entire towns had been destroyed.

Arvo knew that passengers on commercial flights into Lagos were sometimes robbed of their possessions as they disembarked, so he planned his trip carefully. He converted nearly all of his dollars into Traveler's Checks. He took nothing of great value with him. Even the clothes in his battered backpack were mostly cheap tee shirts from K-Mart. To make himself look less important, he let his hair and beard grow long and ragged. "You look like a tramp," one of his daughters told him.

"That's the idea," he said. His daughters were going to stay with their mother until he returned.

In mid-August he departed Michigan for Nigeria. He hoped to visit the bush village where he had been a Volunteer. He remembered again the stricken faces of the villagers on the day he left them, more than thirty years earlier.

On the plane, Arvo was befriended by a Nigerian who was returning home after completing his Ph.D. at Michigan State University. The Nigerian, an Ibo, was from Eastern Nigeria, the region that had seceded from Nigeria when Arvo was a Peace Corps Volunteer. The secessionists had called their country Biafra, but after a long and bitter war, a holocaust really, Biafra and many of its people had died. Talking to his fellow passenger, Arvo recalled his last full day in Nigeria. He and his pregnant wife had risen early to visit her doctor, a Catholic missionary nun, on the other side of the River Niger in Biafra. Rather than cross the only bridge, which was mined and guarded by soldiers with machine guns, they'd crossed into Biafra by canoe. His wife had seen the doctor, and they'd returned to the river. This time they'd decided to cross the bridge, but Arvo had been arrested. The Biafrans had thought he was an English businessman they'd detained earlier. The businessman had had a suitcase full of large-denomination pound notes. Arvo had been led down to the river bank and placed in a line of frightened people awaiting interrogation by a young Biafran officer. Some people ahead of Arvo had been quickly sent on their way, while others had been arrested. A few had been taken down the river and shot. When Arvo finally reached the front of the line, his interrogator had spoken perfect English. He had asked Arvo where he was from, and Arvo had explained that he was an American Peace Corps Volunteer. The officer had asked Arvo where he had trained, and Arvo had told him about Michigan State. The officer had asked Arvo the name of the MSU football team and had then admitted that he had gone to school there too. "How did the team do this year?" the officer had asked, and Arvo had told him. Later that officer had almost surely died, along with the rest of the officers in the Biafran Army.

By the time the two flew into Lagos seventeen hours later, the Nigerian passenger and Arvo were like old friends. As the plane taxied to a stop and the passengers disembarked, all were accosted by mobs of official-looking men exclaiming loudly the ways they could be of help. Some even had badges and uniforms and oversized hats.

"Get out of our way! Leave us alone!" shouted the Nigerian as he and Arvo pushed their way through the crowd. "These people just want a dash, a bribe," said the Nigerian. "They make their living off unwary travelers."

At customs there was a long line, but the Nigerian handed a customs officer some dollars, and he and Arvo moved magically to the front of the line. "Be sure to tell them that you do not have many dollars," said the Nigerian.

"Actually, I don't," replied Arvo. "I have Traveler's Checks."

"Those are safer, but hide them in the bottom of your socks or in your underwear," said the Nigerian. "Better to be safe than sorry."

As a customs officer checked the passport and personal belongings of the Nigerian, Arvo slid most of his Traveler's Checks out of his pocket and slipped them inside his underwear. He felt awkward with the booklets pressing his testicles. Finished with the Nigerian, the customs officer waved the man through and he departed, leaving Arvo on his own.

"Do you have dollars?" asked the customs man as he briskly stamped Arvo's passport.

"Fewer than five hundred," said Arvo.

"Let me see," said the customs man. Arvo withdrew his wallet, and the customs man reached for it, but Arvo pulled it away. He took out the dollars and counted them.

"Four hundred and six," Arvo told the official.

"You will sell them on the black market," said the customs man.

"No," said Arvo.

"You must register them," said the customs man, "You can bring dollars into Nigeria but you can't take them out. I will give you *naira* for the dollars. Otherwise, they are useless to you."

"I will exchange them at the bank,"said Arvo,

"I will give you a special rate," said the customs man.

"But that would be like the black market," argued Arvo.

"I am a government official," said the customs man. "It is okay." He winked broadly at Arvo.

"I will exchange them at the bank," insisted Arvo and handed the customs man twenty dollars. "This is payment for your good advice," explained Arvo.

The man quickly pocketed the money.

"And do you carry any technology?" asked the customs man. "Computer?"

Arvo shook his head no.

"Cell phone?"

Arvo had brought an inexpensive cell phone in case something terrible happened and he had to call for help. He had the phone number of the American embassy in a document case on his belt. Arvo showed the customs man the phone. The customs man reached out very fast, yanked it from Arvo' s grasp, and hid it somewhere behind him. "You could sell it on the black market. It must remain here," he said.

"I must have it to call friends," said Arvo. "How much is the customs fee?"

"Fifty dollars," said the customs man.

Arvo bargained him down to twenty.

"I want a receipt," said Arvo. "I don't want this to happen again."

The customs man laughed uproariously, winked, patted Arvo on the shoulder, and generally acted like they were old friends. He wrote out an official-looking receipt and handed it to Arvo. "You can pick up your baggage over there," he said, pointing to the far side of the terminal. "Welcome to Nigeria," he added.

Arvo joined other passengers as the baggage arrived. His friend from the plane had already picked up his only bag and was departing with a man who appeared to be his brother. As Arvo grabbed his backpack, dozens of young men tried unsuccessfully to wrest it from his grasp. They were all shouting at once, trying to earn a dash by being helpful.

Arvo succeeded in crossing the terminal without incident. Outside a mob of hawkers and beggars approached, but they were driven off by another mob of men who insisted on leading Arvo to a taxi. All of them expected a dash. Arvo selected a middle-aged man out of the mob. The man was wearing an official-looking uniform. "Get me a taxi," Arvo said and handed the man two dollars.

"Only two, sir?" said the man.

"Taxi," said Arvo.

From out of the mob a taxi appeared, and dozens of hands reached madly to open the door. Arvo dropped a dollar bill behind him, and the mob began to scream, push, shove, bite, and kick each other as they fought over the dollar. While they were distracted, Arvo threw his pack into the taxi, slid in himself, and shut the door. "Take me to the Commodore Hotel," he told the driver, who began the process of nudging the taxi through the crowd. Palms thudded on the roof, and voices shouted but soon they were clear.

The taxi wound its way through crowded streets, stopping often. At every stop someone tried to sell something to Arvo or the driver. The driver frequently screamed out the window.

After forty-five minutes, the taxi swerved suddenly into a narrow alley. They were somewhere in the endless poverty and filth of Lagos. A crowd of men appeared and surrounded the taxi. The driver got out and disappeared. The mob yanked open the taxi doors and pushed and pulled Arvo onto the street.

"Give us all you have," said one of the men, who seemed to be the ring-leader. Or maybe he was the only one who spoke English. "We will take your bag," The backpack had already disappeared. "Give us your clothes," said the man. "Leave everything in the pockets. We want that, too."

"No," said Arvo.

"Then we will kill you," said the man. He took a large knife from another man and shook it menacingly in Arvo's face. Other men waved machetes.

Soon Arvo was standing in the alley, wearing nothing but his underwear and socks. The mob had disappeared. The fake taximan had driven away. Dozens of people passed. None spoke to him but one must have gone to the police, for soon a policeman appeared. He sympathized with Arvo but indicated it was Arvo's own fault. "You should have insisted on a number-one taxi," explained the policeman. Only number-one is safe." The policeman led Arvo to some vendors who sold Arvo a tee shirt and some shorts and sandals. The tee shirt was from K-Mart and had been in Arvo' s pack a few minutes earlier. "This is guaranteed to fit," said the vendor as he sold Arvo Arvo's shirt. The shorts had also been Arvo's minutes earlier. The sandals were new.

The vendors followed Arvo and the policeman to a nearby bank, where Arvo cashed a Traveler's Check and paid them. The vendors laughed and winked to each other as Arvo removed the checks from his underwear. "You go with God," said one of the vendors as he took payment. The other vendor laughed loudly and slapped his thigh. Arvo bribed the policeman for his courtesy, and the policeman explained how to get to the American Embassy. The policeman also got Arvo a taxi and threatened the driver. "I want no harm to come to my friend," he told the driver. "Do you understand me?"

Arvo spent two days at the Embassy, waiting aimlessly and sleeping in the lobby, until his new passport was ready. The Embassy was like a fortress, and Arvo felt safe there. The Marine guards looked capable of repelling an army. Arvo knew now that he could not go back to the Nigerian village where he had spent part of his youth. That village would be gone. *Everything becomes memory*, he thought. Life passes into pages if it passes into anything. He felt like a gnarled and hollowed-out old apple tree. Maybe I can still bear fruit, he thought. Even a twisted apple has sweet spots.

On the morning of the third day, Arvo took a taxi to the airport, bought a new ticket, and awhile later boarded a flight back to America via London. On the plane he felt depressed but oddly exhilarated. He had faced hell and survived. His life in America awaited him. He had his daughters, his job, his writing. There was always the possibility of love. Love always appeared unexpectedly. Plus, Arvo was a Finn. He had *sisu*. He could rely on his own strength, his own ability to overcome adversity. "Which is worse?" he wondered aloud. "The inferno of Nigeria or the self-centeredness of Tiltu? It's a tie," he said aloud to himself.

He felt disconnected from the people around him. He felt old. He would not age well. "I hope I go down kicking and screaming," he said to himself.

"You're a queer one," said the British passenger beside Arvo. The man was on his way home to London.

"I don't normally talk aloud to myself," explained Arvo. "It's Nigeria. When I was here before, we called it WAWA—West Africa Wins Again."

"Nigeria does strange things to people," said the man. "I'm glad to be out of it."

"So am I," said Arvo.

"Are you a businessman or government?" asked the British passenger.

"A tourist," said Arvo.

"A tourist? To Nigeria?" The British passenger was shocked. "Nobody goes there as a tourist, not even you daft Americans."

"I did," said Arvo. "But it was a short trip."

"And what did you see?" asked the man.

"The heart of Lagos, the heart of darkness," said Arvo.

The British passenger looked more shocked. "Well . . . did you learn anything?" he asked.

"I certainly did," said Arvo. "I learned that I'm like an old tree."

"Bloody hell!" said the man.

"Yes," said Arvo and he closed his eyes. He was tired. He hadn't slept well at the Embassy. Moments later he was asleep.

Arvois Grandmother

The Portage Gazette, March 11, 1892

Last Saturday in Houghton the abandoned wife of Erkki Erkkinen was arrested for selling homemade liquor without a license. On Monday morning in circuit court Mrs. Erkkinen announced to the court that she wouldn't tell a soul that the judge was one of her best customers. She was sentenced to ninety days in the county jail and must pay a fine of twenty dollars. Mr. Erkkinen was sitting in the back of the courtroom with Miss Sonya Heikkinen. He paid the fine.

Loviisa received her coal-black hair, high cheekbones, Mongoloid eyes, and short stature from her Lapp mother, whose ancestors had herded reindeer on the tundra of the high arctic. Loviisa, however, was unaware of questions of race when, at ten, she raced laughing across the back field with her seven-year-old brother, Reino, in hot pursuit, a stick in his hand. In Reino' s imagination, the stick was a sword, and Loviisa was an ogre. At the edge of the forest, Loviisa, who imagined herself a princess, reached out with her left arm, palmed a birch sapling, and, letting her speed do the work, swung herself around the tree, reversing her direction, but her little brother couldn't stop. He plunged forward into the trees, tripped over a root, and fell forward onto the stick, driving it into his left eye socket. The eye itself popped out and struck the ground, which was covered with a thick matting of twigs and leaves and new seedlings struggling to find light.

Reino screamed and kept screaming. He was on all fours in the dirt, his eye lying on the ground among yellow birch leaves below his distorted face. The eye was still attached by the optical nerve. With difficulty Loviisa got Reino to sit up. She prayed loudly for Heavenly support. "Please, God, help me to help my brother! Please!" Then she tried to pull the stick from his eye socket, but he wouldn't let go. "You've got to let me pull it out!" she cried.

"No!" he screamed.

She tried to reason with him. "If you leave it in there, Mother will punish you!" she told him. "You'll have to stay in the pantry all day."

"No!" he screamed again, but his voice broke into a wail, a sign that he was weakening.

"I asked God to help us. Let Him do His work."

"No!" he screamed again, with renewed vigor.

Loviisa grabbed the stick with both hands and yanked as hard as she could against Reino's resistance. The stick popped out, and blood streamed from the wound. The soft flesh inside the socket was the color of fire. "We've got to clean you up," Loviisa told him, but he was crying too hard to listen. "I'm going to get a clean cloth. You wait here and I'll be right back."

Reino's shirt front was already drenched in blood, and it was leaking into his pants. His screaming had slowed to hard crying as she left him there by the edge of the field and raced to the small storage shed by the barn. Father kept containers of kerosene there. She took a jar from a shelf, spilled out the nails it contained, and half filled it with kerosene. Then she ran to the well pump and half filled a bucket with water. She put a dipper into the bucket and then raced back across the field to Reino, spilling kerosene and water with every stride.

Reino still sat helplessly where she had left him. He was groaning softly and rocking his upper body back and forth. The eye hung against his cheek. It was coated with blood and bits of dirt, grass, and leaf. A single large, black ant was scurrying aimlessly over its surface.

"With God's help, we're going to put your eye back in," she reassured him. "But first I have to clean it." She had forgotten a cloth. She took Reino's bloody stick, which had been sharpened at one end, and she thrust it against the hem of her skirt until she had started a small rip. With her hands, she tore off a ragged square of cloth. *I'll tell Mother I caught it on a nail,* she said to herself. In her most adult voice she ordered her brother to remain still. She dipped a corner of the cloth in the kerosene and tried to swab the eyeball, but Reino began to scream hysterically and thrash around, so she pushed him down and sat on his chest, with her legs wrapped tightly around his head. He tried to kick her but his legs thrashed only the air. He tried to knee her in the back but she sat firmly on his chest, and he could barely breathe. His arms were useless under her weight, and his head was locked in the vice of her legs. She swabbed the eye, careful to rub every part of it with the kerosene. Reino tried to scream in terror and pain but couldn't. Then she dipped another corner of the cloth in the water and rinsed the eye.

"This next part will hurt the worst. Try not to scream. We don't want Mother to hear."

Reino desperately wanted to scream, but his sister's weight prevented him from filling his lungs. He wanted to attack his sister and beat her terribly. But he couldn't move. She picked up the jar of kerosene and poured some into his eye socket. The pain was instant and unbearable, and his body shook with spasms. She put down the jar and pressed on his head firmly with her hands and turned it, and kerosene ran down the side of his face. She then turned the head back so that his face, with its one pleading eye, again looked straight into her own. She relocked her legs around his head, picked up a dipper of water from the nearby bucket, and poured the water into the socket. She kept pouring until she was sure that the kerosene was all out. With the cloth she removed from the socket several tiny bits of splinter and bark. She inspected the socket and then re-inspected it. It appeared to be clean.

"Now I'm going to put your eye back in. Don't be a baby," she told Reino. She redipped the cloth in the water in the bucket, squeezed out the excess, folded the cloth into a rectangle that fit into her palm, and then picked up the eye with the cloth. She lined the eye up carefully with the socket and then, with her cloth-covered palm, applied force. The eye popped back in.

"There. You're okay. Don't tell Mother or I'll beat you," she said.

By suppertime the area around the eye was puffy and purple, and the eye itself was bright red and burning. Loviisa told her parents that Reino had fallen and struck a rock. Reino remained silent.

A few days later the swelling and redness were gone and the eye was normal. Reino still had his sight.

From then on, Loviisa knew that she could handle whatever life threw at her. She had faith in her own abilities and faith in God. The only thing she truly feared was cancer, which took her mother when Loviisa was fourteen. By then there were four children in the family, and Loviisa's father, a tenant farmer on parish land, had to ask the parish for help. The church board auctioned off the children to local landlords, and they became *huutolainen*.

Loviisa only occasionally saw Reino and her other siblings after that. She became a housekeeper and laundress for the minister and his wife and their five children. Often she also helped the cook. Loviisa asked for and received the rent of a small strip of parsonage land. Working at night because the parsonage kept her busy all day, she cleared a garden plot. She grew a mixture of vegetables and a little rye for flour. She sold the vegetables and her homemade bread at a farmers' market in the town. With the profit, she bought herself tailoring tools and, late at night, while often exhausted from long labor at the parsonage, she sewed beautiful dresses for the ladies in the town. She herself every day wore the same rough homespun clothes of the cheapest materials.

Shortly after her nineteenth birthday she set out for America via Christiansted in Norway, where she boarded a ship for New York. From there she followed other folk from Kurikka to the slate quarries of Monson, Maine. On the journey she met a Matti Viitala from Vaasa and agreed to marry him because four arms were better than two. But before a wedding, they needed to survive. He stayed in a boarding house where she got a job as a cook, maid, and laundress. He worked all day in the quarry, hoisting great blocks of slate that had been cut from the wall of the pit two hundred feet below.

At night he returned to the boarding house exhausted and short of breath. The slate dust had begun the steady, slow process of eating away at his lungs.

But Loviisa and Matti earned more money than they had ever dreamed of having when they were in Finland. Out of every check they saved a little, and eventually, one fall, they bought themselves a sizeable farm lot three miles north of town. Almost all of their money had gone into the purchase of the land, but they had enough left over to buy lumber for a rude shed and a ruder sty. They kept a cow in the shed but it froze during a subzero January blizzard. Their three pigs survived and thrived on the garbage from the boarding house. In the spring, they hired Veikko Pentti and his team to clear a garden plot. "What kind of home begins with a sty?" he wanted to know.

That summer, with the help of a bank loan and their many friends in the Finnish community, they built themselves a home. The walls and floor were insulated with newspaper and sawdust, and the homemade braided rugs that covered the rough floorboards were thin, but eventually the house was livable. They used kerosene lamps for light, wood for heat, and a single pump at the well for water. A week after the family pictures from Finland were hung on the wall, they married at the Lutheran Church on Pleasant Street.

In ensuing years they had six children, including Arvid (Arvo's father), but Matti was wearing out. All day he did backbreaking work in the quarries, and much of the night he cleared land, improved their home, constructed outbuildings, built fencing, fed and watered animals, threw manure, drained the garden area, shoveled snow in winter, made wood in the fall.

When Matti slaughtered the pigs, he filled a barrel of brine with fatback. He constructed a rude smokehouse and smoked the hams. Loviisa joined in, as she often did with his never-ending chores. She pickled the hogs' feet and cut off the head flesh to make cheese. She washed the entrails with a small, hard brush until her hands ached. Then she made sausage by cutting up the meat, grinding it, spicing it, and packing it into the casings. From the blood she made more sausage, and for breakfast she made pancakes, using blood instead of milk.

Matti had little time for recreation, but he liked to fish and justified it by the thought that every caught fish was free food. In winter he fished through the ice for lake trout and pickerel. In spring he netted smelt from streams. In early summer he fished for brook trout in streams, and in summer he fished for trout and perch in Lake Hebron. Loviisa pickled fish, fried fish in rye flour, and baked fish in milk, with lots of dill.

Loviisa made bread every Saturday morning—braided *pulla* and flat *rieska*. For dessert she mixed rye flour, molasses, and orange rind and baked the mixture for three or more hours to make *mammi*. For winter she canned the garden vegetables. Matti and she picked wild apples from abandoned orchards to make sauce and jam. They picked wild strawberries, blueberries, and raspberries for pies and jams. They picked elderberries and dandelions to make wines. Along riverbanks, Loviisa picked fiddleheads for greens. They bought several cows to replace the first one that died. From the milk of these, Loviisa periodically made yogurt and *juustoa* cheese.

Loviisa had brought her sewing tools, including a sewing machine, from Finland. She made the family's clothes and sewed for her neighbors.

◄ • ►

In Monson, Maine, forty-five-year-old miners took short, rapid breaths because their lungs were packed with slate dust. In their fifties these miners, often done with mining, whiled away their remaining days struggling to breathe. At night in bed they gasped or wheezed, and in the day they sounded like panting dogs. When one of Matti's lungs hemorrhaged and was removed, the lung felt to the doctor like a leather sack full of large coins. The doctor hefted it several times and shook his head in disbelief. Matti had been breathing because of an open area the size of a grapefruit. The rest of his lung was packed with slate.

After Matti's death from silicosis, Loviisa converted the farmhouse into a boarding house for single miners, most of whom had recently arrived from Finland. Ten miners of the day shift slept in two rows of cots upstairs in what was previously the main bedroom. Ten other boarders were at work in the night shift. When a shift ended, they traded places. Loviisa spent her days racing to create order out of the constant disorder thrown out by twenty boarders. On laundry days she heated double tubs of water on top of the wood-burning stove. She hung the washed laundry on lines that criss-crossed the yard behind the farmhouse. In winter the sheets and shirts were so stiff that they snapped and popped as she folded them.

Meals were an endless chore. The day shift crew wanted a large meal in the morning, before they went off to the quarries. Plus they wanted a prepared lunch of homemade rye bread, *juustoa*, head cheese, meat pie, or *mojakka*. In the evening the night shift crew needed their large meal and wanted another prepared lunch.

The meals took large quantities of bakery and of meats. Several days a week Loviisa rose at four-thirty and baked breads, cakes, and pastries into the afternoon. Loviisa often worried about meat because it was perishable. In winter the slabs of meat were kept in covered buckets outside in the snow or on the open porch. In summer the meats were put into buckets that were lowered on ropes to the surface of the well. The cool water at the base of each bucket kept the meats from spoiling, even on the hottest July and

August days. Other foods in danger of heat spoilage were kept in one of the two root cellars.

And so Loviisa slaved away toward old age while all but one of her grown children left home, married, and began their own families. Her crazy son, Lenni, worked in the slate pits for a while but then quit, remained at home, and did nothing.

When Loviisa grew too old to manage the boarding house, she closed it up and retired. She received a tiny Social Security check each month from her dead husband's account. Soon after she stopped working, the slate industry died, and the town's population dropped precipitously. Jobless miners moved away, and if they didn't, their children did, as they reached adulthood. The only signs that there had ever been mining in the town were the eighteen great holes in the earth and the mountainous tailing heaps.

Arvo's dad, Arvid, remained in the town. He was a butcher and a store owner. He took care of Loviisa and crazy Lenni, bringing food, clothes, and money to the isolated farmhouse. During a January blizzard when Loviisa was sixty-eight, Lenni locked her out, and she froze her legs. One had to be amputated. After that she hopped about on one leg and a homemade wooden crutch.

The fall that Loviisa turned seventy, she hopped into the backyard with a load of washed laundry. It was November and cold but clear. In the middle of hanging one of Lenni's shirts on the line, a hunter's random bullet struck her in the chest, tore open her heart, and killed her instantly. No one ever knew who had fired the shot or from where. In November in northern Maine, the woods contain more New York, Massachusetts, Connecticut, Rhode Island, and Maine hunters than there are deer. One of those hunters (Arvo likes to think it was some idiot from Boston!) had missed a deer but killed an old, half Lapp/half Finnish woman who was still doing the work that she had done all of her life.

Afterwards, Lenni, of course, got crazier. (The author has written about him in other books. He lived alone after his mother's death, guarding what he considered to be his property. He used a pitchfork to terrorize anyone naive enough to approach the farmhouse.)

Arvo's dad, Arvid, paid the property taxes every year and fed and clothed Lenni. Lenni broke windows, threw paint at walls, burned wooden chairs, and repaired nothing. Eventually, as the main rooms of the farmhouse became unlivable, Lenni moved into the pantry, where he had a cot and a wood-burning stove. In the other rooms outside of his pantry, plaster collapsed, wood warped, upholstery became moldy, and mice took up residence. When he turned fifteen and got his driver's license, Arvo brought his Uncle Lenni food several times a week.

On Christmas morning of 1959, Arvo received as presents a black leather motorcycle jacket with orange rabbits' feet dangling from the zippers, a black leather motorcycle hat with a winged-tire logo on the front of the brim, and tall black leather engineer boots. A month earlier Arvo had purchased for one hundred twenty-five dollars a 1950 green Oldsmobile whose rear end was jacked up so that the car always appeared to be nose-diving into the earth. The young Arvo thought the car looked really cool. Plus the steering wheel had a suicide knob for whipping around corners at high speeds. Of course Arvo was disappointed that he had no motorcycle, but he proudly wore his new motorcycle garb out to his Oldsmobile and drove the three miles to the old farm to bring Uncle Lenni a plateful of Christmas dinner.

Arvo parked by the side of the road, climbed over the five-foot bank of snow thrown up by the plow, and pushed his way through thigh-deep snow to the front porch of the broken farmhouse. The porch leaned sharply away from the house while the house itself leaned sharply toward the road. Beams from the collapsed barn propped up the road side of the house and had slowed the building's eventual disintegration. Arvo had to pull himself up onto the porch because the stairs were missing. Then he had to leap across a space and through the front door that was frozen open by the house's tilt.

Inside, everything was in shambles. Wind and snow blew freely through shattered windows. Arvo strode over broken glass and crumbled plaster, through drifting snow, and past unrecognizable furniture. At the back of the house he arrived at the pantry off the former kitchen. He found Uncle Lenni in there, bearded and long-haired and wrapped in many layers of dirty, soot-saturated clothes. He was sitting on the cot by the blazing fire. That fall Arvo and his dad had cut the stovewood and piled it in neat rows in the kitchen.

Arvo handed Uncle Lenni the plateful of food. Lenni took it, but, instead of wolfing it down in his usual manner, he set it beside him on the cot and stared hard at Arvo's hat. Then he examined Arvo's new black leather jacket and his new black leather boots. He reached out and fingered one of the orange rabbits' feet. "What in hell did you do?" Uncle Lenni asked. "Did you join the Foreign Legion?"

Arvo said nothing. He didn't want to set Lenni off. Lenni's pitchfork leaned nearby in a corner. Lenni had sharpened the tines so that they glistened like knife blades. "When they let you out, I want them boots!" Lenni added.

Now, decades later, in 2003, Arvo remembers that long-ago day. The farmhouse that Matti and Loviisa built lives only in memory. The outbuildings are also gone. The fields that they cleared have been taken over by ash and poplar forest. The area where the buildings once stood is now a town cemetery. Crazy Uncle Lenni is buried only a few feet from the pantry where he spent his final years. Arvo' s parents are also long dead. They are buried in another cemetery in that town. The town itself is nearly gone. It became a kind of ghost of itself when the mines closed long before, and, ever since, it has continued to fade away. The school where Arvo found academic and athletic glory is closed. The businesses on Main Street are closed. The buildings that contained them are decaying.

Arvo has lost his roots.

Now he has lived many years in northern Michigan, where street signs are in Finnish and where he teaches in a Finnish university.

Here he raises his daughters and tries to instill in them some echo of their Finnish heritage. Occasionally he takes them back to Maine so that they can see what isn't there. He hopes that he succeeds in making his daughters kind inheritors of their ethnic roots, but lately he feels utterly alone and abandoned in the middle of America. He feels dislocated, fractured. Maybe it's America. It's a continent wide.

And where are the loves we have had and have lost? Where? Arvo wants to know.

Arvo's Confession

The Portage Gazette, June 6, 1889

Miss Inkeri Polkkinen was to have been married to her sweetheart, Robert Asiala, at the Finnish Lutheran church in Calumet on Saturday afternoon, but she died instead. She was buried in her wedding dress on Monday amidst much grieving. She was nineteen.

Arvo is, of course, the author.

"Why do you disguise yourself and everyone else in your life?" asks Arvo's closest friend, Sulo, who is really named Timo. "Over and over again in all of your stories in all of your books, you disguise real people. Why do you do that?"

And I have no answer. I write obsessively of the crises in my own and others' lives. I write of losses—of the long-dead Finnish-speaking grandparents I barely knew, of the Finnish father and New England mother who never understood each other and who sparred often and for a long time, of the third- and fourth-generation children of Finnish immigrants who are gradually losing the old culture but often failing to gain the new.

But that doesn't explain the need to disguise. Recently a student interviewed me for her senior practicum in Human Services. She needed someone to play the role of patient while she pretended to be a therapist. She showed me a chart in her textbook.

The chart purported to evaluate stress levels. "The types of stress at the top of the list are worth lots of points. A therapist adds up the points and knows the level of stress of the patient," explained the student, who was actually Lillian, the wife of my closest friend, Timo. "More points mean greater stress. At the top of the chart is divorce. You've been divorced twice. Next is jail. You've been jailed but actually didn't do anything, and you are still very angry about the unfairness. Next is war. You were in Biafra, in the midst of a holocaust in which millions were slaughtered by being chopped to death by machetes, burned to death in a necklace of tires, or shot to death by the army. You're old enough that you've lost both parents to death, and you've had to sell yourself your own house several times during the divorces; so you have a huge mortgage. Your beautiful daughter Charlotte has diabetes, and you've been hospitalized yourself from traumatic amnesia and high blood pressure. In addition, you're a single parent. My God! If I add up the point values of all of these things, you are way off the chart. Most people in your situation would turn to God or alcohol or drugs or attempt suicide; but you haven't done any of those things."

"No, I haven't," I said.

"Plus, you refuse to take the pills that your doctor prescribed. How do you remain sane?"

"I don't," I said. "For example, right now I'm right on the edge of going nuts."

"Your ex-wife did terrible things to you. Most people would not believe it possible for one person to do all of that to another. Most people couldn't even conceive of half of her deeds. How did you put up with it?" Lillian asked.

"I don't know. I just did," I said. "It's because I loved her. I love her now. I'll always love her. She took my heart with her when she and all of our best furniture went out the door."

"Maybe you need to turn that love into hate and then just forget her," said Lillian.

"Easier said than done," I said.

"Maybe you need a new woman—someone nice and caring."

"Yes," I said.

In class I asked my students how many had been shot at. "Let's count those hands," I said. Most raised them. Many had survived an armed ex. One had been in an Old West-type gunfight inside a trailer. That kind of confrontation leaves permanent scars. I had a Colt .38 rammed against my temple when I was an eighteen-year-old member of a geodetic survey crew on the Maine/Quebec border. The potential killer was Ed Suomi, a crazy World War II veteran who reeked of death because he had fought from Normandy Beach to the Brenner Pass in Austria. He kept repeating those geographic points while he held the gun tightly against my head. I was stretched out on a rough bunk in a logging camp. Moments before, I had been asleep. "I ain't gonna let no eighteen year old push me around," he kept repeating until an engineer from the Korean War tackled him from behind, knocking the gun to the floor.

Hunters have shot at me several times when I was hunting. Those were accidents. A relative blew out the windshield on his own truck when a partridge flew from the roadside across the hood. At the time, he had parked at the edge of a dirt secondary road, had taken his loaded shotgun and gotten out, and had walked up the road a short distance to check out an abandoned orchard that often in the fall contained game birds.

I was walking with that relative when he whirled and fired at his own truck. I was also, on another occasion, unhappily standing under an apple tree of a long-abandoned farm when several partridges flew into the branches just above my head. Three nearby hunters began to blast away at the birds as I dropped to the ground with my hands over my head. I was showered with splintered wood, limbs, and bark as birdshot ripped portions of the tree apart.

Those kinds of events are not particularly stressful beyond the moment, but it took me twenty years to write about the horrors of the Biafran War. Now, of course, Biafra is forgotten. The current generation has never heard of it. It's not even a loss. It's nothing. But millions died, and I was there.

Lately, at odd times and frequently, I feel the nothingness that Hemingway describes so eloquently in "A Clean Well-lighted Place." The nothingness is all that I feel. It's as if there is a hole inside me that can't be filled. That hole used to be filled with Tiltu, but that was before the many affairs, the drunkenness, the verbal abuse, the gambling. Now the hole inside me is a bottomless well. Or it's quicksand that smothers.

"You have to get on with your life," friends tell me.

"Easier said than done," I say.

And so I invent disguises. I create phony fictions instead of truthful memoirs.

"But everyone knows it's about you," Timo says. "Sometimes it's even about me."

"I know," I say. But it doesn't matter. It's as if the full frontal assault of truth is just too painful or too dangerous to confront. So I fabulize. I costume and mask. I add and subtract. I fictionalize. And yet the essential truth is still there. The pain is still there—the emptiness.

"Keep loving those daughters of yours," friends tell me. "Even if every-one else leaves, your daughters will stick by you."

"Yes, they will," I reply. "I'm the luckiest man in the world because I have them."

I can be sentimental about Maine because I grew up there, but the Maine I knew is gone. The slate mines of my hometown have closed, and the town has become a ghost of its former self. The Finns who made up much of the town have either died or moved away, scattered across the continent like me in Michigan, my sister in Illinois, and my brother in California. My par-ents have died. My parents' friends, who disapproved of the way I portrayed my parents (without a disguise) in *Hunting Hemingway's Trout*, have died. Almost everyone I knew in Maine is gone.

I love Massachusetts because it has produced an amazing number of writers I love—Bradstreet, Dickinson, Hawthorne, Thoreau, Kerouac, plus its adopted son, Melville, to name a few. Plus, I love the Red Sox, those definers of angst and existential nothingness for baseball fans. On my desk in a special place of honor, I have a baseball signed by Ted Williams and Jim Piersall.

There are other places that I love with equal fervor. I can create a romantic haze about the Pacific Islands because I taught in Truk Lagoon in the East Carolines of Micronesia. Plus, I have summered in Hawaii. I love Paris because Parisians respect all of the arts and support them. If they knew I was a writer, they'd let me go to the front of the line as a sign of respect for the artist. Plus, they eat well—France produces four hundred and fifty dif-ferent kinds of cheese and an amazing number of recipes for sweetbreads and salads. I have loved the many schools where I have studied—the University of Maine, Michigan State, the University of the Pacific, Indiana University, Cornell, Westbrook, New Mexico, Ferrum, Guadalajara, the University of Nigeria, the East-West Center in Honolulu, Mount Holyoke.

But most of all, for many years, I have loved Michigan's Copper Country. But now, because of the monstrous actions of Tiltu, that love is in danger. Now, when I cross the Mackinac Bridge going north or enter the Upper Peninsula from Wisconsin, I no longer feel a rush of pleasure. An emptiness follows me everywhere I go—even here in the Keweenaw. Right now, as I sit at my desk and type in my office on the fourth floor of Mannerheim Hall at Finlandia University, an emptiness surrounds me, threatens to drown me.

"So, what are you going to do about this emptiness?" Timo asks me.

"I don't know," I say. "Sometimes I just want to die. In fact, I feel certain that I am going to die. But I want to finish this book first."

"That's foolish talk," says Timo. "Seek the mystery."

"I don't even know what that is," I say. And I don't.

In the beginning was the *word*, and I can only hope that the words themselves still carry meaning . . . and hope . . . and love.

Arvois Student

The Portage Gazette, November 16, 1891

On Saturday night Amy Myllyoja of Hancock died after her husband, Uno, used her in an inhuman manner. On Sunday after church a mob beat him and forced him to flee from town. No one knows where he has gone. If you know, contact the authorities.

W hen she was barely fifteen, she became pregnant with the baby of a thirty-five-year-old married neighbor with children. After the baby was born, she applied for ADC, and the State immediately pressed charges against the baby's father. He was jailed for several days and then was listed as a sex offender.

To support herself and the baby, she lied about her age and got a job as an aide in a home for the mentally deficient. By the time she turned twenty, she had gained so much weight that co-workers described her as "huge."

Not long ago she married a fellow worker who was also terribly lonely, but within a month of the wedding, she began a three-month affair with a newly divorced man ten years older than she. Then her husband left and filed for divorce.

This morning she came to work with her recently developed wedding pictures in her left hand and her crisp, new divorce decree in her right. Her eyes shone with light when she showed fellow workers her wedding pictures. She sobbed uncontrollably when she showed them the divorce decree.

Her ex-husband is now dating the ex-wife of the man from her ex-affair.

"I've made a mess of everything," she told her colleagues, her body shaking from hard sobs.

Yes, you did, you stupid woman! They wanted to tell her. "You'll find another," is what they said.

They would have taken her out for a drink if she'd been old enough.

Arvo as a Pond

The Portage Gazette, August 14, 1890

On Friday James Moilanen startled the evening third-level pit crew as he fell past them to his death at the bottom of the shaft. Mr. Moilanen had been drinking earlier. He leaves a wife and three children. Funeral services will be at the Painesdale Lutheran Church on Monday.

The words echo in my head during the silent drive home from Charlotte's Youth Orchestra concert.

"You weren't there, were you, Dad?"

"No, I wasn't."

But Tiltu was, with a guy in a sportscoat. They held hands coming out. Her hair was tinted blonde, and she wore a long, gray skirt I had bought her. She stood out as the most beautiful woman in the crowd of moms, dads, brothers, and sisters.

I had planned to attend my daughter's premier as a symphony clarinetist. I had even driven to the Rosza Center, where I saw Tiltu's car in the parking lot. I could not force myself to park and go inside, where I surely would see Tiltu.

Sulo, that wise man, did it right when he went out the door in Amherst, Massachusetts, in 1972, walked with focus to his truck, got in, backed out of the driveway and, without once looking back, drove to Negaunee, Michigan, to renew an old life and to begin a new one. He hadn't been in Amherst since. Or in Massachusetts. Or in New England. Or on the East Coast.

Because he never looked back and never left a forwarding address after she said she was leaving him, he sometimes joked decades later that he might not be divorced.

But I am. And it's killing me.

I'm divorced from Tiltu, a demonic siren, a succubus. And my life is fractured into bits and pieces. I've lost my soul and my desire to live. I've lost the comfort I always felt in Michigan and I can't return to Maine, where I am a ghost, and I think of the myriad number of other places that I've loved and lost. And I've lost people, dozens of once-were and would-be friends. I've lost . . . lost . . . lost.

And my daughter is slipping away, my beautiful daughter that I'd be willing to die for but am not able to watch in concert because Tiltu is there. I'm a coward, a broken-down old man who cannot face a single, momentous defeat.

And why should I care? I've been places and accomplished things that Tiltu, in her profound and all-encompassing provincialism, cannot even comprehend.

And the disappointment in my daughter's voice is like the sound of rain on the surface of a pond.

And I am the pond.

Arvo, Vaasa, and Sheriff Hatfield

The Portage Gazette, July 14, 1886

On Tuesday a section of the Hecla mine collapsed. Two miners were buried under the rubble and are presumed dead. Kalevi Tahtinen's lower left leg was crushed under a large rock. Rescuers amputated the leg at the knee joint. Mr. Tahtinen was taken to the hospital, where he is recovering.

In 1917 Johani Kurtti escaped the drudgery of the family farm in Vaasa by joining the White Guards. The times were momentous. Finland had just declared itself independent from neighboring Russia, and Russia itself was in the throes of a revolution. But there were workers in Finland, especially in southern Finland, who wanted a Bolshevik revolution in Finland too. The Finnish communists had formed Red Guard units and were trying to assert their authority all over Finland. The Red Guards were a threat to the family farm. Johani both loved and hated that farm. He loved the smell of the grass in the spring and the hay in the summer. He loved the comfort of the farmhouse in the winter when outside temperatures dipped far below freezing. He loved the sauna, which was set among a stand of birches behind the house. He even loved the rude path, often muddy in the spring, that led to the building. Johani was especially proud of the workmanship in the sauna and the farmhouse and even in the barn and other outbuildings. Every corner was square, and every log was fitted snugly against its neighbors.

At the same time Johani hated the isolation of the farm, with its constant chores. It seemed that as soon as one task was completed, at least two more had already sprung into existence. The work was endless and repetitive and physical. There were no days off.

And so Johani had joined the White Guards. His father had grumbled at first because he needed Johani's labor, but Johani successfully argued that his military duties were only temporary and that someone had to protect the new government from Marxist ideologues and from re-integration into Russia. "No more Tsars or Lenins, and no more service in the Russian army!" Johani proclaimed.

And so his father let him go just before Christmas. Johani spent a month in rudimentary training, and by January of 1918 he and two hundred other Guards were manning a blockade of the North/South rail line at Vilppula. Just north of the town was a railroad junction and an East/West rail line that the

Whites used for moving troops and supplies and for communications. Holding Vilppula was essential to General Mannerheim's strategy. Mannerheim visited his Guards at the beginning of the blockade, looking splendid in his white uniform, and spoke Russian to one of the officers and Finnish and Swedish to the troops. Johani was glad the general was on his side.

The blockade was made up of anything and everything that the White Guards could find to throw across the tracks. Mostly it was logs. The men felled them with axes, roughly limbed them, and then used horses to drag them across the tracks. The men then built a crude wall out of the logs and reinforced it with burlap sacks of dirt. Because the earth was frozen rock solid, the dirt had to be heated first—with fires made from the green limbs plus whatever was dry enough to burn—birch bark, boards from outbuildings, rags, bits of paper, the brown lower branches of evergreens. When the fire's heat thawed the earth, it was shoveled into the sacks. Large boulders were dug out of the waist-deep snow and dragged to the middle of the tracks as an added deterrent. "If they bring up heavy artillery, they'll blow us all to hell in a few minutes," their commander told them, but the Whites had some artillery of their own.

Neither side wished to destroy the rail tracks. The Whites wanted to use it to ride victoriously southward to Helsinki if they won. The Reds wanted to use it to ride north to defeat the Whites.

All through January and into February, temperatures hovered well below freezing, and snow fell steadily until the surrounding forest was chest deep in the white stuff. Every morning just before dawn, the Red train chugged north to within a short distance of the White barrier. The Whites always knew the time of the train's arrival because White sympathizers telephoned from down the line to give the train's speed and location. The Whites always fired their artillery to keep the train just beyond its range, and the Reds always fired theirs to keep the Whites behind their barrier.

Every morning, under cover of fire from the train, Red Guards would try to flank the barrier through the woods, but their movements were always in slow motion because of the depth of the snow. Every morning White Guards struggled through the same snow to cut them off. Naturally both sides used the trees as cover. Sometimes they were close enough to chat. "Jesus, it's cold today," a Red Guard might say. The Reds were always complaining about the cold because they spent their nights in the train's uninsulated boxcars, and the small wood-burning stoves in each did not heat them sufficiently; and even if they did, the cold seeped in through the walls. For the Reds the war was a time when they could never get warm. The Whites, though, slept in the well-insulated houses of Vilppula. They had only boredom to contend with—which they fought by playing endless games of cards.

Most of the White Guards were farm boys like Johani. Most of the Reds were factory workers. "Where are you from?" a Red might shout at Johani from behind his tree.

"Vaasa," Johani would answer. "We have a farm there."

"I hear the girls of Vaasa are very beautiful," the Red might shout.

"Yes," Johani might reply.

"Do you have a sister?" the Red might shout. This was, in fact, a common question. If Johani replied in the affirmative, he and his foe might make a temporary truce to exchange photos. Each would weight the picture and throw it within reach of the other. "Your sister is very beautiful," a Red might say to Johani, but Johani would be busy, staring at the picture of the Red's sister. After a few minutes, each would toss the photo back to its owner and then the war would commence.

On a particularly cold and dead-calm day, a Red named Jussi introduced himself to Johani from behind a tree only a few meters away. The Red said that he wanted to meet Johani's sister. "You tell her that after the fighting is over, and we've won. I'll come to see her. She should expect a visit from Jussi from near the piers in Helsinki."

Johani shouted back that he would be the one meeting a sister. "And I'll bed her too," he shouted.

Often the Guards would try to persuade each other to switch sides, but if anyone showed himself, everyone on the opposing side fired volleys. Every day hundreds of rounds were fired, but only rarely was someone hit. Death was rare. The best marksman among the Whites was Andrew Kirkki. If a Red showed even a small part of himself, Kirkki made him pay.

As each short winter day approached its close, the Reds reversed the train's engines and rolled back down the tracks to a communist-friendly hamlet. Then the Whites posted guards and went inside to play cards and drink coffee. Every few days, some of them went to nearby farmhouses to take saunas and to do their laundry. Occasionally one would go home to see his folks.

Near the end of January the Reds increased their forces to five hundred, but so did the Whites. In February each side mustered over nine hundred men. On February twelfth the Reds sent six hundred fifty men to outflank the barricade and to take Vilppula. The Whites used their artillery and blasted the forest. The Guards kept up a withering volley of rifle fire. The Reds suffered dozens of losses, but Juhani and the other Whites remained relatively safe behind the barricade and behind the safety of Vilppula's buildings. As darkness approached, the Reds retreated, loading their wounded and dead onto a rail car marked with a giant red cross. They retreated down the line.

In ensuing days there were no more dramatics—just the usual forays accompanied by ineffectual shooting. Johani grew increasingly bored, especially after White Guard victories in other sectors. An ultimate victory was ensured. In the spring, the Reds either fled or conceded. Johani moved into Helsinki with other Guard units. Within days of his arrival, Johani roamed the pier district in search of Jussi the Red. After many mistakes he located the home of the correct Jussi. A young woman with black hair and blue eyes opened the door to Johani's persistent knock. She verified that her brother had, indeed, been in the fighting at Vilppula. "But he's crossed into Sweden," she said. "He said he was going to America by way of Norway. He had an old flier from a company in Michigan that recruits our people for its copper mines. He said that he could earn good money there."

"I came to meet Jussi's sister," explained Johani. "I told him I'd take care of you. I'm from Vaasa. We have a farm."

◁ • ▷

In America Jussi lived in a boarding house in Calumet, Michigan, and worked for the Calumet and Hecla Copper Mining Company. For a while he kept quiet about his past, rarely went out in the evening or on weekends, and preferred to work alone. He gained a reputation as an overly shy, hard worker. In spite of his self-imposed reticence and reclusiveness, Jussi had a way with languages. From the day he arrived in America, he listened carefully to the English around him and soon spoke the language well.

A few years before Jussi's arrival, Michigan's copper miners had gone on strike. The strike had quickly turned nasty—with acts of violence and sabotage on both sides. The Wobblies had been heavily involved in the strike, but when seventy-two children died at a Christmas party in a union hall, some people blamed the Wobblies for creating the violent atmosphere that led to the tragedy. The Wobblies' influence waned.

Jussi, however, was drawn to the Wobblies. They espoused the same ideas that he had found attractive in the Finnish Communist Party. Jussi returned to his old activist ways. Soon he spent many of his evenings among fellow radicals. They drank a lot of beer together and talked incessantly about revolution. Jussi became a union organizer and gained a reputation as a hothead with a stubborn streak. "You can't talk to him. He already knows it all," said the company men.

By 1920 Jussi' s constant tirades against the company and his frequent threats to blow up company property had become a hindrance. He was no good in contract talks because he refused to compromise. "To hell with the company," he'd say. "What we need is a revolution so that we miners own the mines. After all, we're the ones who do all the work."

When the call went through the union ranks for organizers to go into Mingo County in West Virginia to organize striking coal miners, the Wobblie hierarchy recommended Jussi for the job. It was their way of getting rid of him.

In Matewan, West Virginia, Jussi met a hard-living sheriff named Sid Hatfield. Sheriff Hatfield was a drinker and womanizer who turned a blind eye to moonshining and poaching. A diminutive five-foot-six, Sheriff Hatfield had a streak as stubborn as Jussi's. When the coal company brought in Baldwin-Felts detectives to evict miners' families from their company-owned homes, Sheriff Hatfield confronted the legalized company thugs. "I don't care if you have eviction notices signed by a judge, and I don't care if these people are accused of living illegally in company housing. Most of these families have lived here all their lives, and I won't let you do this. They have nowhere else to go," said Sid. "What kind of men are you?" he added.

"But we have the law on our side," said the leader of the thugs.

"There's a higher law," said Sid. "I'm ordering you men out of my county, and if you come back, I'll kill you." Then Sheriff Hatfield deputized every man in Matewan. "Get your guns, boys. If these gentlemen are still here when you get back, shoot them."

As the men scattered to get weapons, the company thugs retreated. Days later, they reappeared in greater numbers, and Sid met them at the edge of town. The thugs were led by the Felts brothers themselves, who probably thought that their reputations gave them a kind of immunity from the threats of small-town officials such as Sheriff Hatfield. "If you take one step toward my town, I'll kill you," Sid told the assembled mob of company enforcers. A moment later, when one of the Felts brothers did take a step in order to try to hand the eviction notices to the sheriff, without hesitation Sid shot him and his brother dead.

Seven people died that day in the streets of Matewan, most of them company thugs. Jussi himself fired from a rooftop, wounding a thug in the leg.

No jury in West Virginia would convict the sheriff for doing his duty and for doing what was morally right. Jussi had found a man who represented the best kind of revolutionary. Jussi visited Sheriff Hatfield several times after the shooting, and when the first union contracts were signed, he made a point to visit the sheriff and shake his hand. By then the sheriff was married to the mayor's widow. The mayor had been killed in the shootout. A few days later, Jussi boarded a train and returned to his home in Michigan.

Jussi wasn't welcome. The union had given his position to someone else, and the company refused to rehire him as a miner. "You're too much of a hothead," he was told by both workers and bosses.

Jussi had lived inexpensively outside of his union work and had saved some money. He bought some land on Little Moscow Road in rural Tapiola and began to farm and to log. Most of his neighbors were former Finnish Reds who had also fled Finland when their cause was lost. Jussi had no time to talk to his like-minded neighbors, however. He had become bitter and perpetually angry, and he took out his anger in work.

He put in long hours and worked twice as hard as a normal man. Living alone, he banked most of the money. Eventually he invested in more land and in housing. He built several boarding houses on land he acquired near mining locations. He became the landlord of dozens of single miners. He also built rows of cheap, ramshackle houses on the edge of Calumet and rented these to mining families. The families were eager to move in because they preferred to live in anything that wasn't owned by the company.

By the close of the twenties, Jussi was a wealthy man, a kind of Red capitalist. When the stock market collapsed in 1929, Jussi didn't lose a dime because he hated Wall Street and hadn't invested any of his money in stocks. "It serves them right," he said. "Maybe it will bring on the revolution."

In 1930 Jussi's sister's sister-in-law, Ani, emigrated from Vaasa. Jussi met her at the train station, and he fell in love with her the moment their eyes met. From that day, he courted her day and night. "I'm a wealthy man," he told her. "I can give you whatever you want." He built her a log home on a lakeside property he had acquired near the Calumet waterworks.

But she wouldn't marry him. "My family would disapprove," she tried to explain to him. "My brother hates Reds. Johani fought against you in the Civil War. He says you tried to kill him. I think he married your sister just to spite you. Of course, he now loves her, and he's a good husband to her, but our marriage would never work."

"But I'm a rich man," said Jussi.

"I don't find you attractive," said Ani. "You are too thin and too intense. I don't care for your politics or for your hunger for money. There's no one worse than a failed revolutionary." Jussi tried to argue with her but that made matters worse.

And so Jussi's marriage plans collapsed. Ani went to work as a maid for a lawyer and his wife, and when the wife died suddenly from an embolism, the lawyer married Ani.

Jussi became perpetually and forever bitter. He set out singlemindedly to become the richest man in the Copper Country. As the years passed, he became wealthier and wealthier. People learned to stay out of his way. "That man would take the food right out of his own mother's mouth if he could make a profit from it," people said.

The log house that Jussi built for Ani withstood the passage of time. Jussi had put a lock on the front door in 1930, and in 1960 the rusting lock still held. Every time Jussi passed the house, he was reminded anew of his loss— of the emptiness of much of his life. In the ensuing thirty years, America had passed through the Great Depression, World War II, and the boom of the fifties. Finland had had its own Great Depression and had fought Russia twice, in the Winter War and in the war to regain Karelia. Observing Stalinist Russia from afar, Jussi had become disillusioned with Communism. By 1960 he owned plenty of land, plenty of houses, and plenty of stocks. He was known as the Copper Country's number-one slumlord. He put very little maintenance into his buildings, but he filled them with students and with welfare families.

In the fall of 1960, the local paper began an investigation of Jussi's business dealings and of his past. Jussi read every article. The reporter called Jussi "an ex-Communist who has fallen in love with capitalism." In a series of follow-up editorials, the paper implied that Jussi had become rich by taking advantage of the poor. The paper implied that Jussi was a political hypocrite.

Jussi was furious. When he caught a photographer in one of his slummiest buildings, Jussi told the man to leave immediately and not to take the camera. The young photographer continued to snap pictures of the dreary hallway, with its peeling paint and dim lighting. Jussi exploded with anger. He hurried out to his car and from the glove compartment he retrieved the pistol that he had carried with him ever since the long-ago battle for Vilppula in Finland in 1918. He had once aimed that pistol in the direction of Johani but had never fired because Johani was hidden behind a tree. Jussi returned to the hallway where the photographer was still taking pictures. "If you take one more photo, I'll kill you," Jussi told the young man.

The young photographer ignored Jussi and knocked on an apartment door. After a moment a young, single mother opened the door a few inches. She was holding a newborn in her left arm. The photographer introduced himself. "Hi. I'm a photographer from the local paper, and I hate to bother you but I'd like to take a few pictures of you and of your apartment."

Jussi shot the photographer through the heart. He died instantly, crashing in a heap at Jussi's feet. A cloud of dust swirled upward from the hallway floor, causing Jussi to sneeze. He glanced at the dead photographer and then at the apartment door. It was closed. "I've become Sid Hatfield," Jussi thought briefly, and the idea swirled around in his head. He liked the idea—the way it precluded any opportunity to turn away from what had to be done. When the Houghton County sheriff arrived, Jussi handed him his gun without being asked. "He wouldn't stop taking pictures," Jussi said. "I warned him, and then I did what had to be done." Jussi assumed that the sheriff would understand.

In jail Jussi wrote to his sister in faraway Vaasa. "It's Ani's fault," he wrote her. "If she hadn't stood me up in 1930, none of this would have happened. And if you hadn't married Johani in 1918 everything would be different," he added. "You betrayed me."

At the trial, Johani's lawyer argued that the photographer had no right to be on Jussi's property. "He had been told to leave," the lawyer argued. The young mother who had seen the murder never testified because she never came forward.

Without witnesses to refute Jussi's interpretation of events, there was little the jury could do. Jussi got a one-year suspended sentence for manslaughter plus two hundred hours of community service. Jussi asked the judge what the community service would consist of.

"For starters you can paint the walls of that hallway where the shooting occurred," said the judge. "Then you can sweep the floor and change the light bulb to one with greater wattage."

That afternoon Jussi went home a free man, but within a year he learned that he had liver cancer. He died six months after that. On his deathbed his last words repeated the accusation he had written to his sister in Vaasa. "It was her fault," he told the anonymous nurse at his bedside. "She shouldn't have stood me up in 1930."

Arvoís Seventy-year-old Elderhostel Student

The Portage Gazette, June 6, 1885

Last Thursday Janne Kivivouri was sawing logs for Calumet and
Hecla when he accidentally sawed off two toes on his left foot
and ruined a nearly new boot.

For years I worked in Detroit for the Associated Press. Eleven hours north in the Copper Country, we had a stringer whose Finnish name I forget. He used to send us pieces that the Detroit papers would usually bury on page five or six if anyone used them at all. But one morning back in the early seventies, he sent us a piece about a little girl who had probably fallen into a shaft that had been abandoned and capped for decades. It sat behind a line of former company houses in a location somewhere north of Calumet. The little girl was playing hide and seek with neighborhood kids. Rain and wind had eroded a hole under one side of the cap, and she must have spotted it. It was just big enough for a small child to crawl in. Of course no one saw her do it, but where else could she have gone? No one ever saw her again.

My skin crawled when I thought of that child falling through darkness so thick that she wouldn't be able to see her hand if she waved it across her eyes. Then an editor at the New York Times called with some questions. He wanted to know if there was any possibility the little girl had landed on a ledge or had been saved by debris. I asked the stringer, and he said there was no possibility.

Then the Times editor asked for the depth of the shaft. He also wondered what would be at the bottom. The stringer told me it was a mile straight down, and the bottom was flooded. When I forwarded this information to the Times editor, he said, "May God help us."

For a couple of days the local authorities debated sending a team into the shaft to look for her body, but they decided against it. It was just too dangerous. They sealed the hole and reinforced the cap.

My wife and I went up there yesterday, and with local help, we found the site. Someone had left plastic flowers where the hole had been. Later we went out to eat in a nearby bar/restaurant. The waitress was very friendly. She asked us where we were from and whether or not we were enjoying our vacation. We told her why we were there, and she pointed to a man at the bar. "That's the little girl's dad," she said. "He comes in here often."

I didn't go over to introduce myself because I didn't know how he'd take it. If I'd lost a child that way, I'd've been haunted forever. Apparently he and his wife got divorced after the child's disappearance. Now, thirty years later, he's still drinking heavily because of it.

My wife and I have really enjoyed your class, Professor Laurila. I normally don't read poetry or fiction, maybe because of all those years when I dealt with journalism. I'd almost forgotten the power of words. On the other hand, how do words describe what happened to that child?

Arvois Colleague

The Portage Gazette, June 12, 1893

Last Saturday Oskar Myllymaki married Ellen Lampinen at the Finnish Lutheran Church on Pine Street in Hancock. Since then they have taken a serious honeymoon at Torch Lake. Ellen is Oskar's second wife, the other having died within the year of matrimonial bliss.

My first wife and I were twenty-two when we married. We had dated all through college at Concordia, so marriage was the culmination of four years of getting to know each other. We had both gotten our BAs, and life looked rosy. I enrolled in a graduate literature program at the University of Minnesota while she got a counseling job in the local school district. We made several close friends, and I thought we were very happy together but apparently she was not.

In the summer of our third year of marriage, I was working as an itinerant carpenter for a contractor. We were building a new development in what used to be a farmer's orchard. I was feeling jubilant because it was Friday afternoon and payday. Just before the end of the workday, the boss came around with everyone's check but mine. "Your wife picked up yours at the office," he told me.

"When was that?" I asked.

"Not long after lunch. Maybe around one-thirty."

She'd never picked up my check before, but I didn't think anything of it. I thought maybe she'd wanted to save me a trip to the bank because she had plans for us right after work.

A half hour later we put our tools away, and I climbed into an old pickup my dad had given us and I drove home. Home was an apartment near the university. I noticed that the two-year-old car we'd recently purchased was not parked in its usual spot.

When I walked into our apartment it was empty. The furniture was gone. So were her clothes. My clothes were in a pile on the floor. The kitchen was empty of pots and pans, silverware, cleansers, even trash bags. The stuff that my parents had given me—heirlooms from my grandparents— was gone. My father had given me his boyhood hunting knife—his *puukko*— and she'd taken that too. His father had brought it from Finland to America. I hunted for a note, a phone message, anything; but she had simply disappeared, taking everything connected to our lives together. She didn't even leave me a picture of us.

I called her best friend—a woman that I liked a lot. Her phone had been disconnected. I drove over to her place. It was only five minutes away. She was gone without a trace too. I called my in-laws. They didn't know anything about their daughter's sudden disappearance. I called other friends. No one knew anything.

That night I slept on the floor, and the next day I called or visited everyone that I thought might know something about my wife's disappearance. No one could help me. She had cleaned out our accounts, so I couldn't even get drunk because I had spent my pocket money on gas. I called my folks, and they sent me money via Western Union. They told me to come home, but instead, I drove to New Mexico to hunt for a job. I guess I wanted to get lost too. For the next six or seven months I wandered around in New Mexico and Arizona, doing odd jobs—carpentry, roofing, bricklaying, whatever else I could find. I let my assistantship lapse and dropped out of the doctoral program at Minnesota. Every few days I called my in-laws to see if they'd heard from their daughter. Finally they did. She sent them a letter from an address in Bloomington, Indiana. In the letter, she never even mentioned me or the dissolution of our marriage.

The next day I quit my job with a contractor and drove toward Indiana. I tried to drive straight through, but I finally pulled into a rest stop and slept for three or four hours. Then I hit the road again and reached Bloomington hours later. I found her address pretty easily. I still remember it—315 Walnut Street. It was an apartment house. She and her friend lived in Apartment 6A.

I knocked on the door, and a moment later she opened it. She just stood there, staring at me. "Aren't you going to invite me in?" I asked. So she stepped back and I stepped in. She still didn't say anything. It was really weird: looking around and seeing her stuff and my stuff and the other girl's stuff all mixed together in a strange place. "How are you?" I asked, trying to give the question gravity.

"Fine," she said. Her voice was hollow and without emotion.

"I came to find out what's going on," I said. "You didn't even leave a note. I need to know what I did to deserve this treatment. Do you want to talk it over? Do you have any desire to try to start in again? Or do you want a divorce?"

Just then the phone rang, and she answered it. I don't know who it was. "Listen," she said, "someone is here. Could I call you back in five or ten minutes? No, it won't take longer."

So I left. I was out the door before she had hung up the phone. That was the last time I ever saw her. I got a lawyer, and he got me divorced. She kept everything, even the *puukko*.

For a few months I went through the motions of being alive, but I was stunned. I acted like the front of my skull had been caved in by a blow from a sledge hammer. I returned to my hometown in the Iron Range of Minnesota. Then I met Aliina Ranta one evening in a club. We fell in love pretty quickly—really in love—and I returned to school and finished my doctorate. I did my dissertation on Finnish-American poets such as Judith Minty, Wendy Anderson, and Jim Johnson. I got a job in a university in North Dakota. I edit an academic journal on Finnish-American writers. I'm happy. I've started to write fiction. Someday I suppose I'll write about my first wife. I still don't understand what happened. I guess I never will. Some women are like that—a mystery. Yeah—a mystery.

Arvoís Friend Akseli

The Portage Gazette, September 28, 1893

Notice is hereby given that my wife Ellen has left our home without just cause or provocation and is living with Emil Kivioja. I will not pay any debts she has since incurred or will incur. Oscar Myllymaki.

Akseli had just arrived in Michigan from Finland, and his body had not yet adjusted to the time change. "Right now it's 2:00 A.M. in Helsinki," he told Arvo as they sat in Arvo's kitchen, snacking on slices of boiled beef tongue and steamed beet greens sprinkled with balsamic vinegar. They were drinking Guinness. "I've never been away from my family before. My daughter starts school today in Helsinki. My wife and I enrolled her in a special high school where many of the classes are taught in English. Our son will be in a regular Finnish middle school. I'm worried because he's been in an American school the last two years while my family was here with me. Maybe he will find it hard now to study in Finnish."

"It's too bad you can't be there," replied Arvo. Akseli was the director of Fine Arts and Computer Design at Coppertown College. In his office, he was usually very formal in dress and speech, but now, in Arvo's kitchen, he was relaxed but showed fatigue in his eyes.

"I don't like to be away from my children on important occasions such as the beginning of a new school year," Akseli said. "I don't want to be like my father."

"And how was he?" Arvo asked, with that directness concerning private matters that characterizes Americans.

"He abandoned my mother, my brother, and me when I was five," said Akseli.

"He, in turn, had been abandoned by his parents when he was five. He was raised by his aunt but ran away from her home and joined the Finnish Army when he was fourteen. The Winter War against the Russians had just begun. He was too young to be a regular soldier, so they made him a dispatcher. He raced by horse from the front to headquarters, carrying messages back and forth all day long. If the snow was too deep, he skied. He saw lots of death, especially dead Russians. Their bodies would freeze solid very quickly. Their faces would be blue. Once in our kitchen, I heard him telling my mother about dead horses. The horses had fallen through the ice on Lake Ladoga. It was forty degrees below zero, and the horses were frantic to get out. They swam in tighter and tighter circles as the ice refroze and trapped them with their heads still out of the water. In death their eyes were still full of terror, he said. I remember this because he cried as he talked."

"He sounds like a good man who never had a childhood," Arvo said.

"Yes, that's right," said Akseli. "He did a man's job in the army, but he was a child. He stayed in the army through his teens, fighting in the second war against the Russians and then in the battles to drive the Germans out of Finland. They came in when they were invited as allies against the Russians, but when we Finns asked them to leave, they refused. My father was very young when he saw too many terrible things. Then after the war, maybe as a kind of therapy, he taught himself to be a professional artist. That's when he met my mother. Her parents both were famous artists, and she became an artist too."

"She's very good," Arvo said. "I loved her series of oil paintings about the lives and loves of the first generation of Finns to come to America. If I had a thousand dollars to spare, I'd buy one."

"My father could not make a living as an artist, so he got a job as a salesman for a Finnish company that sold its products all over northern Europe. My father made frequent trips to Norway, Sweden, Denmark, and Germany. In all of these places he had other women. Each woman thought she was the only one for him. In the army he had also learned to drink. He could drink a whole bottle of vodka all by himself and wash it down with beer. When my mother found out about the other women, my father promised to reform. He said he would break up with all of them and that he would stop drinking. Just about that time, the company gave him a new car for his sales trips. He drove it from our home into town to show it off, but he stopped at a bar in a hotel and got very drunk. On the way home, he wrecked that new car, so he walked back to the hotel and drank for a week and a half. My mother didn't know where he'd gone but he was just nearby. Then my father called his father-in-law and confessed about the car and his drinking. He also told my grandfather that he owed lots of money to lots of people. My grandfather sent him money to pay for the hotel, the bar bill, and the car. Then my grandfather came to our house and told my mother what had happened. He also told her to pack, that he was taking us out of there. We moved in with my mother's parents.

"I never saw my father again except once, when I was seven. It was at the funeral of my father's brother. After the service I went up to get a cookie. My father was standing by the buffet table. 'Take two cookies,' he told me. Those were the only words he ever spoke to me after I was five. Ever. For the rest of my life. 'Take two.'"

"Did you ever try to find him?" Arvo asked.

"No," said Akseli. "That was his job. I was just a kid."

"When I go home to the little Finnish-American slate-mining town in Maine, where I grew up, the old people tell me I've become my father. They mean that I look like him as they remember him," said Arvo. "Then they add that I should be proud that I've become him—that he was a wonderful man."

"Your memories are very different from mine," said Akseli. "I don't really have any. Most of what I remember was told to me later by someone else— my mother or my grandparents. My memories are actually their memories, not mine."

"That's sad," said Arvo. "I was lucky to be the son of a man who liked to give. He supported his whole family at one time or another—his parents as they grew old, his crazy brother, a sister, his sister's son, another sister. Of course he also supported my mother and us five children. At his store he also gave groceries to the families of miners who drank too much and who, by Monday morning, didn't know where their Friday afternoon check had gone. Did your mother ever remarry?"

"Yes, she did," said Akseli. "When I was fourteen, she married an officer of the Finnish Air Force. He was a good man, but he didn't know how to treat children. He would line up my brother and me each morning. We had to stand at attention while he checked our beds. We had to have the sheets and blankets tucked tight like they do in barracks. Then he'd check our hair, teeth, and hands for cleanliness before we could eat breakfast. We had to sit at the table with erect posture. He would shout at us if we leaned toward our food."

"That sounds terrible," said Arvo.

"Yes. Plus, we had to move nearly every year. He was in the service and every promotion meant a new assignment in a new place. I think he loved us and our mother, but he was always a soldier."

"But you turned out okay, and your mother is a wonderful artist," said Arvo.

"Yes," said Akseli. "I learned what not to do from my father and stepfather. I think of what they did when I was a boy, and now I do the opposite."

"You're clearly a good husband and a good father," Arvo said. "Plus, you are a superb artist. Your work in glass is magnificent."

"Sometimes I wake up sweating in the middle of the night, wondering if my blood father is dead or alive. I'm a middle-aged man, but sometimes I wonder if he has ever thought of me all these years, these decades. I wonder if he too wakes up sweating. How can he not have night terrors when he destroyed everyone and everything in his life? Did he miss me when the darkness closed in?"

"You'll never be able to answer that question," Arvo said. "Not now."

"Never!" said Akseli and he gulped down the last of his Guinness.

112

Disguised as Eddie Maki,
a Young and Single Parent,
Arvo Flees to the Romantic South Sea
and into the Eye of God

The Portage Gazette, December 7, 1913

Three children of strikers were observed stealing food from the Calumet and Hecla company store on Saturday afternoon. The clerk lectured them on their wickedness and let them depart. There seems to be no end in sight for the strike.

Eddie Maki was proud of his backwoods Finnish heritage and was glad that he had grown up surrounded by that heritage in a small town near the south shore of Lake Superior. But northern Michigan was perpetually economically depressed. So, after high school graduation, Eddie fled eleven driving hours south, to Detroit, for college. Later he went to graduate school in Massachusetts, where he met Julie, the daughter of a wealthy Bostonian. Their affair lasted a year. Julie became the mother of their son, Leif, in 1967, but she was young and unfocused and didn't want to be tied down. She received a large allowance that allowed her to do whatever she wished.

Shortly after Leif's birth she abandoned Eddie and her baby and disappeared.

Four years later, in the spring of 1971, Eddie and his son were living in Stockton, California, where Eddie taught English in the community college.

In the last month of school, Eddie became friendly with an Englishwoman who tutored in the Reading/Remediation Lab of the college. The Englishwoman had only been in the country three months. She was living with her in-laws while her American husband served as an officer on a Navy ship off the coast of Vietnam. The Englishwoman and Eddie frequently spent lunchtime together at a corner table in the student union. They talked about students, about their loneliness, about America. The Englishwoman was very proper, and their relationship never moved beyond talk. The woman was very unhappy. She disliked her in-laws and missed her husband. She strongly disapproved of the war. She also intensely disliked America. Her first day on the job at the college, she had been mugged by a gang of black women students. They had taken her purse and had threatened to do much worse if they caught her on her turf again. She had learned from her employer that the campus was divided into zones. The Chinese hung out in one area, the Hispanics in another, the Filipinos in a third, the blacks in a fourth. "If you walk directly from the library to here, you're safe," the employer had explained. "It's a kind of neutral zone."

With several weeks left before finals, the Englishwoman's husband sent a telegram announcing that he had a forty-eight-hour leave in San Diego. He also indicated that he wanted to camp out somewhere—that he needed to immerse himself in nature. "My husband likes Thoreau," the woman explained to Eddie as they drank coffee at their usual table in the Union. "He's very much an outdoorsman. He finds life on a ship terribly confining."

Eddie agreed to take Leif along and to drive the Englishwoman down the coast so she could see her husband. Eddie also agreed to supply the camping equipment. They left early in the morning and drove straight through to San Diego. After they picked up the husband from his ship, they called a number of parks but found all had been booked months in advance. In desperation they decided to camp out in the San Diego Municipal Campground. Everything was a disaster from the moment they arrived. Eddie's old safari tent required trees for the support ropes but the only tree was a small palm stuck in the sand. It fell over when he and Joe, the naval officer, tied a rope to it and pulled. A park custodian dashed over to reprimand them. He attached a DO NOT TOUCH sign to the hapless tree. Eventually they tied the ropes to the L-shaped redwood fence that marked off Camping Area 147 from 148. The tent was lopsided and sagged but at least it was up. Eddie told the Englishwoman and her officer that they could sleep in the tent. He and Leif would share the seats in Eddie's Ford.

Campsite 147's fireplace was a cement ring. The officer bought a processed wood product at the camp store. The store also had a cafeteria, a snack bar, a laundry, and a roof lookout. Eddie had brought along a package of hotdogs and some buns, and he had planned on cooking the hotdogs on sticks over the fire, but there were no sticks, and the processed wood product smelled of glue and other chemicals as it burned. They all ate burgers from a nearby McDonald's and sang Joan Baez songs while the Englishwoman played her guitar, but their neighbors at 148 and 146 couldn't hear their TVs in their Winnebagos. They reported their singing to the security guards.

The Englishwoman, Eddie, and Leif returned to Stockton. During finals week, on Tuesday, the Englishwoman spent two hours tutoring a twenty-year-old Okie who was trying to complete his first college term after a two-year tour in 'Nam. The man read at a third-grade level. At the end of the second hour, the Okie thanked the Englishwoman profusely for her help, scheduled another meeting for the next day and left. In the parking lot he got in his Dodge pickup and began his drive home. At a stoplight he stuck a shotgun out the window and killed both occupants of the car in the next lane. Then he drove home, fried some eggs, and the police arrived. He held them off long enough to eat the eggs. Then he called the Englishwoman and conscientiously canceled their next meeting. "I'll be leaving the area shortly and I don't expect to return," he said to her, his voice sounding oddly small and far away, as if the connection were bad. A moment later he blew out his brains with the shotgun.

On Wednesday in San Francisco, an exotic black gang called the Zebras randomly shot to death two middle-class whites when they answered their doorbell. On Thursday, out in the delta on the edge of Stockton, eleven doped-up teenagers in a van were struck by a train at an unmarked crossing. All were killed. On Friday, one of Eddie's students committed suicide by jumping off a clock tower.

The Englishwoman had had it. She called the airport and booked a flight for Monday. "If my husband ever wants to see me, he can come to Leeds," she said to Eddie. Eddie understood. He was ready to take Leif and flee too.

In recent months, unknown to everybody else except their killer, several dozen contract laborers had disappeared in the nearby town of Yuba City—murdered by someone and dumped into shallow, anonymous graves on farms. Now in June, with summer vacation beginning, the newspapers were screaming about this. Day after day more bodies were dug out of graves in an orchard beside the Yuba River. The number continued to grow until a new world's record for mass murder was set. Because Eddie was curious about how this crime had affected the people of Yuba City, he and Leif drove there one afternoon. The town had become a fortress. Men ran errands with guns on their hips. Farm wives carefully placed rifles on the car seat beside them before they drove into town for groceries.

Eddie and Leif stopped to buy ice cream. Then they walked along the street. The natives gave Eddie suspicious, ugly looks. A gun-toting farmer ambled out of a hardware store, a large paper sack in his arms. The holster of his .38 was tied, quick-draw style, to his leg by a leather thong. "What are you going to do with that thing?" Eddie asked, trying to smile in a neighborly way as he pointed at the gun.

"Let some son of a bitch come up behind me and you'll find out!" the farmer answered, biting off the words hard and cold in Eddie's face.

The fear and hatred of Yuba City was beyond Eddie's wildest imaginings, and Eddie wondered why he had been crazy enough to bring Leif there, but the greatest horror for Eddie was the faceless anonymity of the victims, most of whom could not be identified. No one in the small farming community could recognize the several dozen men who had died there. For a few of the dead, first names were known. For the others, only question marks appeared under their pictures in the paper. How could so many men disappear in such a small place and not be missed, Eddie wondered. And how many more were buried out there and would never be found? What kind of country, Eddie wondered, allowed so many people to become lost and invisible?

Eddie decided to get out of America, at least for a little while. He placed a POSITION WANTED ad in the Paris edition of the *Herald Tribune*. He listed himself as a potential teacher of English, American Studies, baseball and basketball. Eddie was surprised when he almost immediately received an offer to teach English and coach baseball in Cannes if he would fly over for an interview at his own expense. A week later a school in Tehran said they could use Eddie to teach English the following year, but Eddie didn't want to wait that long. A school in Saudi Arabia needed two English teachers, but Eddie didn't want to teach in a country that enslaved women.

One morning the phone rang, and a man named Mathew Waterhouse was on the line from an ecumenical church board in New York. He had seen Eddie's ad while he was visiting Europe on church business. Waterhouse needed a combination English teacher/department chair/ Dean of Boys in a mission high school on the island of Moen in Truk Lagoon in the East Caroline Islands of Micronesia. He wanted to know if Eddie would be willing to go to the Pacific for a year.

The pay was minimal, the place remote. Eddie thought of James Michener's *Tales of the South Pacific* and of Louis Becke's wonderful *Pacific Tales*. He worried briefly about the lack of medical facilities and doctors if Leif should become ill. He told Mr. Waterhouse that he'd prefer a longer stay but Waterhouse explained that the Church had no money to support the school beyond the coming academic year—that the school would close in the coming spring. Eddie mentioned that he had been raised a Congregationalist, but that he had not gone to church for years.

Waterhouse didn't seem to care. "We're looking for a teacher, not a proselytizer," he said.

Eddie told Waterhouse that he wanted time to think it over, that he'd call him with a decision within a week. Waterhouse said in the meantime he'd send Eddie information about the school and Micronesia. Eddie thought about his options. He knew that he needed time away from the United States. He knew that he did not want to work in a Third World country like Nigeria where starvation, exotic diseases, ethnic hatreds, poverty, and violence-prone military and dictatorial governments vied for the privilege of killing the citizenry.

Micronesia seemed to be different, almost removed from the rest of the world. Its people lived on tiny islands scattered over the western third of the Pacific. Some islands were visited by field ships only once in six months. The geography was intriguing. All of the 2000-plus islands added up to a miniscule 728 square miles of land scattered like bits of paradise in three million square miles of ocean.

Micronesia was an American Trust Territory, administered by the Department of Interior but nominally under control of the United Nations. World War II in the Pacific was largely fought in these islands—the Marshalls, the Carolines, the Marianas. Moen, the island where Eddie would teach, was 7.6 square miles of jungle-covered greenery. An extinct volcano, Mount Tonachou, rose steeply from the populated shore. In a long letter received a couple of days after their phone conversation, Waterhouse told Eddie there was a beautiful white-sand beach at a village called Southfield, that Moen was just one of fourteen islands within Truk Lagoon. The lagoon itself was forty miles in diameter.

Eddie was not much of a war buff—the Vietnam conflict had taught him to hate war—but if he desired, he could explore the Japanese fleet sunk in the lagoon in 1944. War remnants littered the islands—rusting zeroes, landing craft, pillboxes. The collecting and selling of scrap iron was the number-two industry, behind the production of copra. When Micronesian farmers cleared land by burning off jungle growth, they had to light the fires and retreat a safe distance since the ground was full of unexploded shells. The lagoon itself was a diver's paradise, full of exotic reef fish and multi-colored coral.

Eddie accepted Mr. Waterhouse's offer. Waterhouse asked for a resumé a picture, a transcript, a signed contract. He required psychological and psychiatric examinations at Berkeley. Finally he asked for three letters of recommendation and an interview by phone. After that Eddie was issued a passport and plane tickets for Leif and himself. The permission form necessary to enter the Trust Territory was delayed and then never received.

At the end of August, Eddie and Leif left without it,

≺ • ≻

On the flight from California to Hawaii, Eddie thought about how odd it was that he, of all people, was now beginning work as a missionary. Eddie had been forced to attend church every Sunday when he was a boy, and he had hated it. He had hated getting up early on Sunday morning and had hated dressing in his best clothes. He had especially hated the uncomfortable feel of dress shoes that he otherwise never wore. Eddie had also hated the service—the boring sermon, the bad music, the hard seats.

Now Eddie remembered in particular a November night when he was fourteen. On that night Eddie had lost his faith forever. Back then Eddie had been at the far edge of childhood but had been often beset with adult questions. He had fallen in love with Selena, a cheerleader for his eighth-grade basketball team. He and Selena together had attended the Youth Fellowship of the Congregational Church. The Fellowship director had been a redheaded stranger in Coppertown—the wife of a recently retired Air Force officer. She and her husband had been all over the world via Air Force bases and, therefore, Eddie's mother had explained to him, could not be trusted. The retired officer had been a self-important drunk, and rumors about his wife, the fellowship director, had circulated frantically among Eddie's mother's church-going friends. They had been horrified that she was a cocktail hostess in a bar in a tourist area north of their little mining town. They had been even more horrified that she ran the Youth Fellowship. Most of all, they had been aghast that she was having an affair with the minister. They had had no proof of this, but they had seen the agitated way she had circled about the man when they were together in a room. She had been like a tigress playing with her favorite food before she devoured it.

At a Fellowship meeting in her home, the woman had expressed her belief in God. She had said He was a tall old man with shoulder-length graying hair, a long flowing gray beard, and a hairy chest. He wore a long, loose robe.

Eddie had been shocked and had squeezed Selena's hand where they sat tightly together on the couch. It had never occurred to him that anyone old enough to begin school could have believed in such a thing. Eddie had not believed the Bible stories of his youth for many years. His belief in burning bushes that talked had disappeared about the same time that he had stopped believing in Santa Claus, but until that moment at the Fellowship meeting, Eddie had not questioned his own basic belief in the existence of God. Now suddenly Eddie had felt utterly alone, cut off from faith in a universal master plan.

The redheaded stranger had been insistent. For her, God was a handsome old guy who rewarded the good and beat hell out of the bad. She had been as shocked as Eddie but for the opposite reason. She couldn't believe that Eddie had questioned the simplicity of her belief. "Don't you believe in God?" she had asked.

Eddie had been forced into the public role of a theological doubter for the first time. "No," he had replied. As soon as he spoke he had wondered if this woman would explode as Eddie's mother had when he had told her that he didn't want to go to church anymore, but nothing had happened. The conversation had died. Eddie and Selena and the others had eaten brownies and had drunk hot chocolate.

After the meeting Eddie had walked Selena the half mile to her home. It had been fall, the air was crisp, the temperature seemed to be falling, the sky was ablaze with stars but dark clouds were encroaching on the northeastern horizon. Under the cold red glow of the fifteen-watt bulb that Selena's father, Eino, had installed above the shed door of the family home, Selena and Eddie had pledged undying love for each other. They had embraced hard, had smothered each other in long, slow kisses, discovering and exploring the mystery of sex for the first time.

Afterwards Eddie had hurried home beneath a darkening sky. He had been filled with wonder by his love for Selena and by the mystery of sex. Snow had begun to fall. Before Eddie reached home, it was snowing very hard, but Eddie had not gone in. He had paced up and down beneath the streetlight, watching glowing streaks of snow falling out of the void above the light. He had contemplated the surrounding darkness. He had thought back to his confrontation with the redheaded Fellowship leader's faith. Ever since Eddie was old enough to remember, his mother had told him that God was somewhere *up there*, that He was Eddie's father, but *up there* then was nothing—darkness out of which snow fell steadily. And beyond the snow were the planets and beyond them the distant stars of the Milky Way and farther out the empty reaches of space and other galaxies. Eddie had known all of this and had known it since third grade when he had begun to read books about the immensity of the Universe. Eddie had been filled with conflict and had cried out to God again and again. Eddie had asked for a sign—anything that would make him believe. The snow had piled up soundlessly beneath his feet. By four in the morning, Eddie was shaking with cold and his soul was sick and empty. Most of all, Eddie had been demoralized by the sudden and overwhelming realization that the adults of the world, the people he had looked up to as mentors and as guides into adulthood, were intellectual infants and, by extension, so were the millions of other adults out there. Eddie had included his teachers, his parents, and the men who labored so dangerously in the mines—most of them had been quick to grab at simplistic answers for over-whelmingly complex problems. Eddie had been stunned.

Now many years later, that night was still brightly alive and real to Eddie—that night in the storm in the circle of dim light given off by the single yellow bulb of the streetlight. Eddie had paced and paced as the snow piled up. It had drifted through his hair in a fine dust. It had banked the shoulders of Eddie's pea jacket. The snow had streamed downward, covering the world with its cold, dead beauty.

With morning approaching, Eddie had entered his home, had climbed the stairs, had crawled into the comfortless cocoon of his bed. He had felt utterly alone and desolate—acutely aware of the fragility of life, acutely aware that he was kept temporarily alive for no purpose by a pump in his chest. The world outside Eddie's bedroom window had been indifferent to him, to his love for Selena. When Eddie finally fell asleep, it had been the sleep of psychic exhaustion. Outside his window, the wind had howled fiercely out of the impenetrable forest and away into the black. Snow had fallen and fallen, invisible in the night.

Eddie wondered what had happened to Selena. After high school, she had gone to a cosmetology school in Green Bay. Eddie tried to picture her as a hairdresser somewhere in Wisconsin or Michigan, but the image wouldn't come. Selena had taken the secretarial course in high school. Eddie had no difficulty picturing Selena as a secretary somewhere. She was probably married, he thought, with two or three kids and with the kind of husband who watched a lot of ball games on TV and drank a lot of heavily advertised beer—Budweiser or Miller's or Stroh's. Eddie wondered now why he and Selena had spent so much time together in their youth. They had been utterly different from each other. Eddie had been a heavy thinker and reader while Selena never showed any interest in anything beyond who was dating whom, who was wearing what, and how much something cost. Eddie had starred on his high school basketball team, and Selena had been a cheerleader, so, at the time, it had seemed natural that they should date. Selena had had a lovely Finnish peasant body—big breasts, broad hips, and a liquidity to her whole body when she walked. *She's probably gained fifty pounds,* Eddie thought. *Jesus, what a superficial bastard I was back then,* Eddie thought. *And sometimes still am.*

Air Micronesia consisted of a single jet, which left Hawaii twice a week at dawn. Island distances were so vast that a late start or a delay enroute meant that some lagoons had to be bypassed since none of the airports had lights. Eddie and Leif's fellow passengers were military personnel on their way to Guam or Kwajalein. Most were grumbling because they had missed a direct military flight. A few Micronesians were on the plane, but the stewardesses were blonde, blue-eyed, and Nordic. The pilot was American.

They left Hawaii as the first patch of pale gray light diffused itself across the horizon. Moments after takeoff, Hawaii disappeared aft while below, an endless dark belt of water stretched to the horizon. Broken wisps of cloud hung like dirty laundry against a lightening sky. Soon the sun's first solid rays frosted the waters below their climbing wings. Clouds began to glow a healthy pink and then a feverish red. Far below, traces of night still steeped themselves in the dappled sea, but moments later the plane rose above the cloud layer, and the whole world became a magnificent peacock blue fretted with pink and red threads of gauze.

Shortly after takeoff, Eddie's watch must have stopped, for when he checked the time, the hands were still. Eddie realized happily that he didn't care. Loss of a watch could be a catastrophe in America, but time had not moved for two thousand years in Truk, so Eddie had no need to worry. He put the watch in the side pocket of his briefcase, where it would remain for a year. Eddie relaxed and immersed himself in the burnished drone of the jet engine. Leif had fallen asleep.

Eddie examined his situation. He had been summoned to a Pacific island to work, to live, and perhaps to love, in a new way. His life would no longer be measured by daily, scheduled tasks. The car had been sold. The lawn mower had been given away. Other possessions had been shipped to his parents' home in Michigan. He was free to indulge in islomania without persecution from the onward rush of America. Eddie closed his eyes and dreamed of emerald isles rising out of turquoise seas.

Their first touchdown was Midway, a rag of coral flat as a frying pan a few feet above water. Waves of heat stewed the runway. The runway *was* the island except for a half dozen buildings squeezed into a tiny space not needed for takeoffs and landings. Midway had never been inhabited until sailors came, but it had a glorious recent history. A major World War II naval battle had been fought nearby.

A few years earlier President Johnson had stopped at Midway on his way to South Vietnam. Extra teams of seabees had been flown in to repaint everything and to hang bits of red, white, and blue bunting across the sheds. For a couple of days the island had had a festive air. The sailors had eaten special rations flown in from Hawaii. Alcohol had flowed freely and people had laughed. On the big day, Johnson's plane had landed, a band had played, hands had been shaken. Exhausted sailors had stayed up all night perfecting their tiny piece of God's earth and drinking. Most had slept through the president's arrival. A few minutes later *Air Force One* had taken off. The paint had quickly faded, the smiles had disappeared, and the island had returned to its perpetual indolence.

Before the sailors came, gooney birds and gulls had had Midway all to themselves. The birds were still there, but now their shrill cries were interrupted by the scheduled roar of jet engines. A tiny contingent of seabees still maintained a human presence on the island.

Leif was still asleep, curled up sideways with his face partially pushed into the seat. Eddie and most of the other passengers disembarked while the plane refueled. There was nothing to see—a few stunted bushes scraped out a bleak existence wherever the tarmac did not interfere. Buildings were typical military architecture—flat, toneless green rectangles. Even the living quarters resembled warehouses.

Eddie and the other passengers soon discovered that they were all on display, especially the women. The island's entire population had gathered around to gawk. "Where are you from?" the young men asked. "Where are you going?"

Leif woke up and came off the plane, joining Eddie on the tarmac. Eddie explained to the sailors that he and Leif were going to an island in Truk Lagoon.

"Of your own free will?" the sailors asked in disbelief.

Everyone was sweating, great beads of perspiration soaking clothes. The excess dripped to the pavement to sizzle. Eddie and Leif looked for a bathroom. They located it on the back side of a building. It was marked HEAD. Soon everyone gathered around the one Coke machine. Cokes were only five cents, and Leif and Eddie drank several. Eddie tried conversation with a sailor who was staring longingly at the women. "Coke is never this cheap in the States," Eddie said.

"Hell, man," the sailor replied, "this machine is so old it's pre-inflation. You think Coca-Cola is going to send some son of a bitch way out here to this Godforsaken place just so they can get more money per bottle?"

Eddie and Leif and the others entered the Trust Territory through Kwajalein, an American missile-testing base in the Marshalls. Eddie was apprehensive because he and Leif lacked a Micronesian entry permit, but when Eddie mentioned his lack of a permit to a fellow passenger, the man replied, "What in hell is that?" Apparently no one else had one either. Kwajalein was a very important base. When the military fired a long-range missile far into the Pacific from the West Coast, the people on Kwajalein fired an anti-missile missile to shoot it down. Kwajalein was America's only base testing long-range interception of missiles. Consequently Eddie and the others were ordered to put all cameras away as they approached the atoll.

The main island was incongruous—a neatly groomed green broken by a long runway and by a cluster of suburban American homes, a cinema, a px, a marina, and all the other paraphernalia of middle-class life.

As the plane touched down, someone to the right whacked enthusiastically at a golf ball. Eddie glimpsed two or three other golf devotees strolling over greens as the plane taxied past the third hole. The golfers wore low-brimmed hats dipped tightly over sunglasses. Behind them a Micronesian caddied.

The passengers disembarked but were not allowed to leave a cordoned-off area. An armed soldier stood nearby. Eddie had done a lot of reading about Micronesia before his arrival. He knew that a United Nations investigating team had condemned the United States for the atrocious living conditions of the Micronesians who worked on Kwajalein in menial positions as servants, grounds-keepers, bartenders. The Micronesians had once lived on Kwajalein, but now they were packed on Ebeye, an inconsequential flyspeck of a sandbar about two miles from the main island. Ebeye's seventy-six acres were bald except for one road, several hundred cars, innumerable single-room tin-and-plywood shacks, and swarms of people. Six thousand islanders huddled together on this sandbar. Only a handful actually worked on Kwajalein. The others were relatives. One employee often supported twenty or even thirty people. In spite of the slum conditions, Ebeyans were the wealthiest Marshallese, although their base pay was much less than the base pay of Americans doing the same work.

Ebeyans were aware of their predicament. They needed the Americans there in order to buy transistor radios, automobiles, beds, and motorboats, but they resented the loss of their home island. They hated living on a sand bar a foot or two above the water. "I used to live on Kwajalein," a Marshallese passenger told Eddie. He was flying on to Majuro, the plane's next stop. "When I was a young man, Kwajalein was covered with forest. We ate breadfruit, coconuts, and fish. I could go anywhere in my canoe. Now I must ask the military police for a transit permit, and they often won't give me one. Americans have turned our island into a country club. The grass is combed by noisy machines. The trees have been cut down and replaced with bushes you Americans call shrubs. There used to be hills—not big but we loved them. Bull-dozers leveled everything. It will never be the same."

On Ebeye there was not one tree. The people ate canned mackerel and canned tuna, caught in these waters by the Japanese. They ate rice, also from Japan. They were malnourished from lack of fruit and vegetables. "All of this will change when we get our independence," the Marshallese said to Eddie as he swept his arm in a long arc that encompassed the entire lagoon.

"How?" Eddie asked.

The Marshallese shrugged.

Thirty minutes before sunset, Eddie and Leif's flight descended toward Truk. The runway, built in World War II, was too short for jets. The pilot, as he had done many times before, landed anyway, reversing engines and braking so forcefully that anything not in a seat belt sailed forward to slam into the forewall. It was raining. The airport consisted of the ridiculously short runway and an eight-by-twelve-foot tent. The tent served as a ticket counter, lounge, and luggage claim area. As Eddie and Leif disembarked, young Trukese women greeted them and other passengers with necklaces and crowns of maramars (flower chains). Dozens of islanders had come to the airport to be entertained by arriving visitors.

Several members of the school staff were waiting by a green pickup to transport Leif and Eddie to the school. The principal was Mr. Finley, a retired Air Force colonel in his mid-fifties. Tall, thin, and awkwardly stiff, he moved jerkily like a gigantic mantis. Mrs. Finley was tall and stately, with a touch of youthful beauty still visible in her fifty-year-old face. Mr. Finley's sidekick was Perry, the vice-principal. Twenty-five-year-old Perry was short, stout, and athletic, with the beginning of a paunch. His wife, Janice, was thin and bony, her chest flat and her legs like sticks. Mr. Finley and Perry wore Hawaiian shirts, loose Bermuda shorts, and sandals. Both wore thick glasses below 1950's crewcuts. Their wives wore floral dresses of conservative length. They too had short, conservative haircuts.

Before the group departed for the school, Perry wanted to watch the takeoff. The plane sat at the very edge of the runway as the pilot gradually increased the thrust of the engines. When the plane was rocking violently, barely held by the brakes and blocks, workers yanked out the blocks and leaped back. Simultaneously the brakes were released, and the plane shot forward as if fired from a catapult. In spite of this, the plane nearly dipped into the water as it left the end of the runway. Perry turned to Eddie and smiled broadly. "One of these days, she's not going to make it," he said. Then he added, "And we all have to leave on that thing."

The school was a half mile from the airport, along a road with more pot-holes than surface. Some holes were deep enough to form small ponds when it rained. The pickup passed the Truk branch of the Bank of America, a quonset hut whose roof was partially torn off. The hole in the roof must have been six feet across—large enough that one could see right inside the bank. Eddie and Leif were sitting inside the cab with Mr. Finley while the others sat on boxes in the truck bed. Eddie commented to Mr. Finley about the pos-sibility of bank robbery, and Mr. Finley laughed. "The roof was torn off in a typhoon two years ago," he said. "It's never been robbed because there's no place for a robber to go with the money. After all, we're a Pacific island hun-dreds of miles from anywhere."

The pickup passed the Truk Trading Company, the Truk Fish Co-oper-ative, a couple of nondescript bars with handmade wooden signs over the open doorways, a tiny hotel behind a salt bog, and a lot of one-room homes with unpainted plywood walls and corrugated tin roofs. The plywood homes were meant to be temporary and had replaced homes blown out to sea by the same typhoon that had torn the bank's roof.

The pickup passed a solid-looking building made of gray, unpainted cinder blocks. "That's the combination police station/jail," pointed out Mr. Finley, as if it were more important for Eddie to know the location of this building than the location of any other. On a bench out front about a dozen policemen sat in a row. A couple of others lounged in the doorway. A half dozen more sat in the bed of an old World War II Army truck which served as a squad car. The ancient truck was still in camouflage coloring but had TRUK DISTRICT POLICE U.S. TRUST TERRITORY OF PACIFIC ISLANDS stenciled in black on the door.

"How many policemen are there on Moen?" Eddie asked.

"About sixty," replied Mr. Finley.

"And what's the population of the island?" Eddie asked.

"Maybe six thousand," replied Mr. Finley.

"That's a ratio of one cop for every one hundred people," Eddie said in disbelief.

"That's right," laughed Mr. Finley. "And they still can't keep order. Every day some islander knifes somebody else or smashes up somebody's home or rapes a girl or whacks somebody over the head with a rock. The police always arrive too late, bungle the investigation, and then fail to make an arrest. As a result, the two island doctors are kept very busy. They're remarkable men, those doctors. They've seen it all—punctured lungs, torn hearts, swollen brains, and every conceivable kind of break."

"Are they Trukese doctors?" Eddie asked.

Mr. Finley gave Eddie a scornful look, indicating Eddie's utter ignorance of the world he had just entered. "None of these people have that kind of education," he said. "Both doctors are ex-military American doctors. They say they've seen a greater range of injuries out here than they ever saw in Korea or 'Nam."

The pickup left the main village, bounced from pothole to pothole along a less populated shoreline, and then entered a second, much smaller village. Just beyond a church made entirely of corrugated tin, Mr. Finley guided the truck up a sloping drive to the school. The school itself consisted of a half dozen wooden buildings tucked against the jungle-covered base of Mount

Tonachou. A two-story boys' dorm sat at one end of the campus, a two-story girls' dorm at the other. Two-story porches ran the length of each dorm. Only a couple of students were lounging on the porch of the boys' dorm. Because many students had to travel for weeks from their homes to the school, those from distant islands in the Mortlocks, in the Marshalls, in Ponape, or in Kusaie had not yet arrived. Many were probably still traveling by outrigger canoe to an outer island served by a field ship. The field ship would take them to an island where they could catch a plane for Truk.

Scattered between the dorms were a guest house, faculty housing, the classroom complex (including a chapel), and an *ut*, a Trukese meeting house. The *ut* was a long, narrow, thatched-roof building without walls. It had a concrete stage at one end and a classroom at the other. The outbuildings consisted of a pig pen and a chicken coop. Between the road and the school buildings were an athletic field and an outdoor basketball court.

At the top of the loop drive, the remainder of the faculty had come out to be introduced to the new teacher. It was obvious immediately that Micronesians were in short supply. Mr. Moses, the history teacher, introduced himself as the only Trukese with a four-year college degree in education. The remaining teachers were all foreigners like Eddie. Fred from Los Angeles was a young, single, and studious-looking math teacher who had come to the islands to escape his old job of teaching remedial math to underprepared ghetto students. Pete, from New York, was a young, single science teacher who used to be Dean of Boys. He was delighted that Eddie had replaced him and shook Eddie's hand with great enthusiasm. Joe, from Pennsylvania, was a skinny and very conservative-looking music teacher who had come out to missionize rather than to have an adventure. His wife, Margaret, taught English. They had a little girl a year older than Leif. Mary was a single Filipino woman in her thirties who taught home economics and religion. She was also Dean of Girls. Tom was a Kansan, married, an ex-Seabee, a community-college graduate who maintained the plumbing and electrical systems and who taught shop. His wife, Janet, took care of their home and three children. The chaplain, Adam, and his wife, Ellen, were one year out of Berkeley. Neither had ever taught before. He would teach religion and lead the daily and Sunday chapel services. Ellen would teach science. Eddie discovered that everyone did double duty, including the principal and vice-principal. Mr. Finley taught math; his wife, art. Perry taught business subjects; his wife, English.

The maintenance man was Fungo, a Trukese from the local village. He understood English but could not speak it. The watchmen were Lastyear, Niuyear, and Tobako. Tobako also cooked. For protection, the watchmen kept a half dozen mangy mongrel dogs on rope leashes. Mr. Finley explained that at night, as the watchmen circled the campus, the dogs preceded them, yapping and milling about at the ends of the long ropes. The dogs were in bad shape, with runny eyes and with raw, fly-covered wounds. One dog limped.

Leif and Eddie were exhausted from the long flight and the radical time change. Perry led them to their new home in the boys' dorm, built of lumber imported from Oregon. The dorm's first floor consisted of the long porch; a recreation room; a laundry; a bathroom, including toilets, showers, and sinks; and a storeroom. The second floor contained four student dormitory rooms plus their two-room apartment. The first room was a combination living room/kitchen. A sideboard extending out from the wall acted as a divider. The bedroom in the back was just big enough for twin beds. The single closet had plywood doors on runners. Off the bedroom was a tiny bathroom with a shower.

The refrigerator ran if the generator was on—usually from 7:00 A.M. to 9:00 P.M. A gas stove, a table that seated two, a wicker chair, and a couch completed the furnishings.

Perry went directly to the fridge as he finished showing Eddie and Leif their apartment. He extracted two Japanese beers, rummaged in a kitchen drawer until he located an opener, opened the beers and carried them back to the couch. He sat down. Eddie dragged the luggage into the bedroom, dug into one that contained Leif's favorite blanket, put it on Leif's bed, helped the boy undress, put him to bed, kissed him good night and returned to Perry. Eddie was exhausted, but Perry made it clear he wanted to talk.

"You've got a very important job here," Perry said as he placed a beer in Eddie's hand.

"I know that," Eddie said as he sipped at the beer to calm down. His nerves were still back on the plane. He wondered what Perry was getting at. "Last year Pete was Dean of Boys. The job made him a bit crazy. By the end of the year, he wanted to expel everybody. He kept his bags packed at all times. He kept his shortwave tuned to the emergency channel so he could call in Marines from Guam if things got too dangerous. He was really nuts."

"I don't understand," Eddie said. "Maybe after I've been here awhile I'll know what you're talking about."

"He still keeps his bags packed. He's ready to fly out of here on a moment's notice. He also has the keys for the school motorboat. He wants to be able to head out to sea if they come for him. Just don't take anything he says as the truth. It's just his paranoia. These are good boys. You'll like them."

Eddie was too tired to question Perry about this peculiar conversation. Mostly he wanted him to go away so he could join Leif in sleep. The time change had really upset his biological clock. The beer quickly affected Eddie, slowed down his jumpy nerves, relaxed his racing mind. Perry went on to tell Eddie how he and his wife had put very valuable items in Eddie's refrigerator—bacon, eggs, juice, and milk. All were almost impossible to obtain locally because of a longshoremen's strike on the West Coast. "Mostly we eat canned tuna, canned mackerel, and rice," Perry explained.

Perry rambled on about himself and his wife. They were recent graduates of an obscure, third-rate, church-related college in Indiana that Eddie had never heard of. This was their first teaching position, but Perry exuded great confidence. He said he would teach all the business subjects, but that he was qualified to teach in twenty-six different disciplines. He was one of those people who thought that if you could read the text, you could teach the subject. He had also apparently played on several athletic teams in college and, therefore, considered himself a potential coach for any sport. He apparently had no idea of the actual amount of knowledge required for anyone to be considered knowledgeable in a given field. He indicated that if one could write, then one could teach English. Perry meant to write in the most elementary sense; that is, to be able to compose a sentence. Perry's wife had a degree in elementary education but would be teaching high school English in Eddie's department.

◁ • ▷

In the morning, Eddie was startled awake by a fist hammering on his door. Eddie staggered from bed, threw on some shorts, opened the door and stood there bleary-eyed and confused. A short, slim man with a blonde moustache was gesticulating wildly, his shoulders and chest heaving from loss of breath. His shock of blond hair bounced crazily. "I ran as fast as I could," the man gasped, the words bitten off between loud sucking for air. "The principal needs you. Trouble. Drunks at the girls' dorm."

"My son is still asleep," Eddie replied. "I can't go anywhere."

"I'll watch your son," the man said. "Just hurry."

"Where's the girls' dorm?" Eddie asked.

"Over that way," the man replied, waving wildly toward the far end of the campus. "Just follow the noise."

"I can't leave my son with just anyone," Eddie said.

"I'm Pete. You replaced me as Dean of Boys. I teach science. Don't you remember? You met me last night. Now please go. Quickly. Before someone gets killed."

This last statement shocked Eddie into action. He threw on a shirt and tennis shoes. "Go!" yelled Pete. "I'll take care of your son. I'll feed him breakfast if you don't get back in time."

As Eddie hurried across the campus, he recalled what Perry had told him about Pete, that the man was crazy. At the girls' dorm a large ring of male students and teachers kept a wary distance from drunks from the village who had come to rape girls. The drunks were very blunt about what they wanted. "Women! We want women!" growled one. Fred, the math teacher, was in the crowd. He ran over to Eddie and pointed out the leader of the drunks, a young but grossly out of shape man named Eper. Eper was trying to mount the dorm stairs, but the principal was blocking his way. Fred told Eddie that Eper had been expelled from the school years before for attacking a girl. The previous year he had been expelled from a vocational program on another island. For the past year, he had been one of Truk's many young loiterers and now, after a night of heavy drinking, he was intent on procuring a woman.

"Eper wants a Marshallese woman," said Fred. "If he rapes a Trukese woman, one of her male relatives will stick a knife in him at the first opportunity. Of course the Marshallese girls have no relatives here."

Eper was one of the ugliest human beings Eddie had ever seen. His eyes were blurred grease smudges lost in his scarred face. His cheeks were bloated, his lips dark and swollen. His matted hair, thick as tar, fell over his shoulders. His trunk was a mass of rolls and folds sliding inexorably toward a swollen and pendulous belly. Eper wore nothing but a pair of black pants several sizes too small. The fly was broken. Eper's feet were bare and scabrous—the nails torn, the toes misshapen. The mass of the man flowed and oozed, his breath dank and swampy and foul as it issued from behind blackened teeth.

Inside the locked dorm, girls' frightened faces peered from windows. Eper looked around at the crowd and quite suddenly gave up. Maybe he was aware of just how tired he was. Maybe he desired sleep more than a woman. After all, he had been up all night.

Eper retreated down the stairs, turned and lumbered away. Mr. Finley followed, jabbing Eper in the back with an index finger. Eper turned, yelled for the jabbing to stop, and continued to retreat. Mr. Finley continued to jab at Eper's back. Again Eper stopped and shouted. Mr. Finley jabbed again.

At the edge of the campus the drunks picked up stones the size of coconuts. They formed a defense line—side by side, no longer retreating. Mr. Finley advanced, stabbed out at Eper, striking him in the middle of the chest with his index finger. Another drunk gritted his teeth and edged behind Mr. Finley. This second drunk was small and hard, athletic and handsome. His hair hung like thick hemp, but his eyes did not smolder. They burned quick and hot. He began to hop about the lawn in agitation, screaming indecipherable Trukese at the students. Then in English he shouted at the teachers, telling them to get out of Micronesia or be destroyed. "You are robbers!" he cried. "This is not your home! It is ours!"

135

"You go home!" shouted Mr. Finley, his albatross arms jabbing, the air. "Sleep it off, and then we'll talk about it!"

But the little man didn't want to go home. He wanted violence. To Eddie this was obvious in the way the man's body shook with fury. The man's whole body seemed to be aching for the impact of stone against head, of body against body, of will against will. An insane, unreasoning passion seemed to burn from the man's eyes. As he swung the stone at Mr. Finley's head, Eddie slammed his full weight into the drunk's back. Together they tumbled into a hole, originally perhaps six feet deep but now nearly filled with rubbish, brush, and a rusting fifty-gallon burn barrel. Eddie felt the irony acutely as he lay on his back underneath the man he'd just tackled. The thought that he'd just plunged directly out of his idea of paradise into a garbage pit was not a pleasant thought. Oddly, he wondered if Leif was still sleeping. He locked his arms tightly around the chest of the drunk, who was struggling to rise. The drunk fell back, pressing once again against the full length of Eddie. Tom, the maintenance man, bent over to try to help, but a third drunk rushed from behind and slammed a stone the size of a basketball into Tom's skull just behind the the right ear. The impact made a sound like a melon being struck by the flat side of an ax. Tom collapsed in an unconscious heap on the edge of the burn pit.

The following moments rushed by in a blur. The drunks disappeared into the village. Mr. Finley ordered the chaplain to find the police. Perry and Eddie carried Tom's inert form to the pickup, laid him down on a blanket in the truck bed and drove the potholed road to the hospital. Moses rode in back with Tom, supporting his head across his lap. On the way the pickup was rammed from behind by a car full of other drunks, who destroyed their car's radiator when they smashed into the truck's rear bumper.

At the hospital Tom revived, was x-rayed, and was found to be suffering from a severe concussion. He was told to be careful for a few days and to report back if he had recurring dizziness. The doctor ordered three days of bed rest. Tom returned with Eddie and the others to the school. In the meantime the police had arrived but had made no arrests. The village mayor had vowed to guard the school himself through the rest of the day and the ensuing night since Eper had threatened to burn it down.

136

The remainder of Eddie's first day in paradise was uneventful. Still adjusting to the time change, Leif and Eddie, went to bed right after supper. In the middle of the night, Eddie heard a loud crash downstairs, followed by a beam of light dancing about and the noise of the night watchman and his dogs. Eddie fell asleep again, but around 4:00 A.M. he was awakened by the rattle of dishes. Cautiously he rose and crept toward the kitchen. As he reached the doorway, an explosive crash rattled the partition. Eddie had visions of a hurled rock and a knife-wielding intruder. He screamed and dived forward, swinging wildly at the darkness. No one was there. Eddie fumbled for matches by the stove and finally lit one. The kitchen sink was full of shards of glass and peanut butter, the remains of a jar pushed out of the overhead cupboard. Two little eyes peered at Eddie from inside the cupboard. The eyes belonged to a bat.

Although he was below the normal age of entrance, Leif was enrolled in St. Cecilia's, a Catholic elementary school. Every morning he and the four other American children from the school, plus Moses' son, rode to St. Cecilia's in the school pickup. All the classes were in Trukese. The food and toilets were also Trukese. The lunch consisted of cold rice and fish wrapped in a taro leaf while the toilet was a *benjoe*, a small outhouse supported by stilts and stuck over the water far from shore. A long, narrow and rickety walkway led to the *benjoe*. Leif said the *benjoe* smelled, that the hole was dirty. There was no paper, so he had to carry his own. He liked to watch the fish through the hole as they nibbled at his feces. He said he wanted to take his fishing pole and catch some, but Eddie told him there were better places to fish.

After a few days, Eddie noticed that Leif was not learning Trukese. Eddie asked him why. Leif explained that the Trukese kids never said anything. During free moments Eddie watched Leif at play on the school campus with village children. Leif was apparently right. The village children didn't say anything. Leif, however, spoke a blue streak in English, and the others listened attentively.

⊰ • ⊱

On a traditional island, the men wore loincloths called *thus* and the women wore wrappers from the waist to the knee. The men had leg tattoos. Everyone worked copra in order to get cigarette and coffee money. They ate only natural foods, lived in natural dwellings, and worked with natural tools. The reef supplied fish and the island supplied water, taro, breadfruit, and fruits. Life flowed with the sun, the moon, and the tides. Everyone was an environmentalist. They knew the proper time and place to fish. They were careful never to overfish. They were careful not to despoil. People did things only when they needed to be done. There were no schedules.

The mission school on Moen was different. Mr. Finley believed absolutely in schedules. He also believed that work was Godly. He was fond of saying that busy students couldn't get in trouble. He checked to see that teachers gave plenty of homework. Every class day students rose with the sun and prepared for an inspection of their living area. Then they ate breakfast and began classes at eight. In mid-morning students and faculty attended chapel. The students led services. Their sermons were invariably about the dangers of sex, alcohol, and fighting. They did not use euphemisms: "You see this cute girl in the village and you want some sex with her. Don't be a fool, man. She will give you little sicknesses on your penis and dizziness in your head."

At the end of classes every student was required to participate in sports and clubs until five. Supper was eaten between 5:30 and 6:30. Every student was then required to attend study hall from 6:30 to 8:30. The students then had fifteen minutes of free time before bed check at 8:45. At nine the generator went off.

On Saturday students again rose with the sun. In the morning they were assigned to work details. They cleaned classrooms and dorms, repaired broken windows, did carpentry, painted, replaced shingles. Many cut grass with machetes. After lunch the students prepared the dormitories for inspection. They were given demerits for unswept walks and floors, cobwebs in corners, dust along beams, dirty clothes, unmade beds, dirty fingernails, lice. Saturday night all had to attend a dance in the *ut*, where the same ten records were played again and again. These ten had been purchased by Tom the maintenance man during a trip to Kansas the previous year. These were the only records on Truk. Again and again "Raindrops Are Falling on My Head" and "Stuck in Lodi" blasted across the campus. The students had recorded these songs on tapes, which they played over and over as often as possible.

Sunday morning consisted of required chapel. Sunday afternoon was free time for any students without demerits. Those with demerits had to work until supper, which was followed by the Sunday night study hall.

As Dean of Boys, Eddie was on call every waking hour of every day to ensure that everyone was adhering to Mr. Finley's schedule.

Before arriving on Moen, the students had probably never seen a bed or a library or a cafeteria or any structure larger than the one-room thatched-roof homes of the outer islands. The students had never worn shoes or ridden in cars or been in a store. The students had never used a Western toilet or worn a watch or written anything outside the classroom.

Many were in culture shock, and so was Eddie and the other teachers. Eddie struggled to teach the students a new way of life, a new way of seeing the world. The students had arrived with little or no English. In class Eddie concentrated on verb conjugations, vocabulary, grammar. Still, the students produced strange constructions, such as this excuse:

> Mr Edie sir
> Will you please excuse me for I can not consentrate on my studing because of this terrible dizziness in my mind.
> > Thank you.
> > Kino yours truly

The students could also be brutally honest:

> Mr. Eddie,
> I'm sorry but I will not come to you class because I never learn anything in your class. I never understand what are you talking about. And I don't understand why?
> > Linda T.

Sometimes the students voiced in writing a totally foreign outlook:

> According to my feelings about Moses, he said, "eye for eye, tooth for tooth, hand for hand, foot for foot, burn for burn, wound for wound, and strip for strip."
>
> This mean if some one does some thing bad to you, you will do some thing bad to him. If someone kills your father or brother you should kill his father or brother. If someone steals your underwear, you will also steal his or her underwear. If someone breaks your leg, you will also break his or her leg, even though the person is a son of a king or she is a princess, president, or pope, professor, or minster, just kill.
>
> These ideas had been found in Exodus 21: verses 24 to 26. These ideas had been given by Moses and it has been approved by our hevenly father who holds our lifes and controls the huge ball which is call the Earth!!!

Early in the term, some students showed signs of acute homesickness. The worst case was that of Wernes, who wore a perpetual look of worry. One Sunday after church Wernes asked the chaplain if he would like to see Wernes' home island of Fefan. Adam said yes, and five minutes later Wernes was at Adam's door, with his bags packed and ready to go. Adam had to explain that it was impossible for either of them to leave the school to visit an island two weeks away by boat. The next day Wernes came to Eddie with tears in his eyes. He said that his brother was dying on Fefan and that his father had come to fetch Wernes.

Eddie had already talked to the chaplain about Wernes's homesickness, so he didn't know whether he should believe the boy or not. He asked Wernes to go and get his father so that Eddie could explain to the man the inadvisability of removing his son from the school.

"My father is waiting in our boat at the dock," explained Wernes.

Eddie agreed to give Wernes a ride to the dock, where they waited for over an hour for the father "He must have gone back to Fefan without me," said Wernes mournfully as they drove back to the school.

The next day Wernes came to Eddie again. This time he said his uncle was waiting at the dock to fetch him to Fefan. Eddie said the uncle had to come to the school to get permission to take Wernes. Wernes then admitted that he didn't have time to go to Fefan. "It will interfere with my studies," he said. "I must go to the dock and tell this to my uncle."

Eddie refused to allow Wernes to leave the school grounds. Wernes went away, looking morose.

A few minutes later he was back. "I understand you like to fish," he said. "I will take you where the fishing is very good."

"Where's that?" Eddie asked.

"It is good at Fefan. When do we go? Now?"

Eddie told the boy that he couldn't go, that he was very busy at the school, that right then he had to go into town to get some groceries at the Truk Co-op. Wernes went back to his room but returned as Eddie walked to the truck. He offered Eddie a Trukese fishing hat if he would go fishing with him on Fefan.

Wernes carried the hat in his hand. Eddie declined the bribe. As Eddie climbed into the cab, Wernes climbed into the truck bed. Eddie noticed that he had his packed bag at his side. He apparently had put it in the truck earlier. Eddie told the boy that he could ride with him to the dock, but only in order to explain to the uncle why he could not go home to Fefan.

At the dock Wernes got terribly upset when there was no sign of either the uncle or the uncle's boat. "My own father's brother has left without me!" he cried rather pitifully.

Wernes and Eddie then drove to the Co-op. Inside, Wernes brought over a reprobate, his thin face beaming from gin, his front teeth brown from tobacco and decay. "This is my father's brother!" exclaimed Wernes happily.

"But I thought he went on the boat," Eddie said.

"Yes, he did. But this is a different brother. My father has a very large family. He has brothers everywhere. This man will be responsible for me. He is a very responsible man." Wernes patted the man affectionately on the back, but the man nearly lost his balance and clutched at Wernes as if Wernes were a lifeboat in a rough sea.

"This man is drunk," Eddie said. The man staggered again, leering at Eddie as if he were desperate to pull off a deception.

"Not so much," answered Wernes, supporting the swaying man with his arm. "On Sunday he has gone to church."

Eddie was beginning to grow tired of Wernes' games, but he tried to remain understanding. Obviously Wernes was desperate to get away from the school. Eddie tried one more tack. "Sorry, Wernes, but I cannot get permission from this man since he speaks no English."

With that, Wernes suddenly surrendered. "Okay," he said. He spoke rapidly in Trukese to the drunk, who looked more and more bewildered with each passing moment. The drunk staggered away and quickly disappeared. "We will return to the school now," said Wernes.

◀ • ▶

Moses, the Micronesian history instructor; Adam, the chaplain; and Eddie were talking after a faculty meeting. Killem Hung, a junior from the Mortlocks, approached Adam and asked if he would marry Killem and his latest girlfriend. Killem was Truk's version of a California golden boy. He was the only male student with blow-dried hair, manicured nails, and an earring. He liked to wear tie-dyed t-shirts that had been slashed here and there to form a pattern of holes. He had already had several island marriages, without benefit of clergy. Adam refused to perform the ceremony, for he knew that none of the local clergy would marry the couple. Apparently there was a question about whether or not Killem was divorced from his first wife. When the chaplain brought this up, Killem quickly defended himself. "Of course I am divorced," he said. "I threw her out of my house. That is how we divorce on this island. It is our custom."

Killem stormed away, visibly upset. Apparently a wedding feast had already been prepared in the village. Moses was equally angry. After Killem left, Moses said that three attributes were common to all traditional Micronesians—a sense of fairness, good manners, and proper language. "Killem is not a Micronesian. He fails at all three," said Moses angrily.

Moses went on to explain that Micronesian language changed according to whom one was talking to—whether it was a man, a woman, a child, an old man, or a man of God. "These things have disappeared wherever you Americans are," added Moses bitterly. "Here on Moen, young people feel free of all restrictions—of all rules of etiquette that govern their home islands. They want to be free like you are, but they misuse their freedom. They drink too much, fight, curse, and generally treat each other badly. Then they feel terrible. Later they realize that they are not Americans, that they will never be Americans, that Americans don't want them to be Americans. They realize that they are second-class people in your culture and that they have dishonored their own culture. They go to school, but the schooling makes it impossible for them to go back home. It opens up too many possibilities. They are in a kind of limbo between two worlds. They are not Americans and are not traditional Micronesians. So what are they?"

"You must feel this way yourself," Eddie said to Moses.

"I used to," explained Moses. "When I graduated from Truk High School, my father insisted that I fly to Hawaii to go to college. I was terrified, especially when I got to the airport in Honolulu. I noticed immediately that brown men like me did all the dirty work. They swept the floor, cleaned the bathrooms, and carried luggage. The Americans gave orders. I thought I had made a terrible mistake by going there. After I graduated, I came back here and vowed to help others like me to get to America and get a degree. We need to modernize Micronesia and enter the twentieth century. At the same time, we must not lose who we are.

"My father taught me to navigate when I was a boy. He was a good navigator. He sailed in an outrigger canoe to Saipan. That was before I was born. Saipan is about a thousand miles from here. My father also taught me to fish. I don't mean what you Americans mean when you say that. I mean much more. My father taught me all about the reef. He taught me the lives of all the different kinds of reef fish. He taught me to think like a fish. He also taught me to be protective of the reef as our heritage.

"During summer vacation, I always go back to my island of Tol with my family. I go out onto the reef with a canoe. I take my son with me. He'll never be a great navigator, but he'll do okay. We put away these useless shoes and shirts and pants, and we dress in *thus*, the traditional wrapping of cloth around our privates. That's all we need. It's always a perfect temperature in Micronesia.

143

"I hope my son will succeed in living in both worlds, as I do," continued Moses. "I don't want him to become a Killem. Young men like Killem are a danger to themselves and to others. Often when they finally realize how badly they have mistreated their own people, they are driven crazy. They commit suicide. They do it by getting into one of your aluminum boats with a motor. They drive the boat out of the lagoon onto the open ocean. Then they keep going until they run out of gas. They don't know how to return because they have no sail and because they never learned to navigate. Imagine! Many of our young people cannot guide a canoe beyond the reef! So they lie down in the bottom of the boat and die. We have the highest suicide rate in the world for young people—boys between twelve and twenty."

In the evening, after lights were out, Eddie sometimes went to visit Moses. The man was an encyclopedia of Micronesian lore, and he always seemed interested in answering Eddie's questions. Leif would play with Moses' youngest children while the men ate raw tuna dipped in hot sauce and coconut milk. Eddie had heard that women Peace Corps Volunteers often left Micronesia early because of the lack of privacy. He asked Moses about this, and Moses explained that privacy was almost impossible. Homes consisted of a raised wooden platform for a floor, corner posts, and a thatched roof. Unless it was raining, there were no walls, for the sea breeze cooled pleasantly. Through the night, parents, children, grandparents, and maybe a couple of aunts, uncles and cousins slept on mats scattered over the floor.

If a boy wanted to meet a girl, Moses explained, he carved a lovestick and somehow passed it to the girl when no one was looking. The girl memorized the pattern with her fingers and passed it back to the boy. In the middle of the night, the boy sneaked out of his home and crept through the forest to the girl's place. He located her mat and stabbed her lightly with the pointed tip of his lovestick. The girl ran her hand along the stick, checking to see if it had been carved by the right boy, for in the darkness, he was only a shadow in the bushes.

The girl crept out, and the two went off together to make love in a secluded spot. If they were caught, the boy was severely beaten. If they were not, they enjoyed each other until dawn approached and then crept back onto their mats before anyone else awakened.

There were no illegitimate children in Micronesia. If a child were born out of wedlock, the girl's extended family accepted the child as its own. The girl's marriage prospects might even have improved since she had proven she could bear healthy children.

At the mission school, the girls were locked into their dormitory every night. Only the Dean of Girls and the principal had keys. Eddie thought this was a terrible practice, especially since the boys were free to roam, but Moses insisted that the girls had to be locked up for their own good. "Otherwise," he said, "they will all get pregnant." Still, one or two girls turned up pregnant every year. The year before, the principal had caught a couple making love behind the chapel altar. The couple were not irreligious. It was just that the chapel was one of the few private places on the campus.

Three village girls came to the boys' dorm on a Saturday in October and then surreptitiously disappeared into the forest at the base of Mount Tonachou. Soon, one or two at a time, the boys joined them. The girls took on all comers, their sexual energy apparently inexhaustible. A religious boy informed the principal, who loped into the forest, awkwardly thrashing about in a near hopeless search for the girls. The girls were frightened by the noise he created—they dashed out of hiding, trying desperately to pull up underwear and adjust dresses and hair. The principal was right behind them as the girls raced down the hill. He waved his long arms like windmill blades and kicked out with a long, sandaled foot at the retreating buttocks of the girls.

The miscreant boys scattered into the bush, circled around and slipped into the haven of the dorm without being seen, but the principal was not interested in them anyway. It was the girls he was after. In long, jerky, crablike strides he closed in on them and flung out that long leg, missing their buttocks by inches. In desperation, he hurled his leg after them one last time, nearly fell, righted himself, cursed them with a raised fist, and then stopped.

He was exhausted. His breath came in short but very rapid gulps. His glasses were askew on his nose. His shirt was soaked in sweat.

The girls reached the boundary of the campus and broke into gales of laughter. Now they were on their territory. Villagers popped out of plywood homes to see what was going on.

Mr. Finley slowly climbed the grade back to the dormitory. He had decided not to punish the boys. He would give them a talk on venereal disease and sexual responsibility at the next dorm meeting. The students would be terribly embarrassed, for beyond sermonizing about sex in church, Micronesians never talked about sex—they just did it. To talk about it made it unnatural, a sin. To talk about it made it the white man's idea of sex—something dirty and humiliating.

Mr. Finley seemed to have an obsession about the village girls' attempts to have sex with the mission school boys, but Eddie was much more bothered by the young village men. Since school opened, they'd been getting drunk in huts on the jungled hill behind the school. In the early morning hours they'd been occasionally breaking into the girls' dorm, and so far they had not been intercepted by the night watchman or the police. A Peace Corps Volunteer from California named Mike West promised to show Eddie the drinking huts. Mike West lived in the school's guest house—a single-room, cinder block building on the same hill. Mike was in his mid-twenties, athletic, and quick-witted. He had a degree in marine biology and was doing a survey of fish populations in the lagoon. The year before, he had been a Volunteer on Puluwat, one of the outer islands still untainted by the American presence. Mike told Eddie that the outer islands were beautiful and peaceful. He couldn't believe the extent of violence on Moen. "This place is crazy! We've really screwed it up! Here everyone is drunk all the time. On the outer islands they have prohibition." Mike told Eddie never to go near any of Moen's bars. "There are two reasons," he explained. "First, the local church people consider drinking a sin against God. Those people support your school by sending their children here. Second, the Trukese in the bar might kill you. At the very least, they'll threaten you."

When Mike West had been first transferred to Moen, he had stayed with three other PCVs in a Trukese home, in a small room just large enough for the four to sleep. One night they had been awakened by screams outside the wall, followed by the splintering of the door to the other room. There were more screams as the Trukese family fled. The invader had been the oldest son, drunk. He had smashed all the furniture, food, and goods in the room. Then he had pounded on the door where the Peace Corps Voluteers lay. He had yelled obscenities in Trukese and English, had cursed the Peace Corps, Americans, and America in general, had wandered away, had fallen into a pond out front, climbed out, had wandered off into the darkness and had disappeared for two days. When he finally returned, he apologized.

At the end of October drunks from a drinking hut came to Mike West's place because they were out of vodka. They wanted to know what Mike had to drink. He told them that he didn't drink and that they should leave. The next day the same five returned with guns, but Mike was not at home, so they shot holes in his door and window sill and wandered down the steps leading to the main campus. The teachers' children, including Leif, were playing on the steps. Janet, the maintenance man's wife, had heard the shots and was on the alert for trouble. When she saw through the window the drunks approaching, she yelled for the children to get off the steps. Her husband had also heard the shots and now came running. He scooped the children up in his arms and carried them into his house. The drunks passed by without incident, but when they reached Moses' home, they smashed the porch screens and broke chairs. Moses' terrified wife ran screaming out the back and fled toward the classroom complex. When Mr. Finley and Perry hurried over to try to prevent more damage, the drunks threw rocks at them and fired their guns into the air. Then Moses appeared from where he had been tutoring some slow students, and the drunks ambled off into the village. The following day Eddie left Leif with a girl student while he and Mike West climbed to one of the drinking huts. The one they visited was hidden within stone-throwing distance of the girls' dorm. The hut was camouflaged by small pineapple plants, several sprouting green pineapples. There were also some banana trees with bunches of half-formed fruit. Discarded cans and bottles littered the surrounding jungle.

"They sometimes go from here to the girls' dorm," Mike said,

"But it's always locked after nine," Eddie told him. "The Dean of Girls has the only key."

"They get in anyway," said Mike. He had been with these men while they were drinking. He had listened to their conversations in Trukese. They had not thought he could understand because his spoken Trukese was much more limited than his understanding. "They go to a window and threaten the girls in some way. Then the girls let them in. They don't want to, but they do it anyway."

"How can they threaten the girls if the girls are safely locked in? I need to know so we teachers can stop the men in the future."

"They have ways," said Mike. "If the girl is Marshallese and has a brother here at the school, the men may threaten to kill him unless she complies. She'll believe they can harm her brother because she knows that on Truk the Trukese will always defend another Trukese in any inter-island squabble, no matter whether the Trukese is the guilty party or not. And who would identify the assassins? Trukese will not turn in a murderer if all he's done is to kill a Marshallese or a Ponapean. If he happens to kill a Palauan, they'll cheer. Trukese hate Palauans."

"What if the girl they desire is Trukese?" Eddie asked.

"Then it's a bit more complicated. If she's from another island in the lagoon or, even more so, if she's from an outer island, she might feel just as isolated and frightened on Moen as the Marshallese girls. Maybe she's from Tol. The villages on Moen have been at war with Tol ever since anyone can remember. That's why the drunks tore up Moses' porch and smashed his chairs. Moses is from Tol. Maybe the Tolese girl has a male relative who works in an office on Moen. The men will use that against her. Somehow they'll force her to let them in. Then they'll rape her. The girls won't say anything because they are afraid and ashamed. Nothing like this could happen on their own island. A conservative moral code is very strictly enforced on other islands, where there are no Americans other than the occasional Peace Corps Volunteer. It must be terrible. Imagine! And the other girls are there while this happens. If the girls say something, their relatives are honor-bound to kill the offenders. That could start an inter-island feud or, at the very least, a feud between families. Many would die—mostly the young men."

Eddie picked up an empty vodka bottle and examined the label. The stuff had been bottled in California. Eddie made a vow to himself to try to stop this horror but felt isolated and trapped by his white skin. He was an outsider, forcing his own sense of fairness on a world he couldn't comprehend.

Mike understood Eddie's feelings. He felt the same. "We have caused the problem," he said. "Before the American administration, each island group lived pretty much in its own chain of islands. Micronesians traded with each other and even visited each other, but they didn't live all crowded together on a few islands." Mike explained that there were eleven languages in the islands and that life on a low island was quite different from life on a high island. The Marshalls were all low islands, formed out of coral and rising only a few feet above the ocean. The highest point in the Marshalls was thirteen feet above sea level. Truk was a high island, formed by the peak of a volcanic mountain originating on the ocean floor.

Mixing Palauans, Marshallese, Ponapeans, and Trukese was sort of like mixing Englishmen, Frenchmen, Italians, and Germans in one country. Before Americans changed things, Marshallese went to school in the Marshalls, Yapese in Yap, Trukese in Truk. It could be broken down even further. In Truk were people from the Mortlocks, Nama, Puluwat, Satawal, and so on. It took many days in a canoe to get from one of these places to another, and yet they were all within Truk District. Now many people from these places had moved to Moen because Americans had made it an administrative center, complete with schools, a hospital, a jail, and jobs. Young people came to Moen to go to school, but after they graduated, only a few could find jobs. They hung around, living off relatives. They were bound to a strict social code on their own islands, but here the code was set aside. Anything went. They drank, fought, robbed. They no longer treated older people with respect. They broke things. Eventually they got disgusted with themselves and straightened out. Or they committed suicide.

◁ • ▷

Leif came home from school with several pieces of the rubbery outside skin of coconut in his pocket. Eddie asked him where he had gotten it. He said the teacher had given it to him. "I use it in the *benjoe*," he explained, exasperated by Eddie's ignorance. "At school they have no toilet paper."

Eddie asked Leif how it worked. "It's just like toilet paper," Leif explained. "Only I like it better. It feels good on my bum."

He gave Eddie one of his patented smiles—partly full of mischief and partly full of an overwhelming excitement about life. Leif obviously loved Truk. When he was not at St. Cecilia's, he seemed to race through the days—exploring every corner of the campus with his Trukese and American friends, inventing games that required lots of running and shouting. The students adored him—showered him with little gifts and lots of affection. His skin was turning a rich brown beneath the hot sun and his hair had bleached almost white. By nightfall he was always exhausted from all the activity, but it was a good kind of exhaustion, the kind that allowed him to sleep deeply. He was beginning, finally, to speak Trukese. He joined the local children as they used slingshots and sticks to knock down mangoes from the big tree in front of the dorm. The children ate all of the mangoes while they were still small and green. Eddie worried about Leif participating because of the flying sticks and stones.

◁ • ▷

One afternoon between classes Leif and Eddie climbed into the hills where Eddie found a wild papaya tree with green fruit. They returned with a papaya, which Eddie mixed with canned pineapple and copra coconut. With the salad they ate tuna cooked with a packaged sweet-and-sour sauce. They considered this humble meal a real feast, since now in November food had become a real problem. In the midst of one of the world's most fish-rich lagoons, they ate imported canned mackerel, canned tuna, canned sardines—all of the cans from Japan. No one at the school had time to fish, for all had to adhere to Mr. Finley's zealous, very American schedule. Apparently the Trukese on Moen did not fish either, for there were rarely fresh fish at the outdoor market.

On the West Coast longshoremen were still on strike. That meant no bread in Micronesia. It meant no frozen hamburgers, no potatoes, no noodles, no spaghetti. On the shelves of the Truk Trading Company and the Truk Co-op were only Bisquick, rice, the ubiquitous canned fish, canned fruit cocktail, and canned peas and beets. The previous year's typhoon had destroyed the island's local food supply—breaking breadfruit trees, uprooting pineapple plants, inundating taro patches with salt water, as well as blowing down the public elementary school and many homes.

Eddie experimented with exotic combinations of the few foodstuffs available. Leif and he ate rice boiled in fruit cocktail syrup. Then Eddie added the fruit. The combination tasted awful.

Eddie mixed canned mackerel, tomato paste, and peanut butter as a sauce for rice. It too was awful.

Eddie mixed herring and tomato paste as a sauce on rice. It was not too bad.

Eddie opened a can of mackerel and poured it, oil and all, over rice. This was a Micronesian favorite. It was edible.

Eddie opened a can of mackerel and poured it, oil and all, over breadfruit that had been pounded into a gray paste and then buried for days in a rock-lined hole in the ground until it was bubbling and frothing from fermentation. This too was a Micronesian favorite. Eddie forced down small quantities of the stuff. Leif didn't eat any, but he rolled the stuff into little fish-paste balls and lined these up beside his plate. Eddie asked Leif what he was doing. "I'm making snowballs," Leif replied.

"And what do you plan on doing with them?" asked Eddie.

"I'm going to throw them at my friends," replied Leif.

Eddie outlawed the idea and never served the stuff again. Instead Eddie mixed canned tuna, Japanese Ramen soup, and canned peas as a sauce for rice. It was quite good.

For breakfast Eddie sometimes mixed instant Turkish coffee, condensed sweetened milk, and crackers. It was okay, but both he and Leif were hungry by ten o'clock.

The second Saturday in November a Japanese fishing boat docked downtown and Eddie bought two tuna. One he baked. The other he gave to the students, who sliced it into thin strips to eat raw with tabasco sauce. Eddie tried it. It was okay as long as there was plenty of tabasco sauce to hide the fishiness. Leif, however, loved the sushi. He gobbled down one long strip after another.

The boys found this hilarious. They encouraged him to eat more and more. They laughed and said that one day, if he ate enough raw fish, he would turn into a Micronesian.

On Monday morning a bat defecated on Eddie's wrist while he was teaching in the *ut*. The acidic, gray liquid had spattered all over the face of Eddie's watch. Eddie had bought the watch a couple of days after his arrival in Micronesia. The watch was an Asian-made, stainless-steel affair that had only cost four dollars at the Truk Co-op. The stainless steel had quickly rusted in the humidity. Monday evening the watch got Eddie in trouble. Evening study hall was scheduled to end at 8:30, but Eddie's watch said it was 8:40 and Eddie was not going to wait any longer for Mr. Finley to ring the dismissal bell. Eddie rang it for him. Mr. Finley was furious. He went by the electric clock in his office, and that clock was never correct because the school generator frequently sputtered and stopped. "The real time doesn't matter!" Mr. Finley shouted at Eddie in front of the students. "The electric clock is school time! We must go by school time. Time in the rest of the world doesn't matter! Your watch doesn't matter! Get rid of it!"

Eddie was disgusted by Mr. Finley. Eddie was tired of the endless, repetitive pattern of every day—a pattern created and governed by Mr. Finley. Eddie had now been on Truk for three months but had rarely been off the campus, and then usually to shop or to do some other school-related duty.

He and Leif lived without privacy—surrounded by students and colleagues. Yet Eddie knew neither. The students kept their distance, for Eddie was the disciplinarian, the punisher. He was the voice of Mr. Finley in the dorm.

Eddie's colleagues were also practically strangers. He recognized their faces and waved hello as they passed on the way to classes, but he was just too busy with students and with Leif to spend much time with them. Twice Tom, the maintenance man and shop teacher, and his wife, Janet, had given pot-luck dinners in their home. Each time Fred, the math teacher, had brought as his donation the same canned plum pudding, which had been returned to him unopened at the end of the evening. Pete, the biology teacher, brought nothing. Janet supplied an extra tuna casserole and pretended Pete had made it. Janet also did Pete's laundry and prepared Pete's meals. Janet was a traditional Christian wife who didn't believe men could or should do such household things, and Pete was happy to play the role of the dependent, single male.

Mr. and Mrs. Finley had connections in the military community on Guam. They received care packages once a month of food from the PX. To the potluck, they brought dishes made of foods not available on Truk—stuffed artichokes, corn on the cob, roast turkey, Hostess Twinkies, Wonder Bread. Adam, the chaplain, and his wife, Ellen, were the most interesting. Adam was a California ex-hippie whose personal history mirrored the movements and fads of the sixties. He had already gone through the Berkeley versions of Zen Buddhism, Hare Krishna, Scientology, and Hopi Peyoteism. Now he was a chaplain with an M.A. in Theology, but when he was upset he could curse as fervently and as often as any sailor. His wife was extremely intelligent and sophisticated. Her father was a Nobel Laureate in physics. She had grown up in an atmosphere of intellectualism. On Moen she was painfully bored.

The colleague Eddie most wanted to get to know was Moses, but he remained aloof from Eddie and the other Americans except for attending faculty meetings and committees. Son of a chief of Tol, he was energetic and extremely bright. His eyes glistened with excitement when he was caught up in a stimulating discussion. He loved to discuss the most recent books he had ordered from the States. Because there were no history texts for Micronesia, Moses had written his own, but so far, no one had published it, so he made mimeographed copies for his students. Moses had a son in fifth grade and a daughter Leif's age. He was insistent that his children be able to move freely between the Micronesian and American cultures.

Eddie was lonely. He missed the companionship and intimacy of a woman. The girl students were too young, and fraternization between faculty and students was forbidden. The American women were married. Mary, the Filipino, was single but was a kind of nun without a habit—extremely religious and conservative. As Dean of Girls, she was also as busy as Eddie. The women from the village spoke no English and seemed to be from another world. They had no education and no knowledge of a larger world beyond Moen.

Since his arrival on Moen, Eddie had had no moments alone, away from the petty problems, deceptions, dissensions of students and faculty. Eddie longed to escape. He planned to take the school truck the following Saturday and drive to the end of the road. Then he planned to hike with Leif along a less populated shore.

Saturday morning arrived. It had been pouring since before dawn. Sheets of water drenched the island. Eddie walked over to the *ut* to check a leak in the roof. The roof seemed to be leaking everywhere. Eddie squeezed water from the erasers. The chalk was a milky pool. Books were shredding. Lizards scurried down beams from the thatch, trying to find dry spots. The lizards were almost as numerous as the leaks.

The downpour continued all day, turning the ball field into a quagmire. Eddie had planned that after their hike, he and Leif would visit Southfield Beach but the rain had destroyed that. Leif was restless, trapped on the island of the dorm. Eddie slouched at the table, staring disconsolately at a heap of uncorrected compositions.

The afternoon arrived, but time still hung heavily. All of Moen was liquefaction. Tree trunks oozed moisture. Saturated soil trembled beneath a mildewed sky. Students moved restlessly along the porch, their thoughts turning inward to avoid the streaming rag of air. One of them turned a bleak eye in Eddie's direction as he came onto the porch to pace with them. The boy's nasal voice whined like that of a hurt child. "Do you suppose, Mr. Maki, that we could play volleyball?"

Eddie sucked in his breath and stared past the student at the unceasing downpour. The boy was urging action, urging physical combat to overcome the dreariness. A moment later the boy slipped away, wraithlike, a gray shadow against the mass of runlets. The sea of air rolled to the beat of wind gusts circling the porch. The road sloping down into the village had turned into a gushing, mud-red flowage heading for the sea.

For something to do, Eddie hoisted Leif onto his shoulders and splashed across the grounds to the classroom complex. Mr. Finley was there, arguing loudly with the night watchmen, Tobako and Lastyear. The previous night someone had taken several of their dogs for a village feast. Dog meat was considered a great delicacy on Truk. Mr. Finley was not sympathetic. He hated the dogs—said they frightened the students and carried diseases. He saw no reason why night watchmen needed dogs.

"But they keep away the drunks!" argued Tobako.

"Damn your dogs!" shouted Mr. Finley in reply. "They've nipped at my heels too many times. It's about time some gourmand turned them into shish kabob!"

"What is gourmand?" asked Tobako.

"What is sheesh kaybob?" asked Lastyear.

Early Sunday morning the rain stopped. In the afternoon Leif and Eddie went for a walk. They rode the truck to a World War II seaplane launch and then hiked along an old Japanese road which soon narrowed into a path. They passed a cave maybe one hundred feet deep and thirty feet high. It was partially filled with supplies from the war—boxes of ammunition, artillery shells, spare parts for weaponry. Two big, round metal pieces were being used as a diving board by local children, but the water was brown and fetid.

In a second cave the water was peculiarly milky, but the mystery of the color was solved when Eddie noticed clothes on a ledge. Someone had been doing wash.

A third cave was partially immersed in the lagoon. A rusting fleet of PT boats formed angular shadows against a low ledge in the far recesses.

The path wound to the top of a high hill where Catholic and Protestant churches stood back to back, one facing toward Xavier High School and the Catholic population of Moen and the other toward Eddie's school.

In an isolated hamlet, Eddie bought a necklace made of berries, shells, and fishing line. He gave it to Leif, who wore it with delight. They drank California orange juice at a small shop at the end of the path. Beyond, the jungle, the mountain, and the sea converged to make the way impassable.

Christmas arrived without a break in the school schedule. True, there were no classes that day, but Eddie was required to cook both breakfast and dinner for his allotment of students (the rest of the faculty had to do likewise), and he and Leif had to attend a choir service in the morning and a communion service in the afternoon. In October Eddie's parents had mailed Leif a box of gifts. The package arrived two days before the holiday. It contained Tonka trucks, dominoes, a toy pistol, and an erector set. They got Eddie an airmail subscription to *Newsweek*. Eddie's mother sent a long, bitter, and frightening letter in their Christmas card. While she was driving to church, the Dodge had slid on a patch of ice through a stop sign directly into the path of an oncoming municipal sanding truck. The front end of the Daytona had been demolished, but she had escaped unharmed. Neighbors had brought over lots of food, and their insurance covered all damages. Still, Eddie's mother launched into a long tirade about the driver of the sanding truck and about the policeman who had handled the accident.

The last paragraph brought happier news. Paavo had started over again, she wrote. He had a new wife and a new business as a tree farmer. He'd harvested his first Christmas trees for sale in Detroit, and he'd made a considerable profit.

Eddie was overcome with a mixture of pain and nostalgia as he read the letter. He longed to be in Michigan. The snow would be a yard deep in the woods now. He wanted to ski through birch stands, to listen to the wind playing through the branches. He wanted to be there to console his mother and to congratulate Paavo. Someday, he knew, Leif had to get to know his grandparents and his dad's roots.

◄ • ►

Nineteen seventy-two began ominously. The chief of Moen died at 2:00 A.M. on New Year's Day. Mr. Finley called the faculty into assembly the following morning, and Moses explained that the week would be very quiet all over the island. "But next week," he warned, "everyone will get drunk. We must confine the students to the campus or they may get hurt."

Prisoners cleaned around Chief Petrus's house in preparation for an elaborate funeral. Eddie found the presence of police and prisoners at a place of mourning very strange. Among the gang of Trukese prisoners was an American, the son of an Air Force colonel living in the Philippines. The colonel's son and a buddy had kidnapped an underage Filipino girl and had stolen a yacht owned by an American friend of the colonel. The young men had sailed for weeks in the north Pacific, anchoring at uninhabited atolls and enjoying the good life supplied by the yacht's bar and pantry. At some point during a sail between atolls, the men had become jealous over the girl. A fight had broken out. The colonel's son had shot the other man. He could have thrown the body overboard, but he didn't. Remembering a scene from *Moby Dick*, Eddie surmised that the colonel's son had seen the power of God in the immensity of ocean stretching from horizon to horizon in every direction. Perhaps, Eddie thought, he had sensed for the first time his own inconsequence. Perhaps it had been a vision of the terrible anonymity of his friend's body in the depths of the sea. Whatever the reason, he had buried the body in the hold. Eventually the alcohol and food had run out. The colonel's son had run the yacht into Truk Lagoon. The Coast Guard had run its registration through its files and had discovered it was stolen. They had asked questions. The girl and the colonel's son had denied there had ever been anyone else aboard. The Coast Guard had searched the yacht and had quickly located the badly decomposed body.

The girl had been flown back to the Philippines, where she had rejoined her family. The colonel's son had been tried for first-degree murder, had been found guilty, and had been given life imprisonment in the Truk jail. Now the colonel's son slept behind bars and spent his days doing roadwork and other civic improvements. Mostly he filled potholes and cut grass with a machete.

Periodically he complained in a letter to the editor of the Guam newspaper that the food was awful, that he was not treated with the respect due an American, and that the guards once again had stolen his latest *Playboy*.

◄ • ►

At the funeral of Chief Petrus were Seabees in whites, the High Commissioner of the Trust Territory, an ex-High Commissioner, a congressman, a bishop, and thousands of Trukese. The chief was buried in a cement mausoleum, open so his spirit could wander the lagoon and cause people to do good.

◄ • ►

For several days after the funeral, the water was off because it hadn't rained for several days and the water supply of the school depended upon constant renewal by rain. Mr. Finley wanted a faculty meeting to discuss what to do about the drunks. In the pre-war days, he pointed out, alcoholism was not a problem, for the Japanese had only allowed Japanese to drink. Micronesians had lived under prohibition, and habitually drunk Micronesians had been beheaded. Moses had taken affront at the tone of Mr. Finley's voice as he mentioned beheading. "The Japanese, like all outsiders in these islands," said Moses, "either ignored or misunderstood the beauty and complexity of Micronesian culture."

158

After the faculty meeting, in which no solution to the drunks was voiced, Moses gave Eddie a brief history of Micronesia. He said Micronesians had possessed maps of the Pacific long before Europeans knew the Pacific existed. Micronesian maps consisted of long, thin sticks tied tightly together by grass fibers. The sticks criss-crossed each other in a mosaic that Micronesian navigators could read with great detail. The sticks and fibers indicated islands, distances, currents, wind patterns, and wave patterns. Using these maps, Micronesians had sailed thousands of miles across the Pacific, setting up elaborate trade routes between distant atolls.

The first Europeans to visit these islands, Moses explained, had been the crews of whalers. The sailors had brought immorality, a propensity for violence, and venereal disease. They had been closely followed by traders, who had brought guns and alcohol and a taste for Western amenities. Along with the traders had come missionaries—Congregationalists, Catholics, Lutherans. They had brought a hatred for each other, paternalism, Mother Hubbards, the Bible, and evangelical zeal. They had also brought schools.

Many of the missionaries had been American, and many of these had been New Englanders. They had rarely gotten along well with the political authorities. The Spanish had been the first to colonize the islands, needing Guam as a way station between their possessions in the Americas and their possessions in the Philippines. They had ignored all the islands except the Marianas. On Guam they had administered so cruelly that they had nearly killed off the native population. Then they had depopulated the other islands of the Marianas chain by shipping everyone to Guam to replace the manual laborers and servants who had died. The Spanish soldiers had frequently taken island women as mistresses or wives. Eventually a new race had been born. The native language of Chamorro had become so corrupted by Spanish that it, too, had become something new.

In 1898 Guam had become an American possession, and the rest of Micronesia had become German. The Germans had set about trying to make the islands profitable and orderly. Since Micronesians had had little or no money or other resources, they had been required to build roads, public buildings, and docks in lieu of paying taxes. In Yap the natives had refused to work, and, when they had been rounded up at gunpoint and put into work gangs, the gangs had run away at the first opportunity. The German governor had ordered his soldiers to drive around the islands and take the Yapese money from the front yards of Yapese dwellings. "Yapese money is huge doughnut-shaped stones weighing hundreds, and often thousands, of pounds," said Moses, laughing at the absurdity of this custom and at the image of the German soldiers trying to move these gigantic coins. "The stones were brought from faraway Palau by canoe and their value depended upon the size, the difficulty in chopping the stone out of the rockface and shaping it, the difficulty in transporting the stone the 900 miles back to Yap, and the number of men killed in the process." Moses went on to explain how each stone represented a traditional island property and was a kind of deed. But because the stones were so huge and heavy, they had never been transferred when ownership changed. The old owner and the new owner had merely agreed that a transfer of ownership had been made. The stone had still rested in its original spot. As German soldiers grunted and heaved at Yapese money, struggling fiercely to load the great stones into trucks for transfer to the governor's mansion, the Yapese had stood around watching and giggling. Later, when the governor had announced that he now owned all the money because they had not worked, the Yapese had found the pronouncement a terrific joke. "Today a lot of Yapese money still rests in front of the former governor's mansion," chuckled Moses, "but the governor is gone. So are all the other Germans."

The Japanese had taken the islands from the Germans in World War I, sealing them off from the rest of the world and fortifying them in preparation for World War II. The Japanese had found the Micronesians in the way. The Japanese government had sent Japanese settlers by the thousands to the islands, and the Micronesians had been disenfranchised from their own homes. Sometimes, in order to make room for more Japanese, the islanders had been pushed into crowded settlements on remote atolls. Micronesians had become second-class citizens in their own islands. The Japanese had run everything. Micronesians had served as common laborers and servants for the masters.

In 1944 the American Navy had sunk a Japanese fleet in Truk Lagoon and had isolated Truk from re-inforcements. The 30,000 Japanese in the lagoon had slowly starved. Dwindling food supplies had to be conserved for the Emperor's soldiers. The Trukese had been forbidden to eat upon pain of death. "Of course we knew how to find food and how to eat it unobtrusive-ly," said Moses. "We survived as the Japanese died."

"Those years must have been very hard," said Eddie.

"Of course," said Moses. "Educated Micronesians had a harder time than anybody because the Japanese didn't trust them. I had an uncle who was educated in an American mission school. He had visited the States before the war during a choir tour. He spoke and read English. In 1943 the Japanese put him on a list of Micronesians to be executed if the American Navy attacked here. In the middle of the night in 1944 a Japanese execution squadron came for him. He heard the soldiers and fled out the back of the hut into the jungle. He slipped past all the Japanese checkpoints and crawled deep into a mangrove swamp to hide. He hid there all through the remain-der of the war. Our family brought him food."

Moses explained how after the war the Navy had run Micronesia as its personal fiefdom. By 1969 paternal American military control had made the new third-world nations of Africa and Asia angry. Through the United Nations, they had voiced that anger. President Kennedy had been embar-rassed. He had transferred control of the islands to the Department of the Interior. He had also made Micronesia a kind of laboratory for his new invention, the Peace Corps. One thousand PCV's had gone to the islands to build schools, to teach, to be nurses and community developers—one Volunteer for every one hundred Micronesians.

Now there were schools and teachers on every inhabited island, but there was nothing for the graduates to do because there was no modern economy. Most islands still had subsidiary economies—if you were hungry, you caught a fish and dug up a taro. The better high school graduates had been given offices and desks and fake jobs subsidized by the U.S. government. The entire econo-my was a peculiar kind of welfare bureaucracy that drove the paper pushers crazy. They knew the whole thing was fake, that they often had nothing to do, that their salary was donated directly by the U.S. Congress. Their anger came out on weekends. They got paid and immediately bought hard liquor for themselves and for their many unemployed relatives and friends. Everybody got drunk. Some got into knife fights. Others broke down the doors of their own or neighbors' homes, smashed up the furniture, and attacked the women.

Eddie knew what he'd be doing on the weekend. He'd sit on the porch of the dorm as he did every Saturday evening, and he'd listen to the mayhem in the village—the screaming, the breaking wood, the thud of bodies. Every Saturday he waited tensely for the drunks to turn their wrath on the school, on the students, on himself.

⋖ • ⋗

From the library Eddie took out a book about the fate of Amelia Earhart. The author insisted that Ms. Earhart had been a spy for the American military—that her plane had been secretly prepared for an overflight of Micronesia. The author insisted that Ms. Earhart's plane had gone down on an obscure atoll in the Marshalls, that her co-pilot had not survived, that she had been brought to Kwajalein and later to Saipan in the Marianas, and that she had been executed while a prisoner on Saipan.

To prove his thesis, the author had made several trips to Micronesia. Because the U.S. Government was secretly using the islands to train Chinese fifth columnists who were later air-dropped into mainland China, the author had run into interference from government agents. On Saipan the author's life had been threatened. In the middle of the night a machete-wielding Micronesian had tried to kill him while he was sleeping.

Eddie told Moses about the book—about how fascinated he was with the whole mystery of Amelia Earhart's death.

"Why?" Moses asked. "Everyone knows Amelia Earhart crashed in the Marshalls and was taken to Saipan. That is common knowledge."

"Not to Americans," Eddie replied.

"Americans are pretty dumb sometimes," said Moses. "There were lots of witnesses. The man who tried to kill the author is well known to us. He was a collaborator before and during the war. He caused the deaths of many Micronesians. Many people still hate him. He worked at the jail on Saipan when Amelia Earhart was there. Maybe he killed her."

Eddie was surprised by the matter-of-fact way Moses told him about this. He had erased all elements of mystery surrounding her death. "On Saipan," he continued, "the Americans captured intact all of the Imperial Navy's records. They had the answer to every question right there in their hands. They transferred the records to Washington. All somebody had to do was to read them, and they'd know all about Amelia Earhart. They'd also know about all Japanese operations during the war. But your government didn't have people to translate Japanese. So after the war, they returned all the records unread.

"Now the Japanese are a world power again. They come to Micronesia in their huge ships and catch our fish. We make laws to prevent them, but they do it anyway. If the fish in our waters are depleted, outer islanders will starve. They depend absolutely on the sea for food. They are clever, these Japanese. They are like pests—like mosquitoes. No matter what you do, they are still there. The author of your book is not clever, however. He has written many pages about what everyone already knows. He should write about a real mystery next time."

"And what would you suggest?" Eddie asked.

"Maybe he should write about how a little people like us were able to figure out how to make voyages greater than Columbus's and much earlier. Maybe he should write about how we were able to find all these islands in the first place. Maybe he should write about how we designed the perfect canoe thousands of years ago and how oar navigators knew the routes to Japan, Hawaii, Tahiti, and California even though they've never been there. All of that is a real mystery. Not Amelia Earhart."

≺ • ≻

On Guam in late January a farmer glimpsed the last member of the Imperial Japanese Army in Micronesia fishing at a stream with a homemade trap. Local authorities organized a search party, and the soldier was trapped in the hole he had called home for twenty-eight years. Twenty men surrounded the narrow twelve-foot-deep shaft, which had a fifteen-foot tunnel running off it. Hidden in a bamboo thicket, the hole reeked of decay and smoke. Sergeant Shoichi Yokoi's cave contained coconut shell dishes, a small Japanese Army-issue stove, firewood, and bales of rope made of coconut fiber. Yokoi had lived in the cave since July 21, 1944. Until a year before, two other soldiers had also shared the hole, but they had died from eating toxic toads.

Everyone treated Sergeant Yokoi with great respect, as if he were a priceless archaeological find that might disintegrate unless handled with care. Sergeant Yokoi refused to surrender to anyone other than his commanding officer. The only surviving officer of his regiment was located in Japan and flown to Agana. Sergeant Yokoi surrendered. "We Japanese have great spiritual power, but America has more weapons," he said as he boarded a plane for home.

"Crazy son of a bitch!" said Moses when Eddie showed him the articles from *Newsweek*.

Eddie joined Moses and the students in not comprehending the fanaticism of Sergeant Yokoi. He also joined them in not comprehending the fanaticism of fundamentalist preachers, who had come to the islands since the nineteenth century, or Big Bang theorists, who had tested the atomic bomb on Bikini. One of Eddie's students wrote an essay attempting to interpret these two groups, but he succeeded only in showing his inability to comprehend their foolishness:

> The creation that I have learned was about the earth. The scientist and Genesis gave us the information about the creation of the earth. Both of these two had different ideas of creation. Scientist took a long time to create the moon the sun and the etc. Genesis took only a short time when he created the world. And

their ideas were different because Genesis created only man and plants but scientist created man, plants, and animals, and the reef. Scientist can blow up the reef with A-bomb. Genesis call this apocalypse and say good.

Micronesia is best without scientist or Genesis.

February arrived with another all-day downpour. The gods of the heavens seemed to be intent upon washing the island into the lagoon. Rich, brown streams of water dug gullies into the road and overflowed the school's drainage ditches. Because the *ut*'s roof leaked badly, Eddie had gotten soaked while trying to teach his senior class. When he returned home, he discovered that his apartment roof was also leaking. Brown stains ran down the wall behind the kitchen sink.

That evening Eddie played cards with Leif, sent the boy to bed, corrected student compositions, and then went to bed himself. Shortly afterwards, a two-inch roach raced across his face from under the pillow. It got entangled in Eddie's beard. Eddie mashed it and then ran into the bathroom to remove the corpse and to wash out the scattered entrails.

As soon as Eddie got back in bed, he heard a loud rattling. Eddie used a flashlight to discover an invading army of roaches all over the kitchen—in the wastebasket, on the floor, on the sideboard. Eddie guessed that their nest had been disturbed by the downpour. Maybe the leak in the roof had had something to do with it. For an hour, Eddie killed them with roach spray and wadded newspaper. He found hundreds more in the cupboards, in the oven, and under the burners. The spray made Eddie dizzy and nauseated. His arms grew tired from swinging at them. Finally, when he couldn't find any more, Eddie surveyed the battlefield. He spent another fifteen minutes sweeping up the dead with a broom and picking them up with toilet paper. Then he heated water on the stove, poured it into a bucket, mixed in Spic and Span, took a rag, and scrubbed the entire kitchen. Then Eddie washed all the dishes. He completed his task, exhausted, around midnight. He crawled back into bed.

An hour later, a senior student named Gaspar woke up screaming. Eddie hurried to see what was wrong. The other boys were trying unsuccessfully to calm Gaspar. Finally his screaming stopped. A ghost had been after him, he explained. Now the ghost had left, and he was ready to go back to bed. So was Eddie.

At three Gaspar woke up screaming again. This time the other boys were able to calm him. The remainder of the night was quiet.

The next morning, Eddie told Fred, the math teacher, about Gaspar's nightmare. In the afternoon Fred strolled over to the dorm, ostensibly to help a student with homework, but actually to tease Gaspar. Gaspar was playing table tennis in the recreation room, his shoulder-length hair flying with each attempted return. Gaspar was losing badly to Mataichy, an excellent player. Between volleys, Fred told Gaspar that he had dreamed about Gaspar around one and again, around three. Gaspar was shaken. He threw down his paddle, abruptly ending the game. He wanted to know about Fred's dream. Fred was happy to oblige. "I dreamed I was chasing you through darkness."

Gaspar gulped and then became indignant. From the distant Mortlocks, he didn't like it when someone tried to play him for the fool. He was older than the other students, and the Mortlockese already respected him as a long-distance navigator. "You are a skinny white guy who teaches math," Gaspar said to Fred. "The ghost of my dream is a long-dead chief of my people. He has long, flowing hair and tattoos on his legs and chest and arms. He is angry because I am in an evil place like Moen. He chases me with a green warclub."

"It was only a joke," said Fred, shaken by Gaspar's fierce anger. Fred tried to be friendly but to no avail. He smiled and reached out, but Gaspar pulled away and continued to glare.

"If you were the ghost in my dreams, I would not be afraid," said Gaspar. "I would laugh!"

"I'm sorry," said Fred.

"Tonight, in your dream, you had better be careful," warned Gaspar. "You have insulted my dead chief, and he may seek revenge."

Now Fred looked the haunted man. His face was ashen and his lips quivered. Again he apologized and walked away. Mataichy and Gaspar resumed their game.

◄ • ►

Although still young, Gaspar was already a man of stature in Micronesia, for he could navigate a canoe. Gaspar had begun to learn navigation when he was a child. Eventually he had initiated proof of his ability within the lagoon, but under most difficult circumstances—when seas were rough and winds changeable. The old navigator who had spent years preparing Gaspar was on the canoe as an observer. The boy Gaspar had changed direction on command, had increased or decreased speed, had passed over the reef into the open ocean and had returned. After years of training, the final proof of manhood had occurred when the navigator took Gaspar as a crewman across open ocean to another atoll. On the return, Gaspar had become a navigator himself. He had used his knowledge of stars, sun, currents, winds, wave action, fish, and birds to locate precisely his own tiny island, a few hundred yards long, after a voyage of nine hundred miles.

Eddie had learned the details of Gaspar's apprenticeship from Moses, who was in the early stages of teaching his own son traditional navigation.

Eddie admired Moses for keeping the tradition alive. Eddie recalled how his Finnish grandfather, who had been inseparable from the geography he inhabited, had taught Eddie's father how to live off the land—how to trap and hunt wild animals, how to take care of domestic animals and how to butcher them, and how to net and smoke fish from Lake Superior. But Eddie had learned little of these things. The apprenticeship had broken down. Instead Eddie had mostly learned to dribble and shoot a basketball, to hit a baseball, and to ski. He had also read books of a kind that his father would never read, and he had dreamed dreams of a kind his father would never dream; yet he had lost something that was essential.

Maybe that's what it means to be an American, Eddie thought. The process involves a separation from the earth. Eddie recognized that at least his father had always been there as someone to be admired and loved. Eddie knew that too often too many sons were raised by their mothers in single-parent households. Those mothers often had to work, so the children grew up alone.

Leif was fortunate that he had a dad, but each morning after Eddie flicked roach waste off the toothbrushes, Eddie cringed and wondered if he had done the right thing in bringing Leif to such an isolated and unhappy place. One morning as Eddie sipped his coffee, Leif heard a scratching in the oven. As Leif pulled open the door, a huge rat leaped onto his shoulder, leaped again, landed with a thump on the floor, skittered against the base of the counter, dashed into the bedroom with Eddie in hot pursuit. It crawled out a hole in a window screen. Eddie was shaken by the rat, but Leif seemed to have taken the event in stride. Eddie checked the boy's shoulder and neck and found no bite marks.

"If you see another rat, run away!" he had urged the boy. "They are filthy creatures full of diseases!"

The following night the rat reappeared on a beam above Leif's bed. It was late, and Leif was sleeping, but the rat awakened Eddie with its scratching. Eddie rose stealthily from his bed, careful not to frighten the creature. His heart pounding in his ears, he gathered the flashlight in his left hand and the corner broom in his right. Aiming the light at the floor, Eddie turned it on. The reflected light silhouetted the rat, which sensed something was wrong. It hunched up, all of its muscles tensed to spring. Ever so slowly, Eddie lowered the flashlight to the floor on its side, grasped the broom handle tightly in both hands, and swung mightily. The flat side of the broom struck the rat squarely, sending it sailing over Leif's sleeping form on the bed. The rat landed on its feet in the corner. Then it dashed into the closet and Eddie slammed the plywood door shut. Then Eddie went back to bed, but all night he could hear the rat gnawing at the base of the door.

As the first rays of dawn broke into the room, Eddie went to the closet door and opened it, but the rat had hidden itself among the clothes. Eddie went to the kitchen, got a trap from the cupboard beneath the sink, baited it with cheese and placed it in the closet. Then Eddie closed the door and waited. Leif was still sleeping. Eddie watched the boy for a while and then the trap snapped, and Eddie heard a loud thrashing as the rat tried to break free. When the thrashing stopped, Eddie opened the closet door and found the trap demolished and the rat gone. Eddie set a second trap, reclosed the door, and waited. Again the trap snapped within seconds, and again the rat thrashed about, but this time the trap held. Eddie opened the closet door and killed the rat with a blow from his Louisville Slugger.

About five minutes later, Leif woke up.

Leif loved to go to Kristy's Tempura Store to get a doughnut and fresh bread. The inside of the store was black with soot. Sooty air burned the eyes. Fifty-pound sacks of flour were piled against the wall, along with trash. At blackened, heavy tables made of breadfruit wood, workers rolled out dough or mixed flour. The Trukese workers were old men. They eyed Eddie and Leif suspiciously when they entered. Their mouths pursed. Eddie always greeted them in Trukese, but they said nothing.

The front of the store had low tables with red-and-white checkered tablecloths. The tablecloths were covered with grease, crumbs, coffee stains, and countless small black weevils. The place crawled with weevils.

The bread and doughnuts were enclosed in a glass case. The glass was brown from caked grease and weevils. A young boy apprentice spoke English and took Eddie's order, but Kristy himself removed the bread and doughnuts from the case. He shook the loaves and doughnuts vigorously, and weevils flew off, a tight dark cloud humming in the air. Then he thrust the order quickly into a paper bag before the weevils could alight.

Kristy's bread had a delicious sweet taste, but his doughnuts were bland. Eddie suspected the same dough produced both. The bag cost five cents extra but was invaluable as a garbage receptacle in Eddie's kitchen. Sometimes Eddie went to Kristy's just because he needed the bag—the bread was an extra. If Eddie didn't want any, Leif always did. Leif gobbled it down with a smear of peanut butter. Some days it was the main fare of his diet.

One evening Moses came for a visit while Eddie was in the middle of trying to repair a leak in the ancient wringer washing machine that former missionaries had left in Eddie's apartment. Moses listened attentively as Eddie raved about the ineffectual and time-consuming machine. "I think you should be introduced to daily life in the village," said Moses. "Such an introduction might give you a new sense of the consumption of time. I'm sure one of the local boys would be happy to show you around. I'll speak to Slugger. He's from this village."

Slugger was in Eddie's senior English class. Slugger had been named by his father, Ted, after the famous bats from Louisville.

Eddie agreed that a trip to the village would be educational. The next day, after classes, Slugger appeared at Eddie's door to act as a guide. "I want to see the village laundromat," Eddie told him. "I want to see how Micronesians wash clothes."

Slugger seemed perturbed by this but led Eddie to Slugger's mother's home where he told the woman to take Eddie to the village washing hole. Then Slugger disappeared. Slugger's mother spoke a little English but was reluctant to take Eddie with her because washing was strictly a woman's job. "No men there," she said. Eddie persuaded her to take him along by picking up her huge bundle of dirty clothes and carrying the bundle into the yard. Mrs. Ted, her eight younger children, and Eddie followed a narrow path for several hundred yards beyond the village limits.

The community waterworks consisted of a shallow trickle flowing imperceptibly from the mountain base along a slight slope toward the lagoon. The trickle widened into a shallow puddle at three points. Each puddle was separated from the others by a few feet and a few coral stones. The first puddle, which would be upstream if the water actually flowed, was a community bath for both men and women, although the sexes never bathed together. The sexes also never bathed naked since the path was a sort of highway for villagers. Men bathers wore Sears and Roebuck underwear purchased through the catalogue and women bathers wore Filipino bras and slips purchased at the Truk Trading Company. As a result of wearing wet underwear until it steamed dry in the ocean breeze and tropical sun, many villagers had fungus growing in their genitals. Penicillin and salicylic acid controlled the boils and prevented serious sickness.

The middle pool was used for washing clothes. The pool was perhaps ten inches deep in the middle, the bottom a layer of gray mud. Clothes were laid on boards and smooth, clean lava stones. Clothes were lathered with coarse Japanese bar soap and then the soapy clothes were twitched back and forth on the surface of the pool to rinse them. If the clothes sank, the gray mud riled the water and prevented washing until it settled out.

Some of Mrs. Ted's children splashed each other, urinated nearby, and then drank from the pool. Mrs. Ted reprimanded them. Apparently there was another waterhole which supplied drinking water.

In the downstream pool, women washed dishes. Eddie asked why. "The dishes are dirtier than clothes," they replied. Eddie didn't mention microbes. What good would it have done? They'd think I'm crazy, Eddie thought.

A couple of days later Slugger gave Eddie a tour through the village and then walked with him along the road from the village toward the airport. On the edge of the village a water pipe stopped but began again six feet further on. "That pipe leads to one of the two hotels on Moen," Slugger said. "But with that six-foot break in the line, they get no water."

Eddie asked Slugger to explain why this was so. "A man from our village owns that strip of land," laughed Slugger. "He will not give permission for the pipe to pass over. He is angry because the villagers cannot afford piped water. He is also angry because the hotel manager cut down a mango tree belonging to the village. Now the landowner lives on Nama with his son, who married a Nama woman. But whenever someone from Moen visits Nama, the man insists again that the pipe not be connected. He is a very stubborn man. I don't think the hotel will ever get piped water."

Eddie asked how the hotel got its water and learned that a water truck filled a tank about once a week. "The water is only for tourists—Japanese and Americans," said Slugger. "Micronesians must use puddles and rainwater from our roofs."

Tom, the maintenance man, and Eddie were summoned to the court-house on February fifteenth to identify the drunk who had struck Tom with a rock at the beginning of the school year. The trial was set for one-thirty, so Tom and Eddie arrived at one but the judge didn't show up until three. Tom and Eddie then waited in an anteroom until three-thirty. Finally a court official brought in the prisoner and asked if he was the assailant. The man's face brought back no memories of the attacker. Eddie explained that he had been in Micronesia only a few hours when the attack occurred. "I couldn't tell one Micronesian from another at that time," he said. Tom explained that he had been struck from behind and had never seen his attacker. "We cannot identify him," said Tom.

Meanwhile the prisoner stared at his feet sheepishly and grinned in embarrassment. Just before he and the official returned to the courtroom, the prisoner shook Tom and Eddie's hands. Tom and Eddie waited until four-fifteen. The official reentered the anteroom and told them that the prisoner had been found guilty. "We gave him six months in jail."

"But we couldn't identify him," Eddie said.

"That's okay," answered the official. "We know he's the one. We asked the people in the village. Also he says he did it, and that the punishment is just. He has no job, and his uncle is the jailer. He says he's tired of drinking and needs a rest. Jail is a good place for resting, and prisoners are not allowed to drink."

"How did you arrive at a sentence of six months for assault and battery?" Tom asked.

"In six months school will be closed, and you two will be gone. This man cannot then get drunk and come after you."

"What if school ended tomorrow instead of in June?" Eddie asked.

"This man would then have a very short sentence—maybe one month," said the official. "Six months is better, though, because this man comes with a high recommendation from his jailer. He has been in jail many times and is known as a good worker. He likes to fill potholes and cut grass and tease the American prisoner."

"I wish him luck," said Eddie.

172

"Thank you," said the official. "I'm sure he wishes the same to you. Unless he gets drunk. Then, watch out."

The last half of February, some kind of psychic dam seemed to break inside the students, and they began to act as crazy as the villagers. While Eddie and Tom spent their afternoon at the courthouse, the students took advantage and joined villagers to drink at the huts on the hill. The next day, Eddie punished all of them with extra work details, but that evening somebody committed minor acts of vandalism—breaking light bulbs and plugging plumbing. No one knew the perpetrator. Early the next morning, someone broke all the light bulbs on the porch, and a pair of sophomores from Kusaie, Titus and Johnran, borrowed a school hammer to smash the porcelain sinks and toilets. While Eddie was questioning those two, a Trukese freshman beat another Trukese freshman over the head with a sawed-off broom handle. The victim came to Eddie's door with his head and all of his shirt soaked in blood. He looked like he had taken a bath in red paint.

"Can I have a band-aid?" he asked.

Eddie left Johnran and Titus with the chaplain and took the boy to the hospital. While an intern was sewing up the two-inch gash on top of the boy's head, the boy's relatives encircled the inside of the room and interrogated him. They wanted to find out who had hit him. The boy refused to tell them because his assailant was from Moen. "If they find out, they'll fight with my friend's family," the boy told Eddie after the relatives left.

The Discipline Committee met to discuss the fate of Titus and Johnran. By school by-laws, the committee consisted of the vice-principal, the chaplain, and the dean. Perry, Adam, and Eddie met in Eddie's living room, and Adam and Eddie immediately voted to expel. Perry said that they should not be rash—that they should think it over. So Eddie and Adam thought it over for a couple of minutes and then voted to expel. Perry said that he would tell Mr. Finley about their action.

"I want to see what he says," said Perry.

Adam and Eddie asked Perry what he meant by "and see what he says."

"Well, I don't think he's going to agree with your recommendation," said Perry. "He wants you to help these boys, not send them home."

"For chrissake!" yelled Adam. "They got drunk and trashed the dorm. We'll have to go the rest of the year without johns."

Perry visited Mr. Finley, who immediately called a faculty meeting. At the meeting Mr. Finley explained Eddie and Adam's decision and indicated he was unhappy with it. "The trouble is not with these boys," he said, taking off his glasses that had steamed over from the nervous sweat beading on his forehead. "The trouble is with some of the faculty. You aren't keeping these boys busy enough. That's why they get in trouble. And they need order. Last Sunday chapel was ruined for me after I found a mackerel can in the grass when I was walking over. That mackerel can told me everything that's wrong with this school. We need cleanliness and order and lots of rules, AND WE NEED TO KEEP EVERYONE BUSY."

"What good are rules when students can get drunk and trash the dorm?" Eddie asked. "We need to set an example."

After two and a half hours of wrangling, the faculty voted to expel Titus and Johnran. Mr. Finley was furious. His long arms flailed the air helplessly. He asked for another vote. The result was the same. Mr. Finley finally conceded and said he would tell the boys himself.

The next day the plane for Kusai left, but Titus and Johnran were still in the dorm. Eddie went to ask Mr. Finley why. "I thought I'd wait a couple of days for you people to calm down," Mr. Finley said. "Then we can have another vote. Titus and Johnran are contrite now. They know what they did, and they are willing to be punished, but not to be expelled."

"It's not up to them to decide their punishment," Eddie said. "It's up to the Discipline Committee."

"We'll see," said Mr. Finley, and he dismissed Eddie with an awkward wag of his long arm.

The next day Titus and Johnran verbally threatened Joe, the music teacher, and his wife, Margaret. Johnran said that his relatives would kill them unless they changed their vote. Adam and Eddie took this new development to Mr. Finley, who admitted that he had told Titus and Johnran how people had voted.

"Why did you do that?" asked Adam, his body shaking from pent-up anger.

"Because I want these boys to know who their friends are," Mr. Finley replied. "I view this school as a family, and I'm the father. I'll admit it. In this case I made a mistake. I shouldn't have told them. I'll see that they are put on the next plane."

◄ • ►

And the craziness continued. A drunk student hurled a burning kerosene lamp across the dorm, setting the floor and a wall afire. Other students put out the blaze with wet blankets. Another student fell asleep with a cigarette in his hand and set his bed afire. Both times Leif and Eddie were asleep just on the other side of the wall. Eddie was furious. No one would talk about the lamp incident, but the burned bed belonged to Bellik from the Marshalls, and Eddie asked for his expulsion.

Instead the faculty followed Mr. Finley's advice and voted to give the boy daily work details for the rest of the year, an unrealistic punishment that Eddie, as Dean, was supposed to enforce. "This is ridiculous," Eddie told the faculty. "You're punishing me as much as you're punishing Bellik since I'll have to worry every day about whether or not the boy has completed his tasks."

The following night a Trukese boy from the village, Wantus, slept behind the altar in the chapel because another local boy, Rio, wanted to knife him after an argument over food. Rio then disappeared, and no one could find him. Eddie assumed he was wandering the island with the other unemployed youths. Mr. Finley contacted Rio's father, but the man didn't seem to care. The father was drunk most of the time, had a mistress in a shack in Sapik Village, and did not support his family.

On Saturday the craziness reached new heights. Perdus, a Ponapean who was president of the senior class and of the student council, and Jacktino, a senior from Fefan, were in a dorm room, lounging on beds and eating rice that Jack had smuggled out of the kitchen. Jack was irked with some of the freshmen from his own island because they had not shown him the respect due a senior. "These Fefanese," he said, shaking his head in disbelief, "they're foolish boys, always giving me a rough time."

Perdus agreed with Jack that the freshmen were not properly obedient.

"When Fefanese come here, they are very ignorant," added Jack.

Suddenly the door flew open, and Keres, a freshman from Fefan, stood there, pale with anger. "What words are you speaking about Fefanese?" Keres' face twisted into a snarl.

"We were saying nothing," replied Jack, unperturbed by a lowly freshman. Keres continued an angry dialogue in Trukese between himself and Jack. Finally Jack, who was short but burly and easily able to handle a younger boy like Keres, rose, pushed Keres out the door, and shut it. Keres angrily ran along the porch, pounding the dorm wall with his fist. Perdus laughed, finding the event a bit of humorous excitement in the middle of a dull day.

About six-thirty Perdus went downstairs for a shower, but as soon as he lathered himself, the light went out. Perdus came out of the shower to see who had turned it off, and Keres was there. "Stop playing games and turn on the light," ordered Perdus.

"You do it," said Keres.

So Perdus turned on the light and went back to the shower, but as he stepped into the stall, Keres turned off the light again. Now angry, Perdus ordered Keres to leave the light alone. Keres wanted to know why Perdus had insulted Fefanese. Perdus said that Keres was foolish since both had heard Jack, a fellow Fefanese, do the insulting. Keres began verbally to insult Perdus and Ponapeans in general.

Perdus came out of the shower stall but Keres warned him to stay away from the light. Perdus turned it on anyway, and Keres pushed Perdus, who slipped on the wet floor and fell on his back. Keres then pulled up his shirt and revealed a machete, which he yanked from his belt. He chopped at Perdus, who rolled away. The machete blade made small sparks as it struck a stone in the rough concrete floor. At that moment Jacktino and some other students rushed through the door and grabbed Keres by the arms and around the waist. Keres tried to wrestle free as Perdus scrambled to his feet. Jacktino bent back Keres wrist until the boy dropped the machete. Then Jack shoved the boy outside the shower area and ordered him upstairs. Then Jack stood guard while Perdus finished his shower.

After dressing, Perdus went into the forest with Jacktino and other senior boys, met men from the village, and got drunk.

Perdus and other drunk students then went to the weekly dance in the *ut*. The girlfriends of the drunks refused to dance with them. About eight o'clock Perdus left the dance, returned to the dorm, found Keres alone sitting on the edge of his bed, and kicked Keres in the testicles. Keres collapsed forward onto the floor, doubled up in pain.

"Why did you kick me in the testicles?" he moaned.

"What testicles? You are from Fefan. You have no testicles," replied Perdus, who returned to the dance where his Marshallese girlfriend again ignored him. Perdus and several friends then headed back to the dorm but Keres barred their way with a machete and a knife.

"Fuck you, Perdus, and your prostitute mother!" shrieked Keres.

Perdus and his friends encircled Keres. "You wait here! I'll be right back!" shouted Perdus, and he raced for the dorm.

He took the steps three at a time, ran into his room, yanked open his locker, and took out a machete he used for opening coconuts and mackerel cans. Perdus came cautiously downstairs. Keres waited at the foot of the stairs, a huge stone in his hand. The machete was back in his belt, the knife in his pocket. The two faced off at the end of the building.

In the meantime Eddie was in his apartment with dinner guests—Mike West of the Peace Corps and Adam, the chaplain, and his wife. They were discussing the breakdown of morality on the island—the drunkenness, the prostitution, the violence.

Not far from where they sat, Perdus told Keres they should fight man to man. "You put down your weapons and I'll put down mine." Keres was no fool. He knew he was just a skinny freshman. Perdus was a senior who would kick Keres' ass if all else were equal. Very slowly, each combatant dropped into a crouch and placed his weapons on the ground, but Keres kept the knife in his back pocket. Perdus asked Keres to put the knife down too.

"I have no knife," said Keres.

"I can see it bulging under your shirt," said Perdus.

Keres bolted forward and kicked Perdus in the chest, falling down in the process. Perdus scooped up his machete and took a wild swing at Keres, who scrambled to his feet and fumbled in his back pocket. Keres managed to get his knife out. Perdus lunged forward and tried to grab Keres' arm but instead closed his fingers on Keres' knife blade. Keres yanked the knife free, slicing Perdus' fingers to the bone. Perdus lunged again and caught Keres in the chest with the sharp point of the machete, which struck bone and caromed off. Other students now joined in. A junior named Simian, who was from the Marshalls and, therefore, neutral in this inter-island squabble, leaped on Perdus' back and locked his arms. Other Marshallese grabbed Keres, but he twisted away and ran down the road.

Perdus and his friends went to their room in the dorm, where the friends bandaged Perdus's hand and tried to calm him down. A few minutes later they came onto the porch just outside Eddie's apartment. Perdus still carried his machete. Keres and his friends were on the lawn in front of the dorm. Perdus and Keres began to taunt each other again. Keres suddenly hurled a stone at Perdus but just missed Langbar, an inoffensive Marshallese that everyone liked. The stone struck the wall and bounded away. Keres rushed up the stairs with his knife, but Perdus's friends knocked him down and disarmed him. Jacktino simultaneously disarmed Perdus by twisting the machete from his hand and throwing it to the floor. Perdus then scooped up the machete and lunged at Keres.

Hearing the commotion, Eddie opened the door and stepped outside. Perdus's machete cut the air an inch from his face. Eddie rushed Perdus and knocked him to the floor. Someone disarmed him. Others grabbed Keres and dragged him to his room. Eddie ordered all the students to their rooms and ordered Keres into his apartment. He sent Perdus with the chaplain to the hospital. As Eddie unraveled Keres' version of events, Keres defended himself with statements like this:

"I swung the machete down at his head just to scare him."

"So I took the knife from my pocket and put it in my hand, and this surprised me."

"So I threw the big rock at his head which I did not wish to hurt."

While Eddie was questioning Keres, a Ponapean named Yalmer, who was a close friend of Perdus, smashed all the screens in his room. Kino, another student from Fefan, tried to start a fight with Yalmer but was very drunk and collapsed into a deep sleep on the floor. Joe, a Marshallese who was also very drunk, tripped over Kino, struck his chin on the floor, and knocked himself out.

The faculty meeting the next day lasted over three hours. Mr. Finley opened the meeting by reprimanding the chaplain and Eddie for acting rashly. "This squabble among the boys should never have come before the faculty," said Mr. Finley. "I could have handled this myself."

Mrs. Finley added that Perdus and Keres were model students and "such good boys."

Joe, the music teacher, said Keres was quiet and withdrawn and apparently dangerous. "He should be expelled," he said. "He's a danger to the students, to us, and to himself."

Joe's wife, Margaret, disagreed with her husband. "We Americans are trying to impose our values on another culture," she said. "This culture condones knives and knife fights, so maybe this isn't a serious situation in the eyes of Micronesians."

Moses strongly disagreed. He pointed out that knife fighting only occurred commonly on Moen. "On other islands, Micronesians do not fight with knives," he said. "In fact, until you Americans arrived, the people here did not do it either," he added pointedly.

Adam accused Margaret of cultural ethnocentrism. He pointed out that in many American schools, kids also carried knives, but no one condoned that.

Perry's wife, Janice, said that the chaplain was generalizing too—that knives were only carried in inner-city schools.

Adam agreed and added that she had proven Moses' point—that Moen was not Micronesia.

Janice then accused Adam and Eddie of not doing their jobs. "If you spent time with the boys," she snapped, her thin face grimacing, "you'd understand their problems. Then there wouldn't be any fights."

Eddie told her that boys knocked on his door at all hours and that he was with them nearly every day until lights were out.

"Well, we all have knocks on our doors," replied Janice.

"You're so full of shit!" shouted Adam. "If you and Perry are such authorities on the needs of the boys, why aren't you living in their dorm?"

"I really wonder why you came out here," replied Janice, making it obvious by the tone of her voice and by the fire in her eyes that she loathed the chaplain. Her face was scarlet, her eyes popping.

"To teach!" screamed the chaplain, thrusting out his chin and leaning his whole body toward Janice. "I came out here to teach, but I don't have time for that. I'm too busy restoring order among our nice boys."

Mr. Finley felt he was losing control of the meeting and inserted himself into the argument. "If we could just set up enough responsibilities among these boys, and especially among the dorm captains, we wouldn't have these problems. Basically these are good boys. They need to learn to sweep floors and to do other useful things to fill up their time. What we need more of is compassion. By example, we've got to teach these people to have some compassion for each other if they are ever going to be on their own. I know it's difficult to raise teenagers, but Mrs. Finley and I have raised four ourselves, and we have experience."

Mrs. Finley added, "All four have been model students and good citizens."

Ellen pointed out that no one was questioning the Finleys as parents. "A student tried to kill Perdus," said Ellen, "and Perdus didn't report it. Instead he went after the student with a machete."

"There's no proof that anyone intended to hurt anyone else," said Mr. Finley, who looked exhausted. He slouched in his chair, his face sallow and his eyes red and watery. "I like both boys, and I'm in favor of keeping them. They should be strongly reprimanded, of course."

"What kind of reprimand?" Eddie asked.

Fred, who had been sitting quietly, correcting a math test, suddenly shouted, "Make them slaves!"

The chaplain sat bolt upright, swiveled, and glared at Fred. "My God! Do you know what you're saying?" he cried.

"Don't curse!" cried Janice. "I can't abide hearing a man of God cursing!"

"I mean it!" said Fred. "Give them a really hard work load. Lots of work. As if they were slaves. If they fail to complete it, kick them out."

"And who would supervise such a program?" Eddie asked. "I don't want to waste hours of my time supervising grass cutting just because Perdus and Keres were crazy enough to try to kill each other."

Moses interceded. He had heard enough. He was visibly upset. "This fight is not over," he said. "If you do not expel both boys, no one in Micronesia will understand. The word will spread that this is a school that allows things like this to happen. The church leaders, the parents, the people in the village—all will be upset unless we expel these two. Also, if you allow Perdus to stay on Moen, Keres' relatives will kill him. They'll be after him tonight. We must be ready."

"Nonsense," replied Mr. Finley. "I'm a kind of father to these boys. A father does not kick out his son."

Pete, who had his own horror stories about the breakdown of discipline the previous year, when he had been Dean of Boys, had been foaming at the bit. Now he charged into the fray. "I'm sick and tired of you and Mrs. Finley always referring to yourselves as parents to these kids! I must have heard you say that at least fifty times! Last summer, when your daughter was visiting, she drank more than the rest of us combined, partied every night, and played around. You're not such model parents."

Mrs. Finley looked stunned by Pete's accusation. She began to shake, as if she were about to become hysterical.

The chaplain asked Mr. Finley to explain himself. "If you're the father of the school family, and the students are the children, then what are we?"

"The family dogs"!" inserted Pete. "Woof . . . woof!"

"Let's vote!" Eddie urged. "We aren't getting anywhere. All we're doing is hurting each other. Let's have a show of hands."

Mr. Finley agreed but said there should be a secret ballot. He worded the resolution like this: "A *yes* vote means we can help these boys the most by keeping them here and understanding their problems. A *no* vote means we can't help them, and they should be expelled."

Expulsion won, ten to six.

Joe, remembering the threats of Titus and Johnran, asked for a unanimous vote so that the boys would not know there had been faculty dissension. Mr. Finley refused. Tom wanted to know why Mr. Finley always cast himself as the good guy and the opposition as the bad guys. Mrs. Finley broke into tears. "You think we're the lowest of the low," she cried, her voice vibrating with pain. "Well, we're not. I'm going home. I won't remain in the same room with you people any longer."

Mr. Finley said that the faculty had kicked him around long enough. He accused certain unnamed people of undermining his authority by writing to the Church Board in New York. He and Mrs. Finley made for the door. They had their arms around each other in mutual support. Eddie found that very touching. He wanted to tell them that he was sorry about the pain that the disciplinary decision had caused them, but he said nothing. At the door, Mr. Finley turned and addressed the others. "I'll tell the boys of your decision," he said. Then he bobbed through the door. Eddie thought he resembled a giant insect that had just escaped from a web of spiders.

That night Keres' relatives invaded the dorm with machetes, knives, and a shotgun. They terrorized the students, but Perdus could not be found. The men searched the jungle for several hours and then went home. Perdus and Yalmer were sleeping in the pigpen, a place no one searched because it was smelly and wet.

The following day, Perdus flew home to Ponape, and Keres moved in with relatives in the village. He became a frequent visitor at the huts on the hill.

◁ • ▷

Leif woke up early on March first with fever and vomiting and with excruciating pain in his groin. Eddie went in search of someone to drive them to the hospital. Just at the foot of the dorm stairs he nearly collided with Moses, who was taking a pre-breakfast walk. He agreed to act as their driver.

At the hospital Leif was examined by a doctor who suspected blood poisoning. Eddie and Leif were sent to the children's ward, which was dirty and crowded. Trukese mothers slept on the floor on mats beside the beds. The mothers were expected to feed their sick children, sweep the floor, knock down cobwebs, and generally do whatever needed to be done. The nurses were there to give shots and to pass out pills. The needles for shots were painfully dull from overuse, and the pills for Leif were large and bitter.

Leif received a shot of penicillin in his butt every morning and evening for three days. Each time he screamed in fear and pain. He refused the pills, spitting them onto the floor. He also spilled lemonade all over his sheets. An orderly used a dirty rag to soak up most of the liquid, but the sheets were not changed.

After each shot, the bloody cotton swabs were left on the stand by Leif's bed. The swabs became a feast for roaches. Twice a day a large bowl of cold rice topped with canned mackerel was left on the same stand. There were no utensils. Leif and Eddie, like everyone else, ate with their fingers. Then Eddie washed the bowl under a cold water tap at the end of the ward. The bowl was left by the tap to dry until its next use.

On the second day, Eddie gave Leif a sponge bath with cold water from a small washing pan. On the morning of the third day, Mrs. Finley brought Leif a stack of books from the school library. After she left, Leif and Eddie read them together. The Trukese women and their children gathered around Leif's bed to listen. A few understood English and translated for the others. One book was about dinosaurs. The pictures fascinated the Trukese. "What strange animals you have in your country!" exclaimed a woman.

In the afternoon, Leif's fever disappeared, and by suppertime he was back to normal. They checked out of the hospital and returned home by taxi. Eddie received two official-looking letters on the day of Leif's release from the hospital—one from the High Commissioner's office on Saipan and the other from an attorney's office in Boston. The one from Saipan contained an official PERMISSION TO ENTER form for Eddie and Leif. The cover letter explained that Eddie had to show the form at customs when he and Leif entered the Trust Territory. The form had been in the mails for months, having traveled to California, to mission headquarters in New York, back to Saipan, and now to Truk. The letter from Boston announced that Eddie had to appear in court on a date set a month earlier. Julie had changed her mind. Eddie guessed she had finally told her husband and her parents about Leif.

Now she wanted custody. Probably on the advice of her highly successful attorney husband, she had taken the easiest, most direct route to accomplish this. In court documents included with the letter, she had accused Eddie of spouse abuse—verbal, physical, sexual. Lawyerly language accused Eddie of threatening her, striking her often on parts of the body not visible to the public, forcing her to have sex against her will. The same lawyerly voice accused Eddie of abusing Leif in horrible ways—of striking him for no reason, of "defecating on his genitals," of causing him bodily harm. An addendum indicated that Eddie was in Micronesia because he was fleeing from his crimes.

America was after him and after his child.

Eddie feared to show the letter to any of his American colleagues. When the accusation was child abuse, people were apt to believe anything. But Eddie needed to tell someone, so he visited Moses in his home. Moses was in his favorite chair, preparing a history lesson. He read the letter with obvious disgust. "What kind of person would make these accusations?" he asked.

"I made love to the wrong woman," Eddie replied.

"Obviously. We Micronesians know none of this is true. You are a good father. We have seen you with your son as you work here and as you travel about the island. The students have said only good things about you as a father. We would know if you were a bad man. This island is very small. Such things cannot be hidden."

Eddie asked Moses for advice. Eddie told him that he had no idea what to do.

"First we will eat and drink," said Moses. "In Micronesia important decisions must be made with deliberation. No chief would ever make a decision that would affect his people until he had sat in every home, had eaten with each family, and had gotten their opinion without asking for it."

"Why doesn't he ask?" Eddie asked as Moses' wife brought them Japanese beer and a large bowl of cold rice with small pieces of reef fish sprinkled over the top.

"A chief must never be bold. Aggressiveness is not condoned in Micronesian society. A direct question could be coercion. The chief must show he cares about his people. As he sits among them, drinks what they offer, and eats their food, he asks about their children, about their relatives on distant islands, about anything that might be happening in their lives. The family knows why the chief has come, but they don't say so. That would be bad manners. Eventually, in the midst of the conversation, they somehow let him know what they feel about the important issue that has brought him. Without ever asking, he learns what he needs to know. After an appropriate interval, he goes home. After many days and many visits, the chief knows what most of the people want. Then he makes his decision, which always agrees with them. Americans think the chief has power. In actuality he has very little. His decisions are always governed by the people."

"We try to accomplish the same thing through elections," Eddie said.

"Yes, but once your Congressmen are elected, they often don't do what you want. Neither does your president. For example, he just increased the national debt to an unbelievable fifty-five billion dollars, a debt that everyone could do without."

Moses reached into the bowl with his right hand and scooped up several fingersful of rice and fish. He popped the mixture into his mouth with satisfaction and then took a long quaff of beer. Eddie followed his example, sprinkling his rice with tabasco sauce and lemon juice from a small tray of condiments. "Your president often forgets he's a hired man in the White House," added Moses.

For a while they ate and drank in silence. Eddie found himself growing nervous. Eddie knew the cause of his nervousness. As an American he didn't like to sit silently and simply enjoy another's company. He felt duty-bound to talk. He threw out a few trivial thoughts, but Moses brushed these aside with a grunt and continued to eat. When he had emptied half the bowl and had finished his beer, he was ready to give advice. "The police on Moen will not come after you unless Americans force them to act. They don't care what somebody said you did in America. Unless you killed somebody or robbed a bank, they'll leave you alone."

"But my ex-lover is very rich, and her family is very powerful in her state," Eddie explained. "She could pay someone to come out here to kidnap Leif. What if they took him from his school while I was here teaching? I wouldn't even know until it was too late."

"What happened in court?" asked Moses.

"I don't know. That was last month. I suppose that since Leif and I were not there, we are in trouble."

"It looks bad," said Moses. "What you need to do is move to a place where there are no police and where no one could harm you or your son."

"Where would that be?" Eddie asked. He didn't believe the solution was as simple as that.

"On an outer island," explained Moses. "Out there crimes are very rare and are very minor. The community punishes miscreants in its own way. Police are not necessary. No one owns much that is worth stealing and everybody has to help everybody else for the community to survive. Life out there is good. Simple, but good. All foods are natural and healthful. Clothes are a strip of cloth. The only addictions from the outside world are coffee and cigarettes. Everywhere Micronesians are hooked on both. But that's not so bad. Every day begins with sunrise and ends with sunset. There's no TV or movies or rock music stations or electricity or modern kitchens. For an American there appears to be nothing to do, and yet everybody is busy all the time, for there is always something to be done—sweeping the living area or mending the fishing nets or sewing or repairing a boat or collecting food."

"It sounds wonderful," Eddie said.

"All the evil of Moen is missing."

"I'm not sure I could spend my life out there," Eddie added.

"I understand," said Moses. "Even I am not out there. But I have an idea. I want you to meet a friend of mine, a woman. Her name is Ann Mikkelsen. She lives on the other side of Moen, near Xavier High School. She has lived in Micronesia many years." Moses told Eddie about Ann—how she had come from Oregon to Micronesia as an eighteen-year-old bride ten years earlier. She, her husband, and their new-born daughter had set up a Quaker school on Nukuoro, one of the most isolated islands in Micronesia. Nukuorans were Polynesians who had migrated into Micronesia for unknown reasons. Separated from the rest of Polynesia by distance and by time and from the rest of Micronesia by language, Nukuorans had eventually developed their own unique language and culture. "There are only about three hundred and fifty people on the island, but it's one of the most beautiful places imaginable," said Moses. "I was there once when I was a boy. My father and some other men went there to trade and to fish. The Nukuorans are very handsome and happy."

"Then why is Ann Mikkelsen now living on Moen?" Eddie wanted to know.

"Her husband drowned in a boating accident. She came here, abandoning the school. She makes a living training Peace Corps Volunteers and sailing tourists around the lagoon on her trimaran. I hear she is a very good sailor."

"But why do you want me to meet her?" Eddie wondered.

"I think she can help you with your problem," said Moses. "I also think you can help her with hers."

"And what is her problem?" Eddie asked.

"Grief," said Moses.

⋖ • ⋗

Ann Mikkelsen was a pretty woman with long, flowing brown hair, penetrating green eyes, a habit of laughing loudly with her mouth open. Her smooth skin was tanned a rich copper, and she was stylishly but casually dressed in a purple blouse, white shorts, and leather Roman-style sandals.

Moses had arranged that they meet in the restaurant of the Maramar Hotel, a tiny eatery with wooden tables topped with the same red-and-white checked oilcloth table cloths found in Kristy's bakery. They ordered the only entree available—tuna and rice. Moses had already informed Ann of Eddie's problem. He apparently had also told her as much as he knew about Eddie. Ann was immediately sympathetic but was not sure how she could help. In order to break an awkward silence, Eddie asked about Ann's boating service.

After her husband died, she had left Nukuoro because she couldn't handle the isolation alone. "I needed someone to share the place," she explained. "Memories began to overwhelm me." She had toured the islands and had settled on Truk because she could make a living there. "Japanese tourists come here to see where their fathers served in the war. A few Americans come for the diving. Truk Lagoon has about the best scuba diving in the world." Ann and her daughter, Teri, had flown to the Philippines where Ann had supervised the building of the trimaran in a boatyard in Manila. Then she and Teri had sailed the boat back to Truk. Since then they had made a modest living sailing tourists around the lagoon. "A Japanese fleet was sunk here in 1944," she explained. "A lot of people ask to visit the ships. Many are still above water. They were torpedoed, sank a few feet, and hit the coral. Walking around on the decks is like going back in time."

Ann and Eddie quickly discovered they had much in common. Both were serious readers, deeply interested in literature and history. Both were physically active, enjoying all kinds of outdoor sports. Both liked good food, music, and travel. Both adored their children. Ann talked a long time about Teri—about how intelligent she was. "She's learned a lot out here—more than she'd ever learn in the U.S. The American educational system is so bad! Out here I tutor her every morning, and in the evening we read together for several hours. She has no distractions—no TV and no rock music. She's only ten but she already likes Mozart and Melville."

Eddie asked how she survived on Nukuoro without all the things of America. "My husband and I had all the necessities," she replied. "We were supported by Quakers back in the States. A few thousand dollars went an incredibly long way because basic needs were taken care of. We had fresh fish, breadfruit, taro every day. Fruit grew all year round. I had a small veg-etable garden. The field ship visited every three months, bringing the condi-ments and spices I'd ordered. We ate gourmet meals out there. We ordered music tapes and tons of books through catalogues. The field ship brought all that stuff, plus batteries. If we wanted to travel, we jumped in the boat. If we wanted exercise, someone would always join us for baseball or volleyball. Or we could fish or dive. Life on Nukuoro was heaven. Someday I want to go back. The Quakers are still willing to support a school out there."

Ann and Eddie agreed to meet again, to take a day trip on the weekend with their children to an old Japanese lighthouse on the uninhabited cliff side of Moen, near the village of Sapuk.

On Saturday rain drenched Moen from dawn to dusk and into the early evening. On Sunday morning, skies were still gray but the rain had stopped. Eddie served Leif and himself a breakfast of pineapple and oatmeal. Eddie searched among their meager supplies for picnic materials. They still had a little Chinese cabbage left over from market day. The leaves had curled and split from the artificial cold of the refrigerator. Eddie shuffled useless cans back and forth in the cupboard until he spotted a nearly empty jar of forgot-ten peanut butter on the back of a shelf.

A bit of green fuzz had popped out on the oily surface, but Eddie scooped this off with the point of a knife and used the remainder for sandwich spread on two-day-old bread. The bread was woody, like the fine, flaking pulp of ter-mite-riddled trees. Eddie sawed it into chunky slices because thinner slices dissolved like ash into small piles. He spread the oily peanut butter, which acted to hold the crumbling mess together. He added the cabbage and voila—peanut butter-cabbage sandwiches. The sandwiches looked awful, but Eddie knew that Leif would eat anything as long as peanut butter was an ingredient. Eddie threw the sandwiches into a plastic sack he'd been saving for weeks. He also boiled the last two eggs from a rare air-freighted shipment from Guam and added these to the sack. What else was available? Eddie reached into the refrigerator and pulled out a special treat boated from California in the hold of some rusting freighter: olives. Eddie threw the sack into a knapsack and added a canteen of water.

Ann arrived in her blue Datsun pickup and they were off. Teri and Leif crouched in the open back while Ann and Eddie sat in the cab. The gray coral roadbed was full of great puddles, some as wide as the road where erosion had broken the road's back and formed treacherous gullies. They lurched and swayed along a twisting route as Ann steered for the safest fording. Black clouds still lingered off Moen, and tiny nearby Osakura was engulfed in a solid black haze. The air was still quite cool, and the puddles did not yet steam.

Because she was afraid it might rain again soon, Ann drove faster than was necessary. Leif and Teri in back clutched at the sides to prevent themselves from being thrown about. They sat on pillows to cushion the jouncing of the truck bed. Ann slowed, and Eddie shouted out the window, asking if they were all right.

They continued at a slower pace. The wind carried salt spray off the surf. The salted wind whipped their hair into bristly mesh. Eddie's beard was so salted that it scraped his skin like Brillo. Periodically Eddie used a little drinking water to dissolve the salt crystals.

They reached the turn-off that led to the tip of the island. The road was only two years old. For the first few hundred yards, it was only a narrow strip of crushed coral elevated inches above an impenetrable mangrove swamp. The route was little traveled and contained few potholes. Ann gunned the truck along the yellow-red roadbed. Unbroken bits of coral snapped and crunched under the wheels, and occasionally a loose piece ricocheted against a mudguard with a sharp crack like a breaking limb. On each side, dead, gray mangrove muck sloshed into a green mass. Broken glass, Coke bottles, beer tins, old tires, and other junk lay in the mud. Eddie thought of the salt flats in Utah when he and Leif had fled across the country. The same refuse of civilization had been scattered across the dunes.

A few moments later, they were in Sapuk. There were no Japanese structures. Homes were unpainted plywood typhoon shanties. Several had thatch roofs. Ann slowed abruptly and slipped the truck cautiously past naked children sitting in the road. In low gear, they veered around a sow and two piglets in a puddle. People lounged by a small store and stared. Eddie waved but received no reaction. The Trukese faces were as expressionless as dough. The truck crept past a waif wearing only a shirt. Perhaps three, he was trundling home with a can of mackerel balanced on his head. He dribbled urine in his path.

The road petered out to a trail meandering into the forest. Ann stopped the truck and they all piled out. Somewhere above them, on the seamost peak of the mountain, was the lighthouse, but it was lost from view in the forest canopy.

The road had ended directly in front of a home, a rather affluent cinder block structure with several rooms and unglassed windows. The carcasses of three automobiles sat in the front yard. This had to be the home of an important man. A short distance from the road sat an even larger building. From there Ann and Eddie heard the murmur of voices. A flock of chickens scattered as young boys dashed from the back of the large building and ran toward them. They stopped at a safe distance and silently observed. Eddie slipped the knapsack onto his shoulders and turned in the boys' direction. The boys stared, watching Eddie's every move as if he were a wild animal that might charge.

"Do you know the way to the lighthouse?" Ann asked. The boys said nothing. One seemed to be trying to swallow his knuckles. Another pretended he was interested in his toes. All three were barefoot and ragged, in direct contrast to Eddie and Ann and the children, in clean and relatively new sneakers, jeans, and t-shirts. The boys, who looked about nine or ten, lacked the insolence common among boys of the village near the mission school. They whispered together and shifted eyes into the forest, toward the massive green canopy. The door of a nearby home opened, and Eddie and Ann were surprised by a beautiful young island woman. She was Saipanese and dressed for Honolulu—red miniskirt, flower-splashed blouse, polished high heels. Mounds of black hair were wound about her head and tied with flowers. The woman stepped with great care through the damp gray earth. The heels left little dik-dik marks. "Can I help you?" she asked in perfect English. "I'm the village school teacher."

"We need a guide to the lighthouse," Eddie explained.

"Of course. The boys will help you. Edwin can speak a little English." She nodded toward the tallest boy and gave a series of commands in rapid Trukese. The inanimate faces of the boys burst into life. They began to gabble excitedly. The tall one thrust his shoulders forward and marched rapidly to Eddie. "My name is Edwin," he said. "I have a Peace Corps friend. His name is Steve. He teaches me English. We will go to the lighthouse now."

They set off, with Leif perched on Eddie's shoulder. Chickens scattered across swept gray earth. The path wound behind an *ut* where old men sprawled on mats, drinking Kirin beer and talking in a low buzz. Behind the tin shacks, the path twisted abruptly into the impacted forest, and they were lost in a profusion of lacy palms, banana leaves, and shoulder-high grass. The trail was a pencil-thin line of brown scribbled into the superabundant verdure. Eddie, Ann, and the children stumbled over hidden roots, slipped on fallen trunks, and constantly caught the harsh slap of leaves and boughs on their arms and chests. Edwin and the other boys led, taking great delight in the Americans' slipping and sliding as they searched for traction in the mud.

Soon they began to climb the mountain, and the trail became a treacherous solution of mud, grass, and water. They struggled up steeper and steeper embankments with the aid of fistsful of grass and shrubbery. The trail became a tunnel hacked through a bamboo thicket. A stream ran at their feet but coconut husks formed a bridge. Under their soaked sneakers, the trail was churned into a viscous mass as slithery as phlegm. Twice Ann fell to her knees, her feet flicking earth as she slid away down the slope. Once Teri fell but caught herself. Eddie found it impossible to keep his balance with Leif on his shoulders. He set him down, but Leif found it impossible to ascend unless Eddie pushed from behind.

All snatched at tiny footholds, their faces locked in concentration. The dank heat was fierce. Sweat beaded on foreheads and darkened clothes. They passed pineapple plants. The fruit was green and hard, the size of baseballs. The claws of pineapple leaves tore at their jeans and left thin, jagged lines on bare skin. From time to time, the group stepped clumsily among jumbled masses of coconuts that formed dry bridges across puddles. At a ledge Eddie and Ann paused and looked back, but only the forest was visible.

Edwin pointed down at the abutment where they stood. "This is the old Japanese road," he said. "It winds around the mountain. We are cutting across it." Ann and Eddie bent low and kicked at the green earth, which was leveled and solidly buttressed against the hill, but vegetation had over-whelmed the road. Eddie located a broad stick and shoveled away mud and grass. Two inches below the surface he struck concrete. How strange it was to find a concrete highway buried in a nearly impenetrable forest. Ann and he located the drainage ditches, which still worked, though impaired by veg-etation.

Again they climbed, and this time they were even more surprised to find concrete steps clinging vicariously to a nearly perpendicular incline. Eddie ducked under a mass of vines and caught himself as the concrete crumbled. Suddenly Leif rushed ahead, and the rest of the party scrambled to catch up. The earth leveled, and Eddie peered into open sky. They were there. The concrete lighthouse towered in front of them, gray and ominous as a prison wall.

The magnificent structure, with its foot-thick walls, had once been a refuge for its keepers and a proud beacon for lagoon-bound ships. Now it was a prisoner of the forest. The base had weathered very little. Bright red tiles were still in place and were still polished to a rich sheen by the constant sea breeze. Yet immense trees had grown right up to the walls, their branches pushing against the concrete. Below, a green wall of forest fell away to the distant ocean. Eddie and his party were cut off completely from the coast with its tin shacks, poverty, and anger.

Eddie and the others scrambled up the winding stairs to the top of the lighthouse. They were above the roiling green forest blanket. The end of the island spread outward and down and into the sea, whole and magnificent and breathtaking. The mountain itself was a great flapping tent of vegeta-tion, a sea of jungle that flowed down everywhere to breakers. There were no clearings, but along the beach wound a ribbon of road punctuated with native homes. In the lagoon turquoise waves rolled toward the island, and way out on the horizon blue. Pacific waters frothed white and green as they broke over the outer reef.

Between their smaller peak and the great knob of Tonachou, Xavier High School sat prim and proper on a napkin of green lawn. From this distance, its massive fortress walls seemed dwarfed and insignificant, huddled as they were on a low saddle of land. Xavier was the finest high school in Micronesia. Cloistered from the rest of Moen, the Catholic brothers and their students did not suffer the problems that beset Eddie's school. The main building had once been the communications center for the Japanese Navy. Its walls were four feet thick. The shutters were two-inch-thick steel. In 1944 during the American bombardment of Truk, holes the size of swimming pools had been blown in the roof, but the building had remained intact. Now it served a higher purpose.

Ann and Eddie submerged themselves in the view. Leif and Teri ran down the steps and raced back and forth below them, exploring the tower base. Ann took Eddie's hand. She rested her head on Eddie's shoulder. Eddie felt wonderfully content. The silence was broken only by occasional cries of the children and by brush strokes of breeze. The sun rapidly dried their clothes and massaged their tired muscles.

Eddie and Ann explored their perch. Names were everywhere—on the ceilings, walls, stairs, floor. Most were single names; many were pairs enclosed in hearts. All were in English or Trukese. No Japanese scrawls remained, but there were other remnants of the Japanese presence. In among the names were neat, round holes left by American bullets. The holes were everywhere—thousands of them. At one end of the lighthouse, the remains of gun emplacements were scattered in the forest. The steel track was still in place, embedded and immovable in the cement. A pocked bunker wall still eyed a pass into the lagoon, but the gun was gone, possibly disassembled by Americans after the war but more likely lugged away by Trukese to be sold as scrap iron.

Eddie held Ann, brushed her hair with his fingers, kissed her lips, squeezed her against his chest. Ann's eyes glowed with happiness. Neither spoke. They immersed themselves in the silence and in each other. Eddie daydreamed of Japanese ghosts, of little men in sailor suits staring intently out to sea. They had waited always for American ships that never came. The

194

little men had found instead the frightening screech of American planes as they rushed in like avenging hawks and splattered the unresisting lighthouse with deadly lead. Eddie wondered if any now lived who once had manned this place. What would they have thought in 1944 if they had known then that Miss Playboy of 1970 would pose seductively in the lighthouse window while a New York photographer snapped her picture? Would they have cared? Did they starve after the supplies from home stopped and the last fruit had been eaten?

Fruit trees still thrust burdened trunks around the tower base. The young guides brought Eddie and Ann green coconuts and oranges. In return, Eddie gave them a peanut butter and cabbage sandwich, and Ann added a bottle of orange pop.

Eddie broke a coconut by slamming it on the floor. Flecks of meat and milk sprayed Eddie's hair and shirt front. The guides found this immensely amusing and fetched another for Eddie to break. Eddie declined. Ann tore open an orange with great difficulty since the skin was thick and leathery. The pulp was stringy like lace, and the meat was bitter. Ann twisted her face into a grimace and hurled the orange over the parapet. Again the guides were amused. They doubled up in laughter. Eddie gave the remaining oranges to the boys, and they used them for a lively game of soccer. Leif and Teri soon joined them.

Time flowed by, the sun dipped, and they began their descent. The path was still treacherous and at times all fell. Leif got great amusement from grabbing breadfruit leaves and dropping them in Eddie's hair as Eddie struggled below him. The guides sometimes sat down and used the trail as a muddy chute. Other times they ran ahead and hid behind logs and bushes. They leaped out as Eddie and Ann approached and shot with imaginary guns. Ann responded by shooting back. Leif and Teri joined her.

A half hour later the group stumbled out of the forest and back to the truck. Eddie felt refreshed in soul and body. Ann said she felt the same. They had dipped themselves in nature and been renewed. Eddie was prepared to endure the school once again.

◄ • ►

Eddie's mother wrote from the county hospital back in Michigan. She was recuperating from another car accident. Eddie's father had driven too fast, had missed a turn and had slammed the car into stacked cordwood. Now Eddie's mother had a new steel rod in her shattered hip, but the wound had refused to heal. She'd been in the hospital nearly a month and still a thin stream of yellow-green pus flowed from the drainage tube at the top of her thigh.

Mother said nothing about why Father had been driving so fast, but Eddie remembered Sunday drives when he was a boy. His father had always driven. His mother had always sat in the front passenger seat while Eddie had usually buried himself in a book against the seat in the back. Mother had usually been angry about something. On these drives, she had always seemed to be angry. Maybe Father had not dressed properly for an outing. Maybe he had not washed the odor of blood out of his butcher hands. Maybe he had extended more credit to some poor mining family that hadn't paid for its groceries in weeks. Or maybe he had loaned some money or a rifle or a vehicle or something else to somebody who needed it. Father had always done that sort of thing. Whatever Father's transgression, Eddie's mother had let him hear about it. Her voice had hammered at him. She had shouted her displeasure again and again. Father couldn't escape.

Eddie remembered his father lighting a cigar. At this point, he had always lit a cigar. Mother hated the smoke. She had voiced her hatred. Father had puffed harder and harder.

Eddie too had hated the cigar smoke but he had said nothing. It would have been traitorous. After all, he had secretly been on his father's side. But he had never said so. He had hidden in the back seat, his face buried in words.

Eddie remembered his mother's voice rising steadily. It had become a demented shriek. Then it had become a clangorous roar, as painful to the ears as a fire siren.

She had been a one-woman mob, Eddie's mother. And there had been no avoiding her tirades. Eddie remembered his father trapped behind the wheel inside the closed trap of the car.

Father had wanted more than anything to escape from his wife's voice—to flee to the peace and quiet of the surrounding forest.

At some point he had always stepped on the gas. Soon he had stepped harder. He was trying to outrace the pursuing beast.

Eddie remembered his mother's voice changing its tone, losing tension, and becoming more liquid. It had begun to plead. "Please slow down. You're going much too fast. Slow down!" Mother had almost burst into tears.

Father had slowed down. So had Mother. The cigar had become a half burned and half chewed stub. Father had unrolled the window and had tossed out the fat, blackened butt. The crisis was over.

In Eddie's memory, yes, but in the present, no. Father had taken her into a woodpile. What would happen next?

"You've got to get off this campus," said Ann. "The place is driving you crazy. You have a sick kind of intensity—unreleased nervous energy that probably is raising your blood pressure." Ann rubbed her hand against Eddie's stomach in a teasing way and moved against him. Her fresh, clean smell, mixed with the faint odor of her perfume, clouded Eddie's mind.

Ann had appeared on a Saturday morning just as Leif and Eddie had finished breakfast. A long line of students was already busily advancing across the lower campus, backs bent and machetes flailing as they cut grass. The math teacher was among them, his skinny white legs glowing in the heat of a sunny day. Perry stood officiously far off on the edge of the outdoor basketball court. He was directing his team as they swept the cement playing surface and washed the backboards.

"I'm supposed to assign students to dormitory clean-up," Eddie explained. "Later I have to check their work."

"They're big boys—men actually. They can handle a broom all by themselves. Let's go to the beach." Ann was wearing a swimsuit under cut-off jean shorts. Her head was protected by a red bandanna tied across her forehead.

"I don't think I should," Eddie told her.

"I think you ought to," she replied. "You're too pale. You're a big, athletic guy who's dying to get outside. So come with me."

"Mr. Finley will flip," Eddie answered as he put dirty dishes into the sink and ran enough water to cover them.

"Do you like this Finley person?" Ann knew the answer—she'd already heard Eddie complaining about the way the school was run.

"Hell no!"

Ann laughed. "Then let him throw a fit. What do you care? Do you believe in all these silly, time-consuming rules and regulations of his?"

"No."

"Then don't enforce them. Tell him to go to hell. What you need is someone like me—a free spirit! Someone who does what she wants to do."

"So you see yourself as a free spirit." As Eddie spoke he sensed the ludicrousness of the situation. As soon as he finished the dishes he would go through the dorm and schedule the students' day. Later he would schedule tomorrow. The weekend would disappear without ever having existed. Eddie would have driven himself and the students a little closer to the edge.

"I've always been a free spirit," continued Ann, watching Eddie carefully for a reaction. "That's why I went to Nukuoro with my husband. He was a free spirit too. Out there we could immerse ourselves in life—no desks, no clocks, no bureaucrats, no Mr. Finleys. Just life—caring people, beaches, fish, mosquitoes, the sea and sun. Everything out there is real. So let's go to the beach. I want to feel *your* realness near me."

The last dish was washed, the spigot was pulled, the dirty water whirled down the drainpipe. "Okay, okay," Eddie said, feeling relief and excitement as he gave in. "Where are we going?"

"We'll take my boat over to a little island called Piis," said Ann. "A few families live at one end, but mostly it's uninhabited. Teri and Leif can collect shells and help us fish.

We can swim, walk in the forest, listen to the surf, maybe read. It'll be fun."

In minutes Eddie had collected Leif, their gear, and some sandwiches. Ann had a case of beer in the boat cooler. Teri was at the boat, waiting for the rest of them.

198

Two hours later, on Piis, Ann showed Eddie how to set a weighted net across a depression in the reef. Wearing snorkels and holding long sticks, she and Eddie herded a school of reef fish toward the depression. At a signal from Ann, Teri and Leif reeled in the net, using a small boom and tackle. They caught about fifty fish of varying size. After they had sorted them on the deck, cleaned them, thrown the guts into a bait box, and put the fish on ice, Ann and Eddie guzzled beer.

"Now I'll show you how Micronesians fish when they're alone," said Ann. Taking a spear, she dove overboard, her long, tan body slicing through the water as if she were completely at home there. Soon she re-emerged with a fish flopping at the end of the spear shaft. She bit the fish at the back of the head and tossed the lifeless form toward the boat. "The bite saves them getting out of the water," she shouted.

"What's that?" Eddie asked from the deck as a long, dark shadow sliced beneath the trimaran and raced toward Ann. She had spotted the movement too.

"Jesus, it's a shark!" she cried and began to swim energetically toward the boat as the shadow rushed beneath her, turned, and began to pursue. Ann reached the boat and clambered up the ladder while the children and Eddie watched breathlessly. "Damn!" she cried as she tumbled onto the deck.

"Are you okay?" Eddie asked as Ann sat on the deck, holding her foot and inspecting her toes.

"I'm fine," she replied. "I banged my toes on the ladder. I was in too much of a hurry. That kind of shark is rarely dangerous, but they still make me nervous."

Later, on the beach, the children collected shells of every shape and size, including a large conch that Leif could barely lift.

"I've slept on beaches like this," said Ann as she and Eddie stretched out in the shade of a palm tree. "It's lovely except for the sand crabs and centipedes. The crabs don't do anything, but it's creepy if they crawl over you. The centipedes leave blisters on bare skin. They come out of the sand at night and will crawl over anything on the beach."

"You're amazing!" Eddie told her. "Most women I've known would never sleep on a beach, not even in a tent."

"Neither would most men," added Ann, laughing. "The way I look at it, we only live once, and we'll never have another chance to experience anything. A truly independent person doesn't divide life into gender roles. I try to learn whatever I need to know. That means I can maintain the motor on my boat *and* sweep the floor and cook. If I don't do it all, who will? Out here there are no service people."

"I agree," said Eddie. "But I'm still impractical sometimes. I'd rather read a good book than learn how to fix a boat motor."

"Books are important too," said Ann. "But we must also function in the real world. If you come to Nukuoro, you'll need to be able to do both."

"Am I going out there with you?" Eddie asked.

"Who knows? We must wait and see. Do you want to?"

"I don't know," Eddie replied.

"I haven't slept with a man since my husband died," said Ann, surprising Eddie with her bluntness. She pressed against him, with her head resting on his chest. The sun was glinting painfully on the nearby water. "None of the other men in Truk have interested me. You, I'd like to sleep with."

"Is this a proposition?" Eddie asked.

"Yes. Can you get off your damned campus tonight and stay at my place? Leif can come along. He can stay in Teri's room. She'd be happy for the company."

"That would be wonderful," Eddie said.

"Mr. Finley will never know," said Ann. "And even if he does, who cares? I'll drive you back early in the morning."

"Fine," Eddie said.

"Do you care if Mr. Finley knows?" Ann asked teasingly. She rose and walked down the beach, stepping gingerly into the incoming waves.

"Not really," Eddie replied. "In fact, I'd like him to know."

"Why?" Ann flipped water at the backs of her legs, trying to get the damp sand off.

"So that he knows I'm not the automaton he'd like me to be," Eddie said.

"All right!" cried Ann as she scooped up water from the incoming wave and threw it at Eddie.

≺ • ≻

Sunday. Ann, Eddie, and the children were returning from Southfield Beach. A jellyfish had left a long blister on Eddie's arm, but otherwise he and the others had had a wonderful afternoon of swimming and beach volleyball.

"There's something I want you to see," said Ann as she pulled her truck off the road in the middle of Southfield Village.

The four walked a short way along a path that led back to the beach from the road. In front of them was a long thatched-roof building with a sharply peaked roof. "This is the canoe house," explained Ann. "In the old days, little boys barely out of the toddling stage would come here to listen to the older men talk about sailing. After that they'd come here nearly every day all their lives. First they'd be students, and later they'd learn to build a canoe and to navigate. Gradually they would grow more and more intimate with the sea until they finally blended into it, thought like it and instinctively acted with it. Now the young ones get drunk nearly every day and control of the sea is slipping away. Soon no one will know how to navigate on long sea voyages."

The inside frame of the house consisted of huge beams carved into elaborate designs. The only outrigger canoe in the building was old and had fallen into disuse. The wood was cracked and dry and worms had gotten into it.

"Leif should learn to sail," said Ann. "Teri is already pretty good at it, but she still needs to learn a lot."

"You're a very special woman," Eddie said, wrapping his arms around her waist and squeezing. "I could love you."

"Of course I am," Ann laughed. "Let's get out of here. I'm not supposed to be here. Canoe houses are forbidden to women."

They left and returned to the truck. "Do you resent that?" Eddie asked as they drove away. "After all, you're a navigator. Why shouldn't you be able to go into a canoe house?"

"I can live with the prohibition," said Ann as she steered around pot-holes in the center of the road. "Men have made the canoe house taboo to women because building and navigating a canoe takes years of knowledge. The men don't want women to interfere with a young man's attainment of that knowledge. After all, the lives of islanders depend upon those canoes and the men who man them. What would happen if a pretty young woman sat in on those lessons? Would a young man's mind concentrate on her or on navigation? Anyway, there are places strictly for women too—where men aren't welcome. In the women's meeting house, the young women learn to weave, to create cloth out of tree bark, and so on. They don't want men interfering with that kind of knowledge. Micronesians place great importance upon passing down such arts to their children. Micronesians value crafts as arts. Americans seem to value wealth a lot more."

"So you have no problem with a differentiation of gender roles?" Eddie asked.

"It depends on whether or not the differentiation is completely fair," replied Ann. "Sometimes the divisions of knowledge make sense, and sometimes they don't. Personally, I'd prefer two canoe houses—one for training women and the other for training men."

"And what's happening on Moen?" Eddie asked.

"On Moen Micronesian arts are dead." Ann sounded angry as she said this. "Did you ever look into people's eyes here? It's like looking at the floor of the Marianas Trench—utterly foreign, devoid of most life, and yet filled with this terrific pressure that implodes everything."

At the librarian's behest, Eddie pried open a library file frozen shut by rust. Inside he found only the yellowed diary of Robert Logan's daughter. Robert Logan had been the first missionary to live in Truk Lagoon. When he arrived the Trukese were killing each other at a suicidal rate with guns bought from white traders. Logan had talked them into expelling the traders, disarming, and destroying the guns. Eddie knew that Logan was still remembered in the islands as a sort of saint, though all of this had happened in the 1880s. After the guns were destroyed, Logan had brought his family to Truk.

Logan's daughter had grown up in Truk but had returned as an adolescent to America to complete schooling. As the diary opened, she returned to Truk to take up her father's work. On Truk she became a lay pastor, school principal, teacher, choir mistress, surrogate mother to her flock.

After the visit of a trading ship, a smallpox epidemic had broken out. Whole villages had died. People had buried themselves in sand to escape fever. They had died all along the beach, only their heads visible. Miss Logan's students had died in droves—sometimes half a dozen succumbing within an hour. She couldn't bury them fast enough, and those who could have helped had died. Somehow she had persevered, prayed a lot, and survived. So had a few others.

Miss Logan had traveled all over the western Pacific after that, visiting remote atolls in the mission sailing ship, *Morningstar*. Miss Logan had been the captain. Micronesians had loved her for her navigational and human skills.

In the Marshalls, her ship had run into a typhoon and had been driven onto a reef by fierce winds and thirty-foot waves. A lifeboat had been lowered. The crew had hoped to use it to pass over the reef to the safety of a nearby island. As Miss Logan leaped from the deck, surging seas had thrust the lifeboat directly under her. She had struck the gunwale with her back and had flopped like a broken fish onto the boat's floor.

Her back had been broken. Her vertebrae had been shattered. She had lain in terrible pain on mats on the floor of a Marshallese home for weeks. Finally a German trading ship had anchored beyond the reef. The captain had agreed to take her aboard, to take her to Djakarta in the Dutch Indies. He had strapped her tightly to the table in his quarters. She had lain there for more weeks while the ship passed through the islands, taking on cargo and unloading goods. In Djakarta, doctors had been afraid to operate, but a ship was leaving for Sydney in a few days. Miss Logan had again been strapped to the table. The trip to Sydney had been arduous. Several fierce storms had caused deck damage.

Miss Logan had gained courage throughout her ordeal by recalling how her father had placed his own body between the warring factions on Truk when she had been a small girl.

In Sydney Miss Logan's back had been examined by a team of surgeons. The back had knit itself, but crookedly. The surgeons had rebroken the back, repaired the vertebrae and put Miss Logan in a body cast.

Eventually the cast had come off, Miss Logan had walked again, but her back had remained very weak. She had returned to America.

The diary ended.

Eddie showed the diary to Ann. It was short—she read all of it in an hour. "Ms. Logan and I have a lot in common," Ann said as she scanned the last page. "She and I are both pretty unorthodox. I'm not sure I would have survived all that she went through though."

"I'm not sure anyone could have unless they had her faith," Eddie added. Ann was a tough, independent loner—had been one since her husband's death. She set out to explain her past to Eddie. Her self-reliance went back to childhood. Ann's mother, Joyce, had come from a large working-class family in Portland. Joyce's father had fallen from a scaffold while his children were still small. His legs had been shattered, and his vertebrae broken. After that he had received a small pension which allowed the family to survive. By the time Joyce was fifteen, she was working forty hours a week as a waitress in a neighborhood hamburger joint. Among the regular customers had been the black-jacketed members of a bikers' club called the Scorpions. Joyce had taken up with a Scorpion named Floyd. They had had a few wonderful weekends together.

Then Floyd and two other bikers had beaten to death an old man who had resisted a robbery attempt. Floyd had gone to prison for life at the same time Joyce had found herself pregnant with Ann.

Ann had never met her father. "He's probably still in the State Pen in Oregon," she told Eddie.

Ann had been raised by her grandparents while her mother had gone through a long succession of lovers. Ann loved her mother but still hated the way her mother had never built anything out of life. "She was always grasping at things," said Ann. "But she couldn't hold onto anything—a man, a job, an address. She just wandered through life searching for stability but never found it. She died in a car accident fifteen years ago. By then I had decided to be just the opposite of her. I studied hard in school, went to church, and held down a weekend job. I got a degree from our community college. At church I met some people who loved to sail. One sailor was in his mid-twenties. He'd grown up in Indianapolis and had attended Earlham, a Quaker college. He'd left the Midwest after college and had hitchhiked to Oregon. He'd fallen in love with the ocean at first sight. I loved his sense of adventure. A year later we got married. A year after that we had Teri. Then we came out here to run the Quaker school on Nukuoro. We were there until his death three years ago."

Weeks passed. Ann and Eddie grew close. Teri and Leif became good friends. The school year was rapidly coming to a close, but the craziness continued. Eddie spent almost every weekend trying to keep order in the midst of student drunkenness and violence.

Out in the lagoon a man from Tol was murdered in his boat. The boat was found with the motor turned off. There was a lot of blood and a pair of sandals, but no body. Two days later, two other Tolese were stabbed to death in downtown Moen. A man from the local village was shot in retaliation.

On a Saturday, the chaplain took a group of students by boat on an overnight religious retreat to a small, uninhabited island a half mile from Moen. The boys smuggled a case of vodka aboard. That night the boys got drunk, fought with rocks and knives, wrestled into a bonfire, and attempted to rape one of the girls. The chaplain was up all night, trying to restore order. At dawn the group returned to school.

At the meeting of the Discipline Committee, Perry and Mr. Finley tried to prevent strong action. "You have no proof that the boys were drunk," said Perry, for Adam had not brought the empty bottles back from the island. "It's just your word against theirs. The boys insisted that they had been frightened by ghosts—that the ghosts had driven them crazy.

After an inconclusive meeting, Adam returned dejectedly to his home. On the way he heard suspicious noises in the tall grass behind the pigpen. He went to investigate. He found two Marshallese sophomores, Gerson and Mersihda, busily engaged in sex. They jumped to their feet as the chaplain stood over them. Adam ordered them to dress and to go to their respective dormitories.

Adam's wife was on the women's Discipline Committee. Ellen asked that the committee meet immediately. The other members were Janice and Mary. Perry had fed Janice a lot of poisonous thoughts about Adam and Eddie. Janice, therefore, detested Adam—considered him a dangerous man out to harm innocent students.

Mary had no such thoughts but saw everyone through the rosy filter of her extremely conservative religious views. A virgin herself and proud of it, she could not imagine one of her students having sex in tall grass by a pigpen.

At the meeting, Janice voiced anger that Mersihda's case had been brought up. She had talked to Mersihda, who had denied everything. Janice saw no reason for further action. Her thin face was ashen as she objected to Ellen's request that Mersihda appear before the committee. "I have other work to do," said Janice.

Ellen pointed out that the men's committee members also had many other things to do but that they had met for countless hours over disciplinary matters.

"I asked Mersihda if she was doing what your husband says she was," said Janice to Ellen. Janice's voice was shaking with malice.

"And she lied, and you accepted the lie," replied Ellen who, in her Berkeley days, had been known for her confrontational political nature. Janice represented all the people Ellen had hated then—the pro-war, pater-nalistic conservatives who either resisted or ignored the idealism of the subculture. Ellen's voice was needle sharp. Her eyes were red with fury, as if she were about to physically attack.

"Well, I don't want to hear any of the details," said Janice.

"But that's the only way you'll ever get the truth," snapped Ellen. "Bring Mersihda in here for questioning."

"We should give the girl at least a week of detention," said Mary. She smiled in an attempt to be conciliatory.

"That's ridiculous!" cried Janice. "She didn't do anything! We have only the chaplain's word that her blouse was unbuttoned and that her skirt was above her hips! He probably just looked up it and now is relieving his guilt by blaming her!"

Ellen was shocked by the obvious hatred in Janice's voice. For a moment, she could not reply. "Janice, she was practically naked, and so was Gerson." Ellen's voice had a quiver, for Janice's dart had struck home.

"You can't say that. Only your husband allegedly saw it, and Mersihda says it isn't true. I prefer to believe her. Not him. For that matter, I don't believe you either. Neither of you is fit to teach. All you want to do is punish. You don't want to understand these young people."

Shaking with pent-up fury, Ellen tried to reason one more time. "You're being unfair," she replied. "You're treating Adam and me as the villains. We didn't do anything. It's not our fault that Mersihda decided to crawl off into the grass with Gerson."

Mary tried to mediate. She suggested that Mersihda receive a two-week detention for being with a boy without permission.

Janice would have none of it. "The girl is innocent," she insisted. "It's the chaplain. He's sick. He's perverted. He's accusing poor Mersihda of being what he'd like her to be—naked and willing in *his* bed."

Ellen wanted to slap her, wanted to feel the crunch of her hand against the pale flesh of Janice's face. Ellen wanted to hear the explosion of sound accompanying the impact. She felt suddenly weak at the knees and sick inside from not acting.

She left the meeting, went home, told her husband what had happened, and began to sob quietly in the chair where she slouched. Adam stayed up all night composing a long letter to the mission office in New York. He detailed all the craziness of the school—the knife fights, the rapes, the damaged toilets, the drinking. He described the incompetence and misplaced fatherliness of Mr. Finley and Perry. He described the tensions that had torn apart the faculty.

Early in the morning he mailed his letter and bought two tickets for the next flight to Hawaii. Two days later he and Ellen were gone. Eddie felt deserted. They had been good friends and supporters through all the pain and turmoil.

A week later Mike West completed his Peace Corps service and flew home to California.

Except for Ann and Leif, Eddie felt alone among strangers. He was delighted when he learned that someone had to sail to Dublon to check on the condition of a mission guesthouse. Eddie volunteered and asked Ann if she would take Leif and him on her trimaran. She agreed.

The trimaran was primarily a sailing craft, but it required at least two experienced sailors to control the canvas. Ann asked a Trukese member of her crew to come along and, on the afternoon they sailed, she designated Eddie the official bailer.

They left about two, plowing through heavy seas under a clear sky during the two-mile crossing. They swung by the point of Dublon and then followed breakers between black coral outcroppings. They passed over the turquoise reef glowing in bright sunlight and tied up at a rock wharf covered with coconut husks to cushion people's feet. Here the island rose abruptly for perhaps two hundred feet.

Beside the dock, an ancient boathouse was nearly falling into the water. Half the roof had fallen in, one window was missing, and the wall had gaps where boards had tipped out of position. WAREHOUSE was scrawled in black paint across one side, the letters as lopsided as the building. A piece of wire looped around the door to keep out intruders. A smaller room in the back still had its roof intact. The room was locked. It contained the local minister's outboard motor and gas tank. One could easily have broken into this room, but Ann assured Eddie that stealing was not a problem on Dublon.

"The people here would never steal," she said. "They have the old values. They respect each other and value the elderly. The owner of the outboard is a very old man." Beside the boathouse sat the orange-and-blue boat of the minister.

Ann was ravishingly beautiful that day, her long brown hair billowing about her shoulders in the steady, warm wind blowing onto the island. She was dressed in a purple blouse that brought out the sparkle in her green eyes. Her white shorts showed off the deep tan of her legs.

Teri and Leif were antsy after the confinement of the boat. They raced up the jungle trail, which climbed the embankment. The Trukese crewman stayed with the trimaran, while Ann and Eddie followed the children. At one place the jungle was torn away, the shrubbery flattened into the earth by some great weight. Ann said a bulldozer had recently leveled the shore near the boathouse, and this was the path it had taken. Teri and Leif scrambled up the bulldozed trail, nearly falling several times.

They came upon the mission guesthouse suddenly at the top of the embankment. The house was surrounded by flowers—huge red blossoms sprouted everywhere around the foundation. Teri picked enough flowers to weave *maramars* for each to wear in their hair. Eddie had no key, but a windowpane in the door was held in place by two bent nails. Eddie twisted them back, removed the pane, reached inside, and unlocked the door. The inside of the building was being hollowed out by termites. Holes rifled all the beams. Several needed to be replaced. The raffia on the walls was frayed, brittle, and musty.

Reader's Digests from 1958 to 1961 were scattered over the living room floor, along with elementary school textbooks for math, social studies, and English. One of the texts was *Arithmetic*, used by Ann when she was a child. She laughed with delight when she noticed it, sat down on the dusty floor, and thumbed through the pages. "I recognize some of the word problems," she said. "They deal with the speed of trains, the height of skyscrapers, and stuff like that. I'll bet they confused the hell out of some poor Trukese kid."

"Why is that out here?" Eddie asked.

"I assume somebody used it to teach arithmetic in a local school," said Ann. "On Nukuoro I wrote my own text. The problems dealt with the relationship between the length of a canoe hull and the height of the sail, or between the size of a taro patch and the number of plants. Stuff like that."

A *World Book Encyclopedia* sat on a shelf, the pages blackened by mildew and bored by worms. Two rusty typewriters, a broken phonograph, a rusty refrigerator, and a tipped-over backless chair completed the furnishings. Ann and Eddie sat on an old desk and surveyed the wreckage. Ann was feeling melancholy.

"Our home on Nukuoro has probably fallen into disrepair even more than this place," she said. "It was once so beautiful. My husband and I worked very hard to make it into our dream home, but the tropics destroy everything very quickly when you go away."

"I'm sorry," Eddie said. He kissed her neck, smelling the clean, faint odor of shampoo in her hair.

"Like all of the outer islands, Nukuoro is tiny, but it gave us everything we needed to sustain life—bananas, mangoes, papayas, and a local fruit called *afour* to break up the monotony of taro and breadfruit. The reef gave us fish, turtle, octopus, lobster. It was wonderful." Ann took Eddie's hand and squeezed.

The adults called Teri and Leif, who had wandered off into other rooms. They all went outside to escape the heat, the disarray, the decay. Eddie relocked the door and replaced the pane. Behind the guesthouse was another house, built by the Japanese during the war. Under the Japanese house was a bunker complex, the gun hole four feet across. In the back wall a tunnel led to two rooms carved out of a nearby bombproof hill. A trench led to what used to be a military hospital but was now a Protestant elementary school. A second tunnel led into the hill and then went straight up like a chimney. Eddie and the others entered that tunnel, and at the chimney, Teri climbed several rungs of the iron ladder embedded in stone. Leif wanted to join her but Eddie said no. A bat fluttered past Teri's face, and she dropped, screaming, to the cave floor.

Leaving the area around the houses, they followed a path toward the former hospital. The white, wooden edifice was perched five feet off the ground on concrete pillars. In front was a massive mango tree, its base swept clean of undergrowth and covered with lava stones. Nearby was a Protestant church. It was locked, but Eddie and Ann climbed in through a window while the children played outside. The inside was painted bright gold and silver. Gold and silver tinsel was wrapped around the altar railing.

The quiet was beautiful. Ann mentioned that the church on Nukuoro was just as beautiful. "They don't use tinsel, though. Everything there is natural."

Near the mango tree, several shirtless children were playing marbles. Teri and Leif joined them as Ann and Eddie relaxed nearby. "Robert Logan is buried about one hundred feet away, in that brush," said Ann, pointing at a low piece of jungle.

Eddie urged Ann to lead the way to the grave but she was hesitant. "Look at the sky," she said. A black cloud had filled half the heavens and was rapidly threatening to fill the rest. "There'll be gusts and rain on the way back. It'll be a rough crossing. We should start back as soon as possible."

Eddie insisted it wouldn't take long to visit the grave. His voice betrayed his excitement, and Ann acquiesced, but already the wind was growing stronger, causing her hair to whip about her face. "All right," she said. "But let's hurry."

Ann and Eddie forced their way through the jungle. Blowdowns lay everywhere, as well as thornbushes as tall as Eddie. Together they nearly stumbled into a hole carved out of the earth for no obvious purpose.

One moment they were pushing through undergrowth higher than their heads, and the next moment they stepped into a clearing about twenty feet on a side. The clearing contained wiry grass perhaps a foot high. The grave marker was in the center—a tapered obelisk of gray granite looking much like a miniature Washington Monument. On the base was carved:

> In memory of
> Reverend Robert A. Logan
> American Board of Christian Foreign Missions
> Who died here on Dec. 27, 1887
> He was 44 years old

As soon as Eddie finished reading, Ann signaled that they had to go. They retraced their route, collected the children and hurried to the trimaran.

The sea was high. White breakers smashed into the dock, sending spray across the trimaran's deck. "It's going to be a difficult crossing," said Ann. "In mid-passage the waves are going to be very high, and the wind is directly against us. We'll have to go without a sail. The motor is small but efficient. It'll take a long time."

The Trukese crewman had already lowered the sails and stowed the canvas. He and Ann shouted orders back and forth as the children and Eddie donned life jackets.

Using the partial shelter of the dock, Ann and her Trukese turned the boat without difficulty and quickly passed through the smaller waves scattering over the turquoise reef. The boat glided between the coral markers and headed into the open channel. Quickly they were battered by terrifying waves rolling toward them from beyond Moen. The trimaran pitched and rolled at crazy angles, riding up over one wave as if it were about to climb to the sky and then dipping down into the following trough as if it were lunging for the bottom. After each trough the next wave battered the bow, sending a shiver the length of the boat.

Eddie's concern was all with Leif. If they were to tip over or if Leif were to fall overboard, he'd drown in the mountainous waves in spite of the life jacket. Eddie ordered Leif to sit on the floor, in the middle, and to hold tightly to a seat screwed to the deck. Teri joined him, and together they huddled in fear.

The trimaran seemed to be making no headway. "This is no good!" Ann shouted to her crewmate. "We'll have to swing east toward the reef. The tricky part will come when we swing northwest and beat our way back to Moen."

The Trukese crewman concurred. "We'll get battered on the reef at the end of Dublon if we continue like this," he said.

Ever so carefully, he redirected the boat, and they struggled on. Hours passed. The sun, hidden by overcast, was obviously setting as the world grew darker. Soon Moen became a looming black patch somewhere to their right. The rain stung their eyes. The lagoon blackened until Eddie had to be within a yard of Leif in order to discern his son.

Ann scurried about the deck, checking every detail of the trimaran. The Trukese directed the boat through each surge and ebb. They were all efficiency while the other three were fear. Finally the outer reef frothed ahead, the surging foam white against the inky sky. At the critical moment, as the trimaran peaked on a particularly huge wave, the Trukese swung the boat around, caught the accompanying wave on the rear, and they began their race with the waves toward the protection of Moen's lee shore.

The motor droned on, a secure sound amidst the screech of the wind and the rumble of the angry sea. By the time they reached calmer waters in the lee, they could still see nothing, but Ann and her crewman could relax a little. They let Eddie navigate. "My husband used to call the Pacific the eye of God," Ann said. The strain on her nerves had faded. "He got the idea from some poem. He used to say that all of us are less than mere flecks on the surface of this immense eye, which stares eternally heavenward. He said that planes were as unimportant as gnats, that ships were little more than nothing. Coming from him, these grandiose statements sounded odd since he was the type of guy who could spend all day examining a single coral formation."

Eddie didn't reply. He sat at the wheel and stared into the darkness, hoping they were still running parallel to Moen. He was gripping the wheel so tightly that his hands had cramped.

"My husband thought often about the meanings of things." Ann's voice took on a deeper tone as she remembered. "Yet his death was absurd and defies meaning. He made a mistake in a storm about the same tenacity as this one. He didn't get his sails down quickly enough. The boat capsized, and he got tangled in a rope as he went overboard. He probably drowned very quickly."

"That's terrible." Eddie wanted to reach out and hold her, but he remained glued to the wheel with the knowledge that their lives depended upon it.

"I should teach you to sail," Ann said. "But carefully. I don't want something like that to happen to you too."

"I'm willing," Eddie said. He liked the idea—the challenge of a new sport and the physical nature of it.

"We'll start next weekend," Ann said. "Nothing fancy. We'll run the boat near Moen. The day my husband died was the worst day of my life." Ann reached over and ran her arm across Eddie's shoulders. Her hand was cold and wet where it touched his neck. "People used to think that we had hardships out there, but we didn't. The lagoon was more beautiful than any other place I've been. Teri had her own mini-outrigger and paddles, complete with safeguards against evil spirits. A couple of the men made it for her. She speaks fluent Nukuoran. Imagine! There are only about four hundred speakers in the whole world!"

"Someday I'd like to go there," Eddie said.

It was too dark for them to notice small breakers slapping against the reef's edge to their right. The first notice of trouble was a slight trembling of the trimaran. They had passed over the reef into shallow water. "Coral!" Eddie shouted but too late.

With a loud crunch and then a tearing sound, the motor was nearly torn from its mooring. The trimaran banged over a second piece of coral as Ann killed the engine. The boat was jarred by another impact. Eddie was tossed forward onto the deck.

The children and Eddie waited while Ann and the Trukese checked for damage. "I think we're okay," Ann said at last. "We scraped her, but she's not taking water. Probably the metal suffered a couple of dents." She tested the motor, and it too seemed to be fine. "We have to find a channel that leads off the reef," she explained. "We can't just leave the boat and walk to shore because it's quite far and a reef can be a treacherous thing at night, especially for the children. Beyond the reef, it's probably a mangrove swamp, and we couldn't traverse that at night either. We'll just have to find a channel or be here all night."

Eddie and the Trukese slipped overboard and pushed the boat slowly forward while Ann sat on the bow with a long pole and directed them past outcroppings. Occasionally they ran the motor slowly where there seemed to be a channel. Ahead Ann could see what she thought were posts, upright shadows in the water. "What are those?" she asked her crewman. He didn't know.

"*Rananim*," answered a post, and Ann broke into peals of laughter. The boat was surrounded by Micronesian fishermen—all young, all with nets, all with bare backs silhouetted against quiet waters. Ann and her crewman spoke to them in Trukese.

The fishermen indicated a nearby channel. Several walked ahead of the trimaran until it reached open sea.

"*Kiri so sapu!*" Ann thanked them profusely, but they said nothing, They slid off into the darkness once again.

The rest of the trip was uneventful. Ann docked below the school. Exhausted, Leif and Eddie plodded up the long driveway toward bed. Ann and Teri drove home.

Eddie's mother wrote from Michigan. The last of the snow was melting with the arrival of May. She said how proud she was that Eddie was serving the church in Micronesia. She mentioned how much she missed him and how much she wanted to get to know Leif. She explained that her most recent accidents plus her diabetes were devastating her health. The doctors had told her that the diabetes was preventing the healing of her broken hip. Now she had numbness in her toes. Worst of all, the diabetes was slowly taking her sight. Her eyes had been perpetually red for months from hemorrhages in the tiny vessels of the iris. The hemorrhages had left scar tissue. The scar tissue had grown. Soon she might be blind. She was not so much frightened as aggrieved. Why, she wondered, had God attacked her with such afflictions? She felt like Job. She wrote several times that she was still a young woman.

When Eddie's father was not working, he was devoting much time to taking care of his wife. He cooked the carefully prescribed no salt/no sugar meals, helped her move around, escorted her to the bathroom, baked bread, did the myriad duties necessary when someone was handicapped.

Eddie's mother did not see his effort as good enough. She complained vociferously throughout the last half of the letter that his meals were tasteless, that he didn't clean the house properly or the bathroom often enough, and that he worked too much and too long, leaving her often alone.

Eddie threw the letter into the trash can. They are still at war, he thought. They will always be at war, but no one will win. The one who lives longer will have the privilege of saying only laudatory things about the deceased. Eddie could imagine his mother exclaiming, "Oh, he was a wonderful man!" He could imagine his father exclaiming "I don't know how I can go on without her!"

But that was in the future. Unknown.

"After we're done here, we'll have to visit your grandparents in Michigan," Eddie told Leif.

Leif was excited by the idea. Eddie had told him often about the lakes and the forest. "I want to build a treehouse and fish," Leif said.

◄ • ►

Ann began Eddie's sailing lessons. Nearly every afternoon Leif and he were on the trimaran. They soon formed rich copper tans. Eddie's body lost its flab—his muscles were growing lean and hard. At night his body ached with the pleasure that came from enjoyable activity.

Ann and Eddie grew closer. He thought of her constantly during the long, frustrating class days. His frustration did not come from the students, who were enthusiastic learners—full of a curiosity that Eddie's American students had lacked. It came from Mr. Finley and Perry. They were in trouble with the mission office in New York. They included Eddie as one of the troublemakers who had caused their demise. A new school director was being flown out for the last month of school. Mr. Finley and Perry would soon be ordinary teachers like the rest. Soon a new principal would be telling them what to do.

In the meantime, Eddie talked Mr. Finley into hiring the most vicious drunk in the village as a night watchman. Spin sat each evening in a chair

216

in the middle of the road at the school entrance. He had a fifth of vodka in his lap He waited for other drunks to try to come on campus. Then he beat the hell out of them. He'd already put several in the hospital. He seemed to enjoy the fights. Eddie kept a case of fifths in his office, just in case Spin ran out. Several times Eddie had brought Spin more. Spin had smiled mischievously and had flexed his biceps. He seemed to be a happy man.

≺ • ≻

In the final week of classes, Moses stopped Eddie on his way to a meeting with the new director. He said that they needed to talk in private. They went to Moses' home where they drank instant coffee mixed with coconut milk. "I have friends in the High Commissioner's office," Moses explained. "You are being extradited back to Massachusetts. Leif might be given to his mother. You will face abduction charges."

"That's ridiculous," Eddie replied. "How can they do that? I wasn't even represented at the case hearing. Leif's mother abandoned him and me years ago." Eddie felt a rush of giddiness, and his face burned as if he had been slapped hard.

"Americans often do dumb things. This is another example," said Moses. "Maybe you and Ann should get in the trimaran and sail somewhere and decide what to do. Maybe the Pacific will give you an answer. Now would be the perfect time. They won't detain you until the school year ends. Maybe the Americans want them to, but they won't. It's not our way. Besides, this is an island. The police can not imagine there's any place for you to hide."

"I don't want to hide," Eddie replied. "Someday soon I want to go back to the States. Leif needs to know his own people."

Moses just shrugged.

"What if we go back to Nukuoro?" Eddie asked.

"There are no police there," said Moses. "None will come. Unless, of course, you commit a very bad crime while you are out there—a crime so terrible that the Nukuorans cannot handle it themselves through traditional law. But you won't do that. Go there. The police won't know where you've gone. They won't care. Only your ex-lover will care, but she'll never be able to trace you. Nukuoro is another world. And a fine one. But be aware that a man in disharmony can never fit into a harmonious place."

◂ • ▸

Eddie told Ann about his conversation with Moses. She immediately suggested that they sail to Nukuoro for an extended stay of at least a year or two. "I've always wanted to go back, but I need to go with someone I love. We can support each other out there."

Eddie wasn't so sure. He didn't like the idea of letting a court date wait while he enjoyed himself. A delay could only cause more problems for him and Leif. Still, Ann was so enthusiastic about a return to the island of her dreams that he said nothing.

On the last day of school they were ready. Eddie had met his last class and had said goodbye. The Quakers had given them the go-ahead to re-establish the school. "A radiogram came this morning," explained Ann as they stashed the last of their gear in the hold. "I also activated a standing order for supplies on Guam. I've thought about returning for so long that I had everything planned before you came with your problem. I just needed a bit of a push, that's all. The field ship will arrive at Nukuoro in a month or two with building materials, extra rigging, seeds, gifts for the islanders, and lots of other stuff."

"But what if it doesn't work out?" Eddie asked. "All that stuff could be wasted."

"Nothing gets wasted on the outer islands," replied Ann. "If we can't use the supplies, the islanders can. Anyway, everything will be just fine." Ann kissed Eddie on the cheek as if she were reassuring him.

Jeban accompanied them. A Nukuoran, he had just completed mechanics and electronics courses at a vocational institute. Ann's trimaran was his quickest transportation home. He was excited about his new knowledge. "Many of my people have outboard motors," he explained. "Also the school has a generator and a shortwave radio. I will be the only repairman for these things."

"Does everyone on Nukuoro use outboards?" Eddie asked.

"Oh no," laughed Jeban, who had the classic features of a Roman God in the coppery skin of a Polynesian. He spoke excellent English and had bright and inquisitive eyes that indicated his innate intelligence. "Fuel is very expensive and can only be obtained from the field ship, which only comes every three months. Everyone uses sail power. We still make canoes out of breadfruit trees and still tie everything together with coconut fiber. It's an art. The many outboards are for special occasions—for very rough seas or for other emergencies. If someone is sick or hurt, we use the motors to bring them to a doctor."

By noon they were ready to push off. Moses came down to say goodbye. "If you stay out there, maybe one day I'll bring my son out to see how you're doing!" he shouted as the trimaran skimmed through the shallows and into the swells beyond.

Jeban and Eddie worked the sail as Ann handled the wheel. Teri and Leif were content to watch. Soon the sail billowed full, and the trimaran skipped toward the southern passage that led to open sea. "We're going to make you into a real Micronesian on this voyage," shouted Ann, her hair rippling as the trimaran rushed through the deepening blue of the lagoon. "I brought food for the children, but we adults will catch ours."

"You're kidding!" Eddie exclaimed.

"No, I'm not. These waters are incredibly rich in fish, especially tuna. We shouldn't have any trouble. Anyway, if you do get hungry, there's plenty of peanut butter."

For the first time since his youth in Michigan, Eddie found himself fishing. When he was a boy he had often fished streams for brook trout. Now, feeling mildly seasick, he found himself perched on the end of a bobbing sailboat somewhere in mid-Pacific while his heavy line disappeared aft into endless blue water.

Ann was napping, and Jeban was at the wheel, quietly singing the trimaran toward Nukuoro. Eddie waited for a fish to take the silver spoon that sparkled somewhere out of sight far behind and below. Eddie watched the flattened waves rise from behind the speeding boat. He could feel something distant rising in himself. The act of fishing had made him mildly homesick. His thoughts turned to his childhood streams, the forest, and Lake Superior. But there was something else too. He felt suddenly anxious, as if he were being hunted. He did not like the thought that he was being irretrievably separated from his self—from the land and the people that defined him. On Nukuoro he suspected he would be a stranger playing at island life instead of participating fully in it. He was not an islander. He would never be an islander. He was a backwoods Finn with a young son that he dearly loved.

A fish struck, and that old childhood excitement instantly returned. The line tightened, cutting into the soft meat of Eddie's palm. He reeled it in, hand over hand. Jeban lifted his head from the wheel and showed mild interest, but when he walked over and gave a sharp tug on the line, he returned to the wheel. "It's little," he said, and he was right. Eddie had caught the world's smallest tuna.

As Eddie boated it, Jeban rose, pulled out his knife, and deftly lopped off the head. He ran his knife lightly and smoothly from the anus to the gills and extracted the guts, tossing them overboard, along with the head. He quickly filleted the fish and tossed the backbone and tail over the side. Then he halved each fillet and motioned for Eddie to choose a piece. Eddie took the smallest. Jeban smiled broadly and chose the largest for himself. He saved the other pieces for Ann and the children.

Jeban ripped off large hunks of raw fish with his teeth, chewed briefly, and swallowed. Soon his portion was gone. Eddie continued to eye his piece, trying to figure out how to eat it without tasting raw fish. Eddie's stomach heaved with the roll of the swells. He raised the fish tentatively to his lips but just the thought of swallowing it nauseated him. He handed his portion to Jeban, who chewed it up and swallowed.

They continued to keep lines over the side for the remainder of the afternoon, but these were attached to the boat, and they paid little attention. The trimaran floated on through a blazing sun. Eddie's eyes throbbed from the reflection, his back ached, his leg muscles were cramped. But gradually his nausea passed.

Toward evening Jeban boated another tuna—a large one. Again he fil-leted it and then chopped the fillets into steaks. Eddie hadn't eaten for hours. Jeban handed him a thick slice of tuna, and Eddie mouthed it. It was delicious—sweet and firm. Eddie wolfed it down. Jeban smiled.

Ann and the kids were up and about. They too wolfed down their por-tions. Ahead lay a chain of tiny atolls—Nama, Losap, Namoluk, Lukunor. Beyond all of these was Nukuoro, in the eye of God.

Ann was in the cabin, rearranging and securing goods. Teri and Leif were playing a dice game on one of the bunks. Jeban and Eddie were alone again on deck. The sails strained under a steady breeze from the northwest.

"Why are you going to Nukuoro?" Jeban asked. He was tying off the frayed end of a nylon cord. The tone of his question indicated he was much more interested in Eddie's answer than in his task.

"I'm going to teach," Eddie replied.

"But you could do that in America," Jeban said.

"It's not the same," Eddie answered.

Jeban mulled over this for a moment and then accepted Eddie's evasion. He finished with the cord, checked their direction and then sat down on the deck. "Do you want a drink to celebrate our departure from Truk? I have a case of vodka stashed under here." Jeban was already unlatching the deck plate that hid his booze. His hurried movements indicated guilt. Eddie real-ized that Ann knew nothing about this liquor.

"I don't like vodka," Eddie said. "I'm a gin and tonic man."

"Gin is okay, but not the tonic," Jeban replied. "It's too bitter. What's your real reason for coming to Nukuoro?" Jeban pulled a fifth of vodka into view and immediately replaced the deck plate. He rummaged in his pocket, brought out a pocket knife, opened it, and cut away the bottle's seal. Then he closed the knife and dropped it back in his pocket. He unscrewed the top and swigged directly from the bottle. All this time he watched Eddie, waiting for his reply.

"There are two reasons," Eddie said. "One, I want to be with Ann. Two, I want to escape from civilization. I don't like life in America very much. Everyone tells me Nukuoro is very beautiful. Ann says it's also a wonderful place to live—that the people are happy."

Jeban smiled mysteriously, his dark eyes glowing in his copper face. "Nukuoro is changing fast," he said. "The old ways are good but only the old people still live that way. The old have a special knowledge, and I respect them for that. They are better than the young people like me."

"Why do you say that?" Eddie asked.

Jeban took a long draught of the vodka and then sealed the bottle and put it back in the storage compartment under the deck. "The young men don't go to the canoe house anymore," he explained. "They don't ask the old men questions about navigation. They no longer know the ocean and the reef. Instead they go to drinking huts in the forest and get drunk."

"That sounds like Moen." Eddie was jolted by this revelation. Were he and Ann taking the children from one place of horrors to another?

"No. Not like Moen. We young people still respect our parents. When we drink, we isolate ourselves out of shame. We don't break things or shout profanities. Life on Nukuoro is still good. But it is deteriorating."

"That saddens me," Eddie said. "The last paradise is dying. Adam is cast from the garden."

The trimaran knifed on through endless blue water, white froth bubbling off the surface as it cut its path. Eddie was beginning to feel melancholy.

"I don't understand," said Jeban. "What does Adam have to do with it?"

"Don't pay any attention," Eddie told him. "It's my disappointment coming out. No man is an island."

"Don't worry," said Jeban as he checked the tension on the sails. "You'll like it out there. Just don't expect more from us than we can give. Ann is like that. She's a nice lady but a dreamer. She sees the good—sometimes when it's not there. You and I, we'll be friends. I'll teach you where to fish and how to use an outrigger. In return you can loan me books and tapes.

Books are hard to find on Nukuoro, but Ann always has lots of them. I guess you will too."

"Yes," Eddie agreed. "I'll be ordering them from the States. I can't live without books."

"I like to read Louis L'Amour and Max Brand. I welcome you." Jeban suddenly stepped up to Eddie and shook his hand. Just as suddenly he withdrew to the opposite railing and sat down.

"Thank you," Eddie replied, and he now realized what he had to do, even if he lost Ann. Yet he couldn't imagine losing Ann, and part of him was sure that she didn't want to lose him either. Eddie called to her, and she stuck her head out of the cabin door. "Come here," he said. "We have to talk."

Ann came out on deck, her hair billowing in the breeze. She was barefoot, wearing the flimsiest of outfits—short shorts and a ribbon of cloth that covered her breasts. She looked delectable, and Eddie ached with love for her. "I'm sorry," he blurted out, "but I can't do this. I can't run away from my problem. I have to return to the States and face Julie. I have to make the truth known. The truth will win out."

"Do you have that much faith in the system?" Ann was not just disappointed, she was very angry. Her shoulders shook, and her lips formed a thin line of tension.

"I have no faith in the system," Eddie said. "But I have faith in myself and in Leif and the rightness of our life together."

"It's your choice!" cried Ann. She looked disgusted. She stood on deck with her feet wide apart like a prizefighter about to throw a haymaker. "Why did you take so long to make up your mind? And what if you lose Leif?"

"I won't," Eddie said, trying to sound confident. "I'm sure of that. And it doesn't matter how long it's taken me. It's done. I can't go to Nukuoro. Not now anyway. I can't make my son a fugitive."

"You can never be sure of the court system," said Ann. "You'd be going against motherhood. The courts support mothers because they know what jerks a lot of men are." Ann began to retreat from Eddie. She hadn't moved, but he could see it in her face. She was withdrawing because he was no longer the person she had thought she knew. He was no longer a man in flight.

Eddie caught her hand as she turned and pulled her toward him. Out of the corner of his eye he glimpsed Jeban nearby. Jeban was watching with nervous attention. "Look, I want to talk about this, and I don't want to be interrupted."

Ann glared into Eddie's eyes. She must have seen his need there, for she sat down obediently and softened her antagonism.

"When Julie had problems with her parents, she ran away—not far, but far enough. If she'd run further, she'd've had to grow up and become independent. She chose to live away from them while still using them and their money. I think she lived with me to spite them. Leif's birth was another step in asserting her separation. Then she found out that motherhood has responsibilities, so she left."

"This is ancient history!" cried Ann. "That was years ago!"

"But it describes an established pattern not just for her, but for me too. And maybe for you, for that matter."

Ann intensely examined Eddie's face for clues to his meaning. Her anger began to melt. "Are you saying that Julie and I are similar?" she asked.

"Let me explain," Eddie said.

"Please do." Ann flexed her shoulders as if she were trying to squeeze knots out of her body.

"When I knew her, Julie was always running away. She took college courses but never graduated. She had her own place but never took care of it. She ignored being a daughter but took her parents' money. She played at relationships but refused to be a mother."

"Get to your point," said Ann, exasperation in her voice.

"Julie and I were similar," Eddie explained. "I escaped from the stifling town where I grew up by going to the university. I was running away from the stress of my parents' marriage and the claustrophobic working lives of the miners. At the university, I escaped from the boredom of classes into the library stacks. I read fiction by romantic dreamers and then fled into the Peace Corps. After Julie abandoned Leif and me, I fled with him across the country. When California didn't work out, I fled to Micronesia. Now I've met you, and I don't want to flee any more. I don't want to go to Nukuoro where Leif will be cut off from his grandparents and from his own culture. And I don't want to be a ghost. I don't want to be out there trying to replace your dead husband. He's gone, and so is Nukuoro and the life you had there with him. I want to marry you, go back to Boston with you, face Julie and her lawyers, and begin our life together. Maybe we could come back here. Maybe we can't. To me it doesn't matter. It only matters if I'm not with you. I love you. Marry me. Help me. Come back with me. It'll be okay."

Ann said nothing for a full minute. She stared into Eddie's eyes and kept pushing her flying hair out of her eyes. Eddie began to worry. Then she stood up, leaned forward, and kissed him. "What'll I do with the boat?" she asked.

A wave of relief passed over Eddie, cleansing him like a shower of water. "For now, nothing," Eddie said. "We'll leave it here in Micronesia in a canoe house or some other safe place. Maybe we'll come back. If not, we can sell it."

"It would be a whole new life," said Ann. "The idea frightens me."

"Everything worthwhile is frightening," said Eddie. "But I'll always be there to support you. We need each other. We can grow together into a new, richer life."

Ann smiled. She brushed up against Eddie and then squeezed him around the waist. "I'll marry you. But I won't be a traditional wife. I've thought about this, you know. I want to go back to school—to study anthropology."

"Sounds good to me," Eddie answered, and he wrapped his arms around her and held her against his chest. She rubbed her cheek against his. In the doorway of the cabin, Leif and Teri were grinning broadly.

So was Jeban at the wheel. "I guess I'll have to catch another boat," he said. "The field ship will be going to Nukuoro next month." He had already begun the necessary steps to bring the trimaran around.

◄ • ►

On the way to Massachusetts they stopped in Michigan to introduce Ann to Eddie's parents and to drop off Leif and Teri. Eddie's mother still had trouble with her hip. She moved slowly, as if she were pulling a great weight. Still, she was delighted that the children would be visiting while Ann and Eddie were in Boston.

In Boston Ann and Eddie did not know their way around. They chose a lawyer out of the yellow pages, and he turned out to be the perfect choice. He was expensive, but he knew Julie and promised to demolish her in court. To plan their strategy, Ann and Eddie met the lawyer in his expansive high-rise office overlooking the Charles River. The lawyer sat at a huge, antique mahogany desk. "We had a sea captain in my family during the clipper ship days," the lawyer explained. "He brought back the wood from Brazil, and the desk was built by a local craftsman. The desk is one hundred fifty years old."

They got down to business. The lawyer insisted that Julie was bound to lose. "It won't be difficult," he said. Through him, Eddie and Ann learned that Julie had divorced her rich lawyer husband—that she was alone and childless. "She probably wants Leif to fill up the void in her life," said the lawyer. "Her ex-husband is a friend of mine." The lawyer had already prepared a long list of Julie's former boyfriends. Her most recent had arrived a few months earlier from Guatemala. "I know a few things about the guy," said the lawyer. "He wants to get a Ph.D. He hopes one day to teach in an American university. He's sure he'll succeed because he's aware that American universities now have minority quotas for accepting graduate students and for hiring faculty. He's an Indian and can use that to his advantage whether he's qualified or not. Right now, though, he's learning English at a community college."

"You don't like him much, do you?" Eddie stated.

"No, I don't," said the lawyer. "He's a parasite. He's with Julie only because she's now independently wealthy."

"I don't understand," said Eddie.

"She got half of her ex-husband's estate. He had a lot of money. I'd guess she's worth close to three quarters of a million. Maybe more."

"And you resent her for taking his money," Eddie said.

"You're damned right I do," said the lawyer. "As I said before, her ex is a friend of mine—a close friend. I know how she mistreated him. She had innumerable affairs while they were married. She's disloyal. She's mistreated every man in her life. She's mistreated her parents, too. For years she's taken their money, but she rarely visits them. From what I hear, she doesn't visit them at all now that she has the divorce money."

"How do you know so much about her?" Eddie asked.

"Through her ex-husband. He's still very angry about the divorce settlement. He rants about her all the time. I play squash with him a couple of times a week, and she always comes up as a topic of conversation. We talk about the Guatemalan too. He's an amazingly ignorant man. He believes in all sorts of trash—seances, weird spiritual stuff. Now Julie professes to believe in all that stuff too."

"She was always like that," Eddie explained. "She tends to mirror the men in her life. And she's always been attracted to Third-World types."

"We can use her instability against her in your case," said the lawyer gleefully. "I may even enjoy hurting her."

On the appointed day, Julie arrived at the courthouse in a bright red BMW driven by the Guatemalan. Julie was in the back seat, which made the Guatemalan look like a chauffeur. The Guatemalan was trying to look American—Levis, a Red Sox sweatshirt, and garish yellow-and-green Nikes. Julie wore the kind of outfit that would look right at home on an Indian woman selling *manioc* in a Guatemalan outdoor marketplace. On her head she had a bright red cotton kerchief covered with a blue flower design and edged with orange lace. She wore a white, elaborately embroidered peasant blouse and a wrinkled, heavy, red cotton skirt that reached to her ankles. Her feet were shod in rough leather sandals. She was extremely thin and very nervous.

She refused to acknowledge Ann and Eddie as they waited on the courthouse steps for the arrival of their lawyer. Eddie felt a pang of sorrow for Julie. After she and her Guatemalan had disappeared inside, their lawyer arrived, and Eddie and Ann entered the courthouse.

On the witness stand, Julie was every bit as pathetic as Eddie's lawyer had said she would be. She tried to tell the judge that she had discovered the secrets of the ancient Mayans, who, she said, had used spiritual power to fly to Mars to build ruins visible through telescopes. She asked him if he had read *Chariots of the Gods*. "The Mayans flew all over the universe," she said, wide-eyed and pumped up by the idea.

The judge bought none of her often incoherent argument. He awarded Eddie sole custody of Leif, without stipulations. Eddie and Ann hugged each other.

The next day they flew back to Michigan.

Timo and the Author Give Their Impressions of Arvo

The Portage Gazette, June 15, 1881

On Saturday while crossing the bridge to Hancock, Oskari Ohtinen lost his hat. He tried to rescue it but drowned instead. The hat later was blown ashore and will be buried today, along with Mr. Ohtinen.

You are so full of shit, Anderson," said Timo, who was a professor of literature but often talked like that. We were sitting in the kitchen of Timo's trailer, where he lived with Lillian. "In this last story you pretend that Arvo is Eddie Maki but Eddie Maki is actually you, and there is no Arvo. What are you trying to pull?"

"I'm fictionalizing," I said.

"But ninety-five percent of it really happened," said Timo. "It's non-fiction, just like the rest of the book. You really did go to Micronesia when you were young. And what's that stuff about single parenthood? You went there with your first wife and your son. You didn't become a single parent until your latest ex-wife, Tiltu, left you with two daughters."

"People write about the trials and tribulations of single-parent mothers all the time," I said. "I liked the idea of a single-parent dad fleeing to a Pacific island to escape a broken marriage. I thought it would make the point that single-parent dads have a tough time too. I also thought it would add drama."

"Well it doesn't," said Timo. "Plus the woman your character meets in the islands is too idealized. No woman is actually like that. They're all so damned complicated that they mostly cause grief for guys like you and me."

"So I should rewrite the entire manuscript as a memoir?" I asked him.

"That's right," said Timo. "That way it will all be true."

"Well, I'm not going to," I said. "I think it contains more truth in its present form."

"Well, to hell with you then," said Timo in his usual friendly way. "I've got some pickled herring, *makkara*, and beer in the fridge. Let's eat and drink and watch the Western channel on TV. They're showing an old Lash LaRue movie. What could be better? I love the idealized mythic world of 1940s Westerns."

"So it's all right for Westerns to have idealized characters," I said, "but it's not okay in my book. You're contradicting yourself, buddy."

"Of course I am," said Timo. "That's what life is—a series of absurd contradictions wrapped up in a mystery. Life is full of irony. Your life and my life—they're disasters. And yet we wouldn't trade them. They've been rich lives in spite of, and maybe because of, the disasters. So let's stop being professors for a while and watch the movie and shut up."

"Lash LaRue was my boyhood hero," I said. "I loved his movies when I was about eight."

Timo turned on the TV.